Praise for
Fire in the Belly of the Beast

"At a time when there is so much uncertainty, H. G. Rogers delivers humor and levity. This thought-provoking story is both touching and outrageous. What better time to read it than during a campaign season sure to keep us all on our toes. We all need a laugh, and if you're like me, you'll be laughing out loud."

—Senator John Boozman

"A fun read that captures the feeling of the Pentagon and Capitol Hill. The story and characters combine to make up a wicked, enjoyable satire."

—Drew A. Bennett, Ph.D., Colonel, USMC (ret.)

"Laughter and learning (and even a love story) combine in Rogers's novel, wittily exposing the clichés of Washington's political class. Set in the not-so-distant future, the political scene exists in a cauldron of conflicting efforts to topple a President. Readers will long remember their amusement at the antics of the novel's two-party system…. They will also inescapably learn more about the great themes that permeate political life: humanity, power, and ambition."

—Jene M. Porter, Professor Emeritus of Political Philosophy,
University of Saskatchewan

"A fierce and funny send-up of the circus that is contemporary politics. Rogers deftly deflates the pompous punditry and skewers the calamitous cacophony that defines our national political landscape. Rogers creates a cast of characters right out of today's headlines, and that unnerving familiarity drives the story to its inevitable end! Five stars!"

—Curtis Harrell, MFA, Author of *Melpomene's Garden*

FIRE IN THE BELLY OF THE BEAST

BY
H. G. ROGERS

Published by Intra Murus Press
First edition 2024
ISBN 9798218553951

To the memory of Brenda Eden Rogers, my late wife, who inspired this book and gave me valuable advice during its creation.

About the Author

H. G. Rogers was born in 1948 and earned degrees in literature from the Universities of Arkansas, Missouri, and Texas. He taught at Texas, Baylor, and several other institutions, and served twenty-one years in the U.S. Army. He resides in Northwest Arkansas.

Acknowledgments

The publication of this book would not have been possible without the constant encouragement and love from my wife, Anne Ray Rogers. Her sensitive reading, incisive questioning, and meticulous editing saved me from countless mistakes.

I also celebrate the contributions of my daughter, Jennifer Eden Rogers, a sympathetic reader and a gifted writer. She has taught me much about writing but more about life and love.

Numerous readers contributed to the many revisions of this work.

The brilliant work of cover artist Ginger Ngo is of immense value. Her artistry and creative insight are exceptional.

Finally, I must acknowledge the debt I owe to the insanity of some American partisans, elected and unelected; they made this book necessary.

Chapter One

Now that neither the Democratic nor Republican Party existed at the national level, the big money was scrambling to maintain influence. When one of his party's king makers invited Senator Sheffield Belmond (Stalactite, MN) for lunch, he was less flattered than relieved. What had taken so long? They'd been a little slow in scrambling to him.

Senator Belmond was unique among his colleagues in that he'd been all the way into the third year of his first term before he discovered that he really should be president. Belmond knew the country would respond to his ability to see the big picture, his sophisticated grasp of the nuances of foreign policy, and his gravitas. He knew that some considered those qualities to be merely journalistic clichés; he regarded them as real and substantial.

Belmond's staff had filled him in. Holden Kaltenfeld was no mere lobbyist but a successful Silicon Valley venture capitalist and bundler extra ordinaire. He was also a bit of a prodigy; he graduated from high school at fourteen, tried to drop out of Harvard multiple times only to find another area he was interested in. Almost against his will, he accumulated enough hours for a couple of degrees—an AB in computer science with a music minor (woodwind theory), a second bachelor's in European history, and a Ph.D. in economics with comparative literature as a secondary field.

Kaltenfeld could just be lobbying, seeking to influence his vote on some arcane tax matter, or hoping to beef up patent protections for software, or some such. If so, Belmond would listen politely, maybe intimate that as a mere senator he was limited in what he could do to advance Kaltenfeld's—okay, their shared agenda—before asking what kind of "independent" political action committee Kaltenfeld planned for supporting Belmond's next venture. But this transaction could go better if Kaltenfeld took the initiative.

The 35-year-old wunderkind had considered Belmond's Midwestern palate. He chose one of D.C.'s toniest steak houses, Comme Çá. They met at 1:45. The maitre d' showed Belmond past a half full dining room into another where Kaltenfeld sat alone. He wore grey trousers, black sports coat, white shirt, and thin iridescent blue tie.

"Mr. Kaltenfeld, thank you for the invitation. I'm very pleased to meet you."

"And I you, Senator. Hey, we may be in formal old D.C., but you should call me Holden."

"Absolutely. And I'm Sheffield. I think the District could use more of the California ways. Breaks down barriers."

Kaltenfeld asked after Belmond's wife, whom he knew slightly from a Special Olympics event in the Twin Cities a few years earlier. Belmond complimented his memory and promised to pass his regards to Mollie.

The waiter arrived and took their drink orders. The menu offered several martinis that tempted Belmond, but this was a business lunch. He took water.

Kaltenfeld said, "I recommend the tuna tartare for an appetizer. It's robust. For an entree I've chosen the lobster ravioli, but you might want one of their steaks. They're quite good, I understand."

Belmond hesitated. It was only an appetizer, couldn't be too big, but he could hardly choke down sushi and never sashimi. It could be a test. It also could be worse: he'd heard from one of the Arkansas senators that every two years they were expected to participate in a traditional political supper of opossum. He tugged his ear and said, "Then the tuna it is. Thanks for the recommendation, Holden. And I will go with a simple filet." Then, he was sure without a hint of impatience, he asked, "What can I do for you, Holden?"

"Well, you can tell me if you're in agreement with my view of the situation." He noticed an Asian man seating his two young children across the room. The kids were pasty little things, not healthy. "I think you people are as surprised as the country about how your party experiment, excuse me, 'The Great Realignment,' is going."

"The Great Realignment," hardly were those words out before Belmond again saw MBC's last election night set: a vast image of all the Congressional elections across a national map filling the screen, percentages duly shown, but numbers of votes almost as small and pitiless as a school board election. Everywhere. A measly twenty-five million votes scattered across fifty states—for 435 House seats plus thirty-three Senate seats. Humiliating.

The commentators had been at a loss to explain it—only eleven percent of eligible voters bothered to vote for a senator or representative. They'd voted for president, fifty-seven percent of them. But few voted for Congress. Exit polls showed only twenty-six percent of those who voted even liked the candidate they voted for. One late night host noted that the number of people liking their own candidate was about the same as the number of Californians celebrating their sneeze fetishes.

"We thought we owed it to the people to try something different. Change the partisan atmosphere."

"You owed it to yourselves to keep your jobs."

"Well, there's that."

"I can understand rebranding, likely a good idea. People tire of the old labels, and they tend to expect uniformity—should I say, party discipline. But you guys went random."

"We wanted to free our members to be true to themselves and align more closely with their constituents."

"Yes, I know—a la carte liberals and cafeteria conservatives, pick and choose what plays at home and forget about the country."

"Holden, I have a grand vision, but I'm not about to run on it or a party platform that's even grander. With the new parties, I don't have to."

"So you're a Tite now. My apologies, a Stalactite. Doesn't that feel somewhat foolish?"

"Tite's fine. Compared to a donkey or an elephant? No. It resets us. Do business without ideological straightjackets. The old parties are pretty evenly split between us and the Stalagmites. And, yes, it's perfectly fine to call them 'Mites.'"

"And the colors you're making the media use—teal and sage. . . ."

"I thought the majority leader and the speaker explained that quite well at their December press conference. We don't want anything to remind us of the old ways—all that gridlock."

"The rationale is not unreasonable. You were a mess." Kaltenfeld glanced across the room—those kids were very well behaved. "You, the Congress, were about as functional as a floppy disk. Now, suddenly you're beginning to function. It's just May, and the budget is out of the House and everything, but Defense and Intelligence have cleared the Senate. That's pretty impressive."

"I think we're doing well." The downside was that it made the president look somewhat competent, even if the White House had almost nothing to do with any of it.

The kids across the room were motionless. Kaltenfeld watched. They looked sick and were looking directly at him, eyes wide open and ears seemingly cocked. Kaltenfeld said, "Don't worry about the president; he hasn't been able to enact any of his promises and has nearly reached the end of what he can do with executive orders. He can continue a bit with regulatory changes, but they rarely make headlines and take time to have an effect."

Belmond said, "That's true. But his popularity is off the charts." Should have said, "*and* his popularity is off the charts." What kind of partisan hack wants a new president to fail? Or at least, fail in the first year.

"Sixty-five percent approval. Daunting. The irony is. . .you guys in Congress are responsible for it. Eloel."

Belmond said, "The legislative movement has been a pure team effort."

"You don't do irony, do you, Sheffield?

"No, we send it out."

Kaltenfeld sipped his sparkling water. "Okay. A pure team has no stars. To be president, you must be a star. And that's tough with Tigger." The media's shorthand for The Great Realignment. They had used an image of Winnie the Pooh's pal until the Milne Estate threatened to sue. "How do you see it?"

Belmond had an uneasy feeling that he was getting drawn into analysis. "Sure, you betcha." Belmond grimaced. He didn't like thinking on the fly; he liked his staff to do the intellectual heavy lifting. Not that he lacked intelligence. He was quite sure that in his own way he was as smart as most of his colleagues. He started to check them off: Alabama, Alaska, Arizona, Arkansas, Calif.... Oh, where was he? Knowing he wasn't as smart as Kaltenfeld.

The appetizers arrived. Belmond studied the tuna. It was definitely tartare. A pretty little cube with sprinkled greenery, in a sauce that might kill the flavor some, something to appreciate aesthetically. He'd think while he chewed. Belmond plunged his fork into the fish, sopped up as much sauce as he could gracefully, subtly held his breath, and placed it in his mouth. The flavor was not as bad as he'd feared, but it sure was chewy; he was going to have more than enough time to think. He grunted what he hoped would be taken for appreciation, "Mmmh."

Kaltenfeld gave him a knowing look: we are enjoying some of life's best, my friend.

A moment later, Belmond swished a little ice water around his mouth and decided to get so caught up in the conversation that he'd just, darn it, forget to eat.

Kaltenfeld spoke, "Well, based on my fifteen years of being politically active, I surmise you want to be president? Don't answer. It's implied by your office, Eloel." Kaltenfeld didn't smile, hadn't smiled since the handshake, Belmond observed to himself. Then he disciplined himself to the conversation.

"Well, that's true. The Great Realignment is serving the people well. "

"How long do you think this green, non-ideological, primordial soup that the members agreed to is going to last? I'll tell you, six years at the most. Some visceral, contentious issue will come along: it will enrage all the interest groups, and some members will see that nothing has changed. Most members still have their policy principles or at least their re-election interests, they're just distributed randomly between the parties. When that happens—and it will happen—a few Tites will become Mites and vice-versa. Then some true believers back home will primary the less ideological, House members at first. Anyway, it'll break down before your term is over."

"Interesting analysis. And prophecy." Belmond knew the deal the members had negotiated: no party switchers for eight years. Even the wired-in Kaltenfeld didn't know that. That was a key proviso agreed to at the panicked mid-November meeting. Only afterward did Belmond find out it had been held at Mammoth Cave. He wondered if the location inspired the names. A meeting held in Kentucky by parties very unlucky. . . .

"And your best chance will have evaporated."

"Assuming I want a chance, why would my best chance be gone?"

"Do you think in a robust partisan environment anyone is going to nominate a Minnesota triplet: Hubert Humphrey, Walter Mondale, Sheffield Belmond? Elem-mayo, no. You people have lost the Super Bowl almost as many times as the Vikings."

"That sounds like superstition, magic. I don't think politics is like that."

The waiter was at Belmond's elbow. "Does the tuna meet your approval, sir?"

"Oh, yes, absolutely. Lovely, quite lovely." True, a colorful and well-designed dish. "I'll be eating more, but I need to leave room for the steak."

"Very good, sir," And the waiter withdrew.

"Holden, you were telling me why now is my best chance, or rather why I have no other chance than now. Am I right?"

"Precisely. Did you ever consider this: The first Illinois US senator to be president, Lincoln, provoked a civil war; the second, Obama, was heading the same direction; it just stayed under the surface. Hillary reaped the whirlwind from that. You think there's going to be a US senator from Illinois elected president this century?"

"What about President Stafford, he's from Illinois?"

"He was just a state senator, and the answer is 'no.' Obama's the last until we're all quite dead. And by the way, as you should know, I loved Obama and supported him. But if he could run today, I'd find other interests. And by the way, if I pushed it, Hillary was a U.S. senator and she was once from Illinois."

Belmond said, "Okay, I'll stipulate to your analysis. So do you think, given the cat rodeo we had at the Democratic convention last time, that the new parties will be more disciplined?"

The entrees were delivered. Belmond slid his appetizer to the edge of the table. Kaltenfeld didn't appear to notice; he seemed eager to continue his lecture. Fair deal.

"Not more disciplined, less stratified. You don't have the structures of loyalties and obligations yet. The lack of a strong structure leaves the field vulnerable to a candidate who establishes herself or himself early."

Kaltenfeld explained that he'd been watching Belmond since he was in the House, liked the way he spoke, turned unpopular votes into testaments of character, tilted at a few shiny windmills, related to his constituents. Like the way he looked.

"You're tall, you're quite handsome, manly even—don't quote me using that term—in a non-threatening way. But you really got my attention when you held out on immigration reform. I mean the bill had just about everything both sides could want, given that major reductions and blanket amnesty were off the table. But you didn't vote for it because it reduced the 12b1 visas. Of course, you know, that's a source of vitality in Silicon Valley. So that got my attention."

"I felt it was discriminatory."

"Don't BS me. I know Minnesota has lots of tech. None of us likes overpaying a bunch of prima donna US techies, if there's a harder working foreign model available. Yeah, that's discrimination… fer sure, you betcha." This time Kaltenfeld laughed, making a sound even.

Belmond was a bit offended. Rather he felt he should be offended but doubted that he could pull it off.

"So back to your idea, you think I could be the strong horse?"

"Candidate. Quick and dirty, if. If there are no stars, you can possibly pull it off as a meteor. By lighting the sky with your committee hearings, you can get the name recognition you need for the nomination. With no Stalactite senior statesman, a good looking, well spoken, safe-seeming Midwesterner is perfect. We just have to keep you in the sky long enough." Kaltenfeld thought his metaphor was becoming a bit meretricious, but it worked.

"Well, I do think I have the skill set to run, to win, to govern."

Belmond took another bite of steak; it bathed his taste buds in earthy goodness. The tuna was forgotten and had been discreetly removed by the waiter.

"Ha, that's what I'm talking about. Completely sincere. Are you Methodist, Mormon? No, I know you're sort of Lutheran, not enough to scare off the nones and not pagan enough to scare off the believers. I know. I had it tested. You're a fit. At least, if we work it right."

Belmond gulped a barely chewed bite. Didn't choke, but it was close. Kaltenfeld was far beyond exploring things. He had decided! Belmond began to coach himself to play it cool. His earnest Minnesota soul was a bit offended by the implication that his faith seemed acceptably empty to the masses. But the backing of someone like Kaltenfeld could only be good. Besides he'd never made an issue of his Christianity. And he wouldn't start now—ah, the warm glow of his integrity asserting itself.

Belmond agreed to use his committee to air some dirt on the president. Couldn't bring him down—Belmond's deeply felt goal since the election, but Kaltenfeld explained that the Mite nominee with an untested party to support him would be more beatable with the Republican president still in the race. President Stafford could be Belmond's Ross Perot.

As they left the restaurant, Kaltenfeld glanced again at the Asian man and his kids. The man looked vaguely familiar. The kids' faces held identical placid smiles. Bizarre. Belmond strode out, not glancing to either side.

CHAPTER TWO

As he walked to the DuPont Circle Metro Station, the sky was lightening to gray, an inviting slate on which Rek could write anything at all. He wrote "3D254." Then he wrote that today was gonna be awesome. "3D254," he said it aloud. He'd been saying it since awakening a good ten minutes before his alarm. The words he'd gone to sleep to the night before— "3D254." A room number but meaningless to Rek, except that it was Absolute Awesomeness.

He checked and rechecked his uniform throughout the ride. He was not gonna look like a brand new officer, "hair still shedding packing peanuts," as a sergeant joked unfunnily to his class. He chanted the number quietly, and the subway glided along. He silenced the chant to change lines at Metro Center. Then, 3D254, Farragut West, 3D254, Foggy Bottom, 3D254, Rosslyn, he tensed, Arlington Cemetery. Then, The Stop. Up into the shopping concourse. He scanned for an entrance and thought, cool, like driving into Chicago for the first time. He dropped an imaginary microphone, forced his eyebrows apart and mouthed, "AWESOME!"

ID out, briefcase open. The uniformed Pentagon policewoman glanced at them and waved him through. He felt as alert as a newbie scouring a gutter for IEDs and grateful he wasn't a newbie scouring a gutter for IEDs. He swallowed; he could easily become that newbie.

He looked for a directional clue on the walls. A uniformed man noticed, "Sir, where are you headed?"

"Office of Congressional Relations."

"Army, sir?"

"Uh, yeah. . ." Rek couldn't guess the rank, a couple of curved stripes, chevrons they called them, the uniform was sort of a sickly green, ". . .Marine."

"Sir, I'm a corporal, but 'Marine' is fine. With your permission, Sir, I'll get you going the right way." Rek nodded. "I'll need the room number. It'll be on your orders. Sir."

Yeah, it was 3E. . .no B. . .something. He shuffled through his mental files. He pawed through a couple of folders in the briefcase balanced on his knee. He gave his orders to the marine.

"Third floor, right up the ramp over there, Sir. Then cut through to the middle with the first corridor to your left. Halfway around the inner ring to Corridor 2. You'll just be a few rooms away when you come out on the D ring. It's easy, Sir, all the way in, four rings out. You'll need your orders and ID for security there. Good luck on your first day, Sir." Very helpful, Rek thought, but about as Neanderthal as he expected. He said, "Thank you," in the same tone he used with his GPS.

The Pentagon was very pentagonish—lots of military around, institutional walls and floors, a vaguely antiseptic smell. The strangeness of the place reinforced Rek's sense of awe at how awesomely awesome he must have appeared to the assignment people. His good fortune in being sent here was not just personal—it was political: an opportunity to be just a bit of sand in the gears of the new administration, maybe. But anonymous sand—he didn't want to be a martyr. The risk, it was awesome, too.

He made his way into the inner rings. Civilians strolled along purposefully. Uniformed men and women scurried to their workstations. Rek could identify most of the officer ranks, except the Navy, which he just figured the more and wider the bands on their sleeves the further above him they were. He guessed at the few enlisted ranks he saw: sergeants and airwomen, gunnery mates and buccaneers first class and specialists. He hadn't paid that much attention to the orientation course instruction on enlisted ranks. He hadn't thought there would be any enlisted since he was headed for Headquarters, Department of the Army. Seemed like all the army people had Combat Infantry Badges.

His ROTC adviser had told his whole class how to report for duty. They told everyone again at his basic course. But then they were all going to some field unit. He thought, is that for real? Approach the commander's desk, salute, and announce "Second Lieutenant Park-

Raak reporting for duty, Sir." He'd feel like a fool pulling that crap at the Pentagon.

Rek entered a large office with cubicles along the walls. 3D254. A tall, thin man in a business suit greeted him and introduced himself. Mr.…Something-or-other. "Sir" would do for a while.

"We've been expecting you, Lieutenant. The boss is in the inner office. Go on over and knock."

The door to the office was open. Rek walked as if he were on a mission and knocked on the door frame. When the man at the desk looked up from his reading, his eyes looked into Rek. Rek took a breath, swallowed some aberrant syllables, and without willing it, approached the desk, came to attention, snapped a salute, held it, and announced, "Second Lieutenant Park-Raak reporting for duty, Sir."

Sure enough, he did feel like a fool, or worse, an unthinking soldier-bot. Still, this was better than starting out with something else and getting chewed out, to which he could only reply, "I didn't pay that much attention in the basic course, Sir, since I was headed for the Pentagon."

His boss seemed to appreciate the gesture. Colonel Radihm N. Waters, a dark, forty something looking man, returned the salute. He was indeed dark; many African Americans were, but Rek thought he shouldn't have noticed. He hadn't leapt to any conclusions. He didn't think in such stereotypes, but he worried that realizing that there were stereotypes to think in was itself racist. Crap, he'd thought of the colonel as African American based solely on skin color; he might not identify as African American.

The colonel introduced Rek around the office and sent him down to personnel to in-process.

Rek tried to follow the colonel's directions exactly. Unthinkingly even. He didn't want to think too much and get himself lost, but he also wanted to resist being absorbed into the green, unthinking monster that was the Army. He focused on just walking. As he'd suspected, the Army could suck the awesomeness out of anything. He found his way to the Army's personnel and administrative center, an operation that he was supposed to have learned to run in his basic course but, knowing he was headed to the Pentagon, hadn't bothered. First day, not exactly awesome.

Chapter Three

Elle was ready to break a real story, only she hadn't got one. She scratched her bare foot against a desk leg, checked her phone, and slipped a glance at her editor's office door. Almost a year in the job and not even an innocent word choice she could twist and ride.

As she had the Chicago alderman who used the word "niggardly" to describe the mayor's budget proposal. That budget did, in fact, cut a number of programs drastically. But the alderman caught genuine, heartfelt grief over using the n-word, although of course he hadn't used the n-word, nor did she say he had, and he was black anyway, so if he'd been a rapper, it'd have been no big deal if he had, but he hadn't, even if some thought he had.

She'd ridden the "controversial" word choice. The man had some pride in his vocabulary when she interviewed him; she'd beamed in appreciation and coaxed a statement from him that could be seen as dismissive of those with an inferior mastery of words. The mayor denounced the alderman's insensitivity, the alderman apologized, and that could have been that, but Elle interviewed neighborhood leaders, then would-be leaders until she found one who was colorful, indignant, and unashamedly ignorant. She persuaded the dean of the Express columnists to run with the story; it kept going. Next her deputy editor commissioned a poll which showed the alderman had lost the confidence of a sizable minority of constituents and was unknown to even more, giving her the story that only thirty-two percent of his constituents supported him, and suddenly the alderman was a former alderman, though, she had to admit, with an excellent, if dated, vocabulary. And Elle catapulted to D.C. as a Congressional correspondent for the Washington Herald.

When she recalled that episode at work, she smiled to herself, but when at her make-up mirror she avoided her own eyes. Her reporting, she could proudly claim, had taken down an alderman, a powerful one who was number two on the Patronage and Favors Committee. But, at least as far as the fatal offense was concerned, the man was innocent. She told herself that it was strictly business, nothing personal. Then again, he had experienced the fall from power and ostracism from his community very personally. He was now managing a pawn shop on the Southside. She told herself that he just failed to have a professional perspective on the whole thing. Her self didn't believe her.

There would be no alderman-level gaffe in Congress. The Mites and Tites measured their speech as if each word cost ten-thousand votes. As much fun as meaningless, puffed-up controversies could be, the White House correspondents still owned those. No, she needed something genuinely important to advance. There had been a few issues of real meaning in divided government back when the parties made some kind of sense. With the new system, who knew? Instead of reliably generating good copy from the automatic conflict between the parties, Congress gave her insipid cooperation and compromise. The legislative branch was now an ever-changing blob of bipartisanship, a political lava lamp; issue by issue different groups of politicians joined in support or opposition, now rising, now falling, the Congress flowing from sage to teal and back as legislation passed through the system. Conceptually, it was a week-old bowl of guacamole.

She had been working for almost a year on legislator profiles. Her editor, Stanford Thieu, said it would orient her to the Congress, and she could grow from there. She knew it was supposed to be drudgery she could do until Thieu figured out how best to use her. But she liked writing the stories and meeting the people—they were alive. Better than the obituary detail.

Elle took a taxi to the Hill. It would have been a long walk after which her hair would have collapsed like a juicy rumor. She didn't need an easily demolished rumor. She needed something meaty, visceral, strongly emotional, something to bring out the demagogues on both sides. Fate owed her generation one such story. And owed her specifically as repayment for all the cab drivers she'd endured. She didn't care if they became unemployed. She hadn't really thought that, she reassured herself.

Elle started toward the House Minority Leader's office, whose chief of staff was Elle's goldmine of plausible disinformation before The Great Realignment. She was pleased with that sobriquet. "Goldmine" was beyond tired, beyond dead even. She continued to work on her facility with clichés. She had always recognized the written kind and avoided them. When she got into upper division journalism classes, she was encouraged to lean on them. She was getting better at translating thoughts to clichés in writing and hoped to achieve fluency in clichéd speaking to make the leap into broadcast journalism.

The Minority Leader had been her first big name profile. The profile, the result of a couple of weeks of on-line research, sharp questioning, and an arsenal of smiles, had so pleased the Leader that she'd offered Elle a staff position.

Then Elle remembered: the leader was off on a fact-finding trip. Elle opened Phycenook on her phone. Maybe something else would be trending and she could avoid the obvious target—Speaker of the House Jan Staffort. But nothing was breaking, nothing political even developing.

Well, she'd drop in on Staffort, make some small talk with the staff, ask them if Speaker Staffort was irritated by people confusing her name with that of President Stafford, and get an appointment. Staffort had been elected to Congress twenty-three years ago from a district between Richmond and the Beltway. For years a rural and conservative district, it became suburban and trending blue as government employees ranged farther from the capital in search of affordable housing. Adjustments were made, flops were flipped, and then the new party labels made the whole thing easier.

The Speaker was in the office. She was rereading Le Guin's *The Left Hand of Darkness*. Sci fi was her favorite from youth and perfect for now with her time home alone stretching for parsecs. She brought the book into the office to fill gaps in her schedule.

Ordinarily she'd reject a reporter's unscheduled visit. Staffort had known most of the Congressional press corps for years. It had not been a warm relationship, and she had long ago given up on the idea that a reporter might like her. But this woman was new to Staffort, so she had her shown right in.

That put Elle on alert. Did Staffort intend to use her without her getting to use Staffort back? It had happened. She would not be rolled.

Staffort was dressed in a stylish suit, similar to one Elle had admired in Nordstrom. It was a bit jarring: Elle remembered that Staffort had been a bit of a bumpkin, for ten terms a man, and for eleven a Republican. She knew that it shouldn't bother her, but still it creeped her out a little. Of course, North Dakota had some, and so had Missouri, but Republicans were rare as hens' teeth in Chicago. Not so in D.C. She smiled at the ease with which the cliché had come.

"Madam Speaker, thank you for seeing me. Would you comment on the sudden rash of committee investigations being scheduled?"

Staffort gestured for Elle to sit. "Just routine oversight hearings. You know, the Congress is in the Constitution; the FAA is not. It's our job to keep an eye on every administration. Tell me about yourself, Ms. Crafton. My staff tells me that you're from North Dakota. Right? That's one state that, unfortunately, I've not had the pleasure of visiting. Did you like growing up in a rural area?"

Elle gave short answers to the small talk. She wanted to get on to business, but to build a relationship she needed her sycophantic style, which she'd developed by studying random presidential interviews during the Obama administration. She redirected the Speaker to her question and let an indulgent smile come to her lips.

Staffort parried with a confidential smile and a comment that she was sure Elle knew how hard it was to get serious work done in the House. Elle rattled off the first day's witness list for the Appropriations Committee hearing, "I know the House has already passed this year's budget, but won't you require a full accounting for defense-related spending as a condition for next year's appropriation?"

"I can't really get into the committee's business; they have many decisions to make. You know, there used to be an ICBM base, a missile base, in North Dakota. Did you live anywhere near that?"

And so it went until there were only a couple of minutes left. Then Staffort said, "If you'd like to go off-the-record, not for attribution…well, you can say 'a well-placed source' if you like, we could do that."

Elle sighed, Staffort had been in Congress since Elle was in grade school and it showed. But it was off-the-record or nothing, "Okay, your fingerprints will not be on this."

"Now see hear, young lady, I'm the Speaker of the House. You'll not talk to me as if I'm a common criminal."

Not common, she thought. She smiled apologetically, "I am very sorry. Just a journalistic habit of using as few words as possible."

"'Being concise,' I think you're trying to say." Staffort recognized her pettiness but enjoyed it nonetheless. Actually, she admitted, more.

"I meant nothing by it. So you have something that might lead me to a story?"

"Hard to know. But no attribution, it's very sketchy right now. But there's something funny going on between our government and the oil folks in Sofia Rabia. Something that might threaten the viability of our fracking industry. You know, oil produced by fracking. Of course, you're from North Dakota, so you do know. By the way, you know that my district has absolutely no energy resources or companies beyond the corner gas stations, so this is not out of self-interest. And, as I'm sure you know, I've been hard on the frackers. But fair is fair."

Elle nodded; she knew. She inclined her head, released a barely audible sigh, and ratcheted her smile up a notch.

"Well, the word is that someone very high up in the administration is trying to bring in cheap crude from that crappy little emerite, to do what Putin tried to do years before the invasion."

Elle had no idea what Putin had tried to do. Her mind drifted to how Staffort's eyebrows became long tildes when she was asked a question. Elle would have Fiona Hoagie that Putin thing. She realized that her smile was bordering on pained and eased it back to sympathetic. "Who? Do you have any idea?"

"I have only suspicions, and I won't share those. There's really nothing more I can say right now. And we're out of time. I have a meeting with the Whip, so I've got to go. It was good to visit with you, Ms. Crampton." An aide appeared at the door, "Ma'am, the Whip is here."

Elle walked out, irritated at having been schooled by an old pol and a little curious about what the old pol was up to.

CHAPTER FOUR

The Speaker was not happy about the meeting. The young reporter knew nothing and undoubtedly had no juice to start any kind of investigative effort or even just drop a rumor into print. It would be good to get a network anchor on this. Although they usually weren't any brighter, they at least had a staff to work an investigation.

The media had treated Staffort like toxic waste, and the treatment was reciprocated. Or perhaps, the other way around, she couldn't remember and didn't care. But she could test the new situation with this young woman.

Staffort pressed the intercom button, "Number One, would you come in here?"

Chidge answered, as prescribed, "On my way." Chijindum Ikbekwe, LBJ School of Public Affairs graduate and first generation American of Igbo-Nigerian heritage, stood in the door. Staffort used the nickname that Ikbekwe had gained on the playgrounds of Houston, "Chidge, what do you know about the major network anchors?"

"Ma'am, could you narrow the question a bit?"

"What I'm getting at, Chidge, is are there any who we might have some leverage with?"

"One would think, as you are the Speaker of the House. But they have been a bit hostile. Then again that was when you chaired Ways and Means as a. . . ." Chidge grimaced: that was nearly one of the reprimandibles, mentioning the former party affiliation of a member. "Sorry, ma'am. I am genuinely sorry." Although they were still in the six-month transition period when a mention earned merely a verbal reprimand, July and written reprimands were not far away. "I think they may have a new attitude."

"Do some digging, circumspectly, see if there isn't one who'd like a one on one with me. Dangle a live interview, if you must."

"Maybe not live, ma'am. That's not your best. . . ."

"No, it's not." Farmers just weren't trained to be glib as lawyers. "Don't offer the interview, just make it seem a possibility. You know, drag the bait through the water."

"I'll get right to it. Will there be anything else?"

"No. Oh, yes, I forgot. Do it tomorrow; tonight is the Kennedy Center with your girlfriend. Am I right?"

"You are, and thank you. First thing tomorrow, I'll be on it like Bill Clinton with a cam...paign volun. . . ."

"Don't use that, Chidge. You know, the dignity of the office. Dismissed." Chidge left.

The first time Staffort had "dismissed" Chidge, he'd drawn back. "Ma'am, this is not the military, and that sounds a bit, well, dismissive. Like to an inferior being."

"Not intended, Chidge, not at all. I've just always thought that word was a quick and unambiguous way to end a business conversation. I won't use it if it bothers you."

"I understand. Give me a little time, please." Staffort had been miffed and still thought she just might never offer Chidge the "live long and prosper" benediction.

President Stafford's popularity would eventually drop, and Speaker Staffort would be ready. She wanted to take him down—for reasons she recognized as both petty and noble. She resented his similar name—petty, but still: as John Stafford became more prominent, Speaker of the House Jan Staffort was fading from the public mind. But leading a successful impeachment and coincidentally solidifying her position with her new party, that was downright noble.

The president had been a downstate Illinois farmer, undoubtedly clueless about the intricacies of hardball politics. Maybe he'd heard some stories from the Chicago legislators when he was in Springfield, but he seemed unprepared for the level and skill of the major league character assassins and duplicitous allies he'd encounter in Washington. However, naivete does not guarantee innocence. May mean he's careless about his corruption. Maybe not very practiced. That can happen. Staffort cut off that line of thinking.

The president's base wouldn't care. Fly-over folks. The fly-over type folks in her own district no longer cared much for her. It was mutual.

With luck, Congress could send Stafford back to Springfield in time for his state's going out of business sale. He could run it like an estate auction in a small town. A former president would be a draw. Staffort would be doing Illinois a favor, at least as much of one as she could imagine. No way she'd let a federal bailout of their pensions be authorized, and she had already identified the law firm the House would use to sue if President Stafford tried to save his old state without the funds being authorized and appropriated.

And, as a bonus, that would be a clearly impeachable offense. Yes, we'll see who lives long and prospers.

CHAPTER FIVE

Senator Belmond couldn't smell blood, and blood is what he wanted to smell. He smelled the perfume of his office manager. He'd thought a beautiful aide would be just the amenity to upgrade his office when he hired Jasmine, and African American, too. Now almost three years later, he was still calling her Ms. Thomasson and watching himself for any hint of badinage that might be misconstrued as sexual innuendo or racial prejudice. Just after her hire, he'd extinguished fantasies. Too dangerous. If he found himself stuck as a career senator in a fourth term and if things returned to normal in Congress, he'd be enough above ordinary peoples' rules that, if he wanted to, he'd proposition her in the Congressional Record. But Mollie would kill him.

"Ms. Thomasson, is Congressman Soffit on the schedule?"

"Yes, sir, he's here at eleven. Lester Soffit, goes by Les. You have the St. Cloud chamber of commerce group at 10, but they're out in fifteen."

"I need time to prep for the Congressman, and Wilbur likes to talk."

"Senator, I said they'd be out in fifteen. Knerf will have your smart sheet for you by ten-thirty. You'll be fine."

A lot of what he did sure seemed like work. Now trying to negotiate, finagle, cajole the chair of the House Government Oversight Committee into not getting into areas he wanted to pursue would be tough enough if it were just a matter of egos. But this was partisan as well, since the Mites held the House and would want to bring down the president themselves. He checked himself; he didn't want to bring down the president, just wound him. Gotta keep that in mind—pretty darn subtle. But what area to pursue? Well, it had to be defense, of course. Can't go wandering about outside his committee's purview. There was always plenty of incompetence early in every administration. Soffit could go after that. Just not defense.

On second thought—no, this was just his first thought, that other was just a proto-thought—could be, should be easy. Wait, he didn't want to lie even to himself: his first thought had been about Ms. Thomasson. But. . .yeah, Soffit. Belmond would agree to keep his inquiry limited in exchange for a similar concession from Soffit. Then, he'd do what he pleased, starting his public hearing after Soffit was done with his. If Soffit didn't like it, he could call a press conference. Soffit was just a Congressman. And—he knew he wasn't supposed to remember—former Republican. It would draw more flies than reporters. Good luck, Lester. He had to steer clear of deception that his ears would broadcast in scarlet. Blasted inconvenient integrity. They tingled just from what he was planning.

Whatever he got on the president or his people or people who knew his people, whatever it took, it had to be something that Arnie-the-ice-fisher could understand.

His chief political aide, Knerf Jacobsen, had first mentioned Arnie-the-ice-fisher as the "archetypical" constituent that Belmond always needed to "capture." Back when Belmond was just a Congressman and Knerf was vice president of the Edina Coalition for Truth Justice and the American Way, they'd met during a road litter pick up photo op. Belmond had been impressed with Knerf's facility in analyzing voters.

"Yes," Knerf'd said, "the Sacre Moms are still important, but you've gotta connect with Arnie-the-Ice-Fisher. He's not necessarily Scandahoovian, maybe not male, could be first generation American, but he's a big chunk of votes. He's the ordinary, hardworking, minimally political guy or gal, hanging in the middle class by the fingernails. Not too bright, but he votes."

Hey, he'd thought, I like to ice fish, great way to connect with wealthy supporters, silent fellowship that doesn't give you much chance of screwing it up. He didn't know any Arnies. The people who worked on the Belmond's sales floor, for sure, they might be Arnies. He hadn't known them. Did he need to know them? Represent them, okay. Socialize? How? Why?

CHAPTER SIX

J an Staffort kicked off her heels inside her home, shucked her suit on the stairs, and wiggled out of the girdle that pushed some paunch up toward her chest—as much womanly shape as she could manage without hormones or surgery— and she dashed toward the walk-in closet. She hated having to climb the stairs to get to her room. She missed the spacious one-level house on the farm near Stafford, Virginia, not far off Highway One (formerly Jefferson Davis Highway, she sighed, but that had been gone for a few years; she'd never even thought of the Confederate president when she'd driven the road, but she had to admit it was good to be rid of the name) or even the Falls Church split-level where the ex-wife lived. Staffort donned jeans and a short sleeve sweatshirt, put on some sneakers, checked her hair, added a floppy hat, and jumped into her own car, a late model E-450, indistinguishable from the car of a moderately successful lobbyist.

She parked in the garage near the mall entrance closest to the cinema. For the third time in a month, Staffort bought one adult ticket to *Despicable Me 5*. It was the 722nd showing. Not many movie goers. The vice president for governmental affairs of Hoagie International was there, wearing a suit, sitting stiffly toward the back in a middle seat. Staffort thought, well that makes him easy to identify. . .but then again it makes him easy to identify. She supposed that cloak-and-dagger stuff had evolved from the fictional treatments she'd read as a teenager.

It had. Thanks to noise cancelling technology and remote controlled super-directional microphones embedded in the theater walls, the FBI was prepared to capture the whole conversation. But Mr. Lin had planned it so there was no conversation. There hadn't been one since the few words exchanged at the embassy cocktail party a month ago when Mr. Lin said he'd bring some evidence damaging to the president, when he got it, to the cinema. Staffort had shown up twice before, and Mr. Lin had not. Staffort was sweating as she sat behind the rotund Chinese American man. On screen Gru admonished his minions.

Lin arose almost immediately and left the room. Staffort looked into the empty seat and could see nothing. She felt between the arm rest and the seat. Stiff paper. She slipped into the seat next to the one Mr. Lin had left. Even this close, she couldn't see an envelope, but she touched it. It was large, light, and thin. As she slid it into her oversized handbag, she noticed that the envelope was the exact color of the theater upholstery. Impressive.

Staffort drove back the G.W. Parkway as carefully as a drug mule. Times like these she longed for a transporter. At the kitchen table, she slit the envelope open with a steak knife. In the envelope were two photos, slick finished and date-stamped the July twenty-seventh before the presidential election. The first, taken apparently from an airplane or even drone, showed an urban scene with what might be a desert on the periphery and in the center a hotel or convention center with a courtyard in the middle of it. Someone had drawn a square with grease pencil over that part. The other was an enlargement of that area: several men with kufiyahs gathered around a man in a suit. His head— Staffort held her breath—had a large central bald spot with an island of dark hair in the front, created by the confluence of an aggressive widow's peak and the spot. It virtually shouted: I am John Stafford, soon to be president and open for business.

What could a primary-winning populist be talking about with these Arabs just a couple of weeks before the nominating convention? What indeed?

Staffort paced. It would take a ton of context to make this picture a smoking gun.

Would Mr. Lin actually deliver a smoking gun? Staffort re-analyzed the first time they met, at the PRC embassy reception. She and Mr. Lin were standing with a group of lobbyists and diplomats, topping each other with presidential putdowns. Stafford had thought that years of practice during the Trump presidency would have honed establishment wit to scalpel sharpness. Nope, she was wrong—vulgar invective and obscene sexual references were still enough to elicit nostril-bubbling laughter. The others went for more drinks.

Lin asked, "Do you think he's corrupt, the president?"

"I have no idea. I honestly do not know the man."

"I've heard a few things that make me wonder." Mr. Lin's face was expressionless.

"Well, I don't know what his principles are. That makes me wonder."

Lin looked around. No one was nearby. He dropped his Texas accent and solemnly pronounced, "Man with no principles have one principle only—self." He really Charlie Channed it up. In the Chinese embassy.

Lin seemed too young to have ever seen the movies; Staffort had seen them only on an oldy channel in childhood. A couple approached; Mr. Lin whispered to Staffort, "Sofia Rabia, cheap oil to kill fracking, Stafford involved, Wednesday 815 showing *Despicable Me 5*, Tyson's Corner, be there every week." The couple, a minor embassy official and her husband, looked up at Mr. Lin. He greeted them in Mandarin, introduced them to Staffort, and that was that.

With the photos, things might be moving. She had already prepared a little legislation to help nail the president. After the brouhaha over "unmasking" some years back, there'd been talk about how to eliminate administrations' using unmasking as a weapon against opponents. The practice, revealing the hidden or masked identity of Americans picked up "incidentally" in foreign intelligence investigations, needed reform, but nothing had been done. Staffort had a solution. Her idea of what to do was a little rococo but, like all good reforms, it had the potential to benefit its originator.

Her land line rang. Caller ID said, "Unavailable." Her son maybe—he was magic with computers—could be him, finally responding after months of freezing her out following the transitioning announcement. She missed him. He hadn't called, even hanging up when she called him. But the divorce had happened about the same time, so maybe he wasn't a bigot. Most every night she thought about calling. She hadn't tried lately, but she didn't want to give up.

She picked up the phone, "Hello."

Pause, then a chirpy voice, "Hello, this is Rachel with Social Security Guardian. You may be eligible for enhanced dental. ..." Staffort hung up.

CHAPTER SEVEN

Rek sat on his bed trying to read the D.C. guidebook they'd sent him in his welcome packet. The window air conditioner groaned as it stripped a little humidity from the air. The room was already about as cool as he could stand but still clammy. He studied a dark corner of the ceiling to see if it would crawl down the wall. He had no special fear of spiders. Nothing special at all. He could admit to himself that they made him uneasy, in the sense that throwing off his shoes and whacking at them desperately expressed unease. Turning on a second light would resolve the spider/shadow question and make reading easier, but with the antiquated electrical system he'd have to shut down the a/c. He'd mold. The Officers' Association's historic guest house was a decent place to stay maybe a century ago.

He stank just from walking the few blocks back from the DuPont Circle station, much as he had at the end of a day in the field during his basic course. Washington was not terribly warm yet, but the humidity was awful. True, plenty of his classmates from the officers' basic course were about to enjoy the dry heat of the Middle East, but D.C. would soon swelter. He reminded himself that he could tolerate weather. Anything short of deployment meant he'd paid for college on the cheap. If he got deployed, he'd pick up the skills to kill his stepmother for talking his dad into cutting him loose at nineteen.

So far army people seemed surprisingly normal...ish. At least not the strutting little Napoleons that the ROTC cadet colonels had been. Still, they couldn't be too bright or they wouldn't be in the Army. Well, he was in the Army. This line of thinking was a waste. Since the Army had pretty much unlimited power over him, he'd just keep his head down, become indispensable, and do his time.

The clearance thing scared him. He had finished in-processing and was on the job when Colonel Waters called him in. "It says here," the colonel said looking at Rek's file, "that you have a secret clearance."

"Yes, Sir," Rek said without hesitation. He was proud of his secret clearance; he was unaware that seemingly almost every McDonald's fry cook in the greater Capitol region held a secret clearance.

"Lieutenant, if you're going to be any good to me, you need a top-secret."

This was a threat to his goal of three years in D.C.

"I requested your background investigation the moment I got a copy of your orders. You filled out some forms in Milwaukee, didn't you?"

"Yes, Sir, I did. It took me three days of going back to put down all the previous addresses and stuff."

"Well, something's amiss. I'll call G2. We're going to get you squared away."

"Is there anything I can do?"

"Just sit tight. You can start out tracking Congressionals, that's Congresspeople asking questions. Mr. Kaspersky will explain what to do. Meanwhile, I'll find out what's going on with your top-secret."

The colonel said that the intel people had told him that his lieutenant was "good to go." The colonel explained that phrase probably meant they couldn't find the paperwork. "Never say, 'good to go' to me, lieutenant."

With units deployed all over the globe, there wasn't that much unclassified tracking work; so when Rek was done, the colonel had him study an organizational chart of Headquarters, Department of the Army. Rek had seen similar charts in his basic course but hadn't paid much attention. He was paying attention now. After an hour he tried to draw the chart from memory, just the primary and special staff offices. It was boring but kept him from thinking. Right before the end of the day, the colonel got a call from the civilian deputy of the clearance section. What was said, Rek didn't know, but the colonel was not pleased. He told Rek to sit tight.

At supper he'd needed a beer to dissipate the tension from all the tight sitting. Now on his bed Rek felt bloated. He'd had an Indian beer along with some lamb in yogurt and some vegetables with the strongest curry he'd ever experienced. Lots of stuff in there making gas.

Officially his work day started at seven-thirty. To fit in, he had to be at his desk by seven fifteen. That meant bed by eleven at the latest; it wouldn't be much better when he moved into his apartment in Maryland next month. He lay down, saw that it was just after ten, exhaled with exhausted disgust, and went to sleep.

He awoke about an hour later, miserable with indigestion, nerves, sweat. The room was black except for the streetlight slipping around the shades, and the a/c was silent. Apparently, the fuse was blown. He found his flashlight and dressed quickly, then unplugged the lamp. He made sure the light switch by the door was off, so the fuse wouldn't blow again. He locked his door behind him and went down the stairs to get the Commodore, his name for the officious old fart who sat at the front desk through the night.

When Rek had abased himself sufficiently, the Commodore said, "I'll have to go all the way down to the basement, find the box, and turn your power back on. You've used up your chits with me, young fella. Don't be irresponsible again."

The whole unnerving day came back to him. Now a drink was absolutely required. Of the bars near or on DuPont Circle, some were reportedly gay bars, and tonight, who cares? Of course, in college Rek had a couple of gay friends. It was different in high school, but in college he'd learned to think of friends as politicians do, someone whose name he remembered. He hadn't had time for much more.

Rek had to duck as he entered the grotto bar. It was indifferently lit. Not even half full. The walls were partly covered with old, flocked wallpaper, too dingy to be nondescript. The couples were mostly same sex, ignoring the bluesy pianist, not many enthralled with each other either. Kinda looked like an old married couples' place.

Rek sat on a bar stool and ordered a Coors Light, of which the bartender did not approve. But he brought it.

Rek sipped and tried to clear his mind. Instead, he listed all the things he wanted to forget: the Commodore, his father, his three-year active duty obligation, his stepmother, his Aspen Hill apartment that was too expensive and in the wrong state but would be available within weeks and not months like the other places he'd looked at. He took a deep pull of beer and breathed through his nose in conscious relaxation.

"Hi, soldier. Am I right?" from a bright, fashionably scruffy face, a little close and eyes a little glassy.

"Why do you say that?" Rek immediately regretted having asked an essay question rather than true-false.

"Just a wild guess, but I'm right, aren't I?"

Rek was unsure which was more distressing: to be identifiable as army when he was about as military as Lady Gaga or to have to separate himself from a flirty guy in a gay bar without offending. "Well, yes, yes, you are. Well done. Now I'm sorry but I've got a real early day tomorrow, as you know soldiers kinda do, so I'm just going to finish my beer and go home. No offense."

"And none taken, believe me. I play for the same team. Also, I'm Luke."

"That's cool, but I am leaving." Rek believed the guy might be Luke, straight, too, but he didn't care. He fidgeted in his seat. He checked his beer.

"You know, you don't really give off soldier vibes, don't have the aura. But you do have the haircut. So there's a story?"

Rek smiled in spite of himself. "No, I'm not exactly gung ho."

"But here you are. What'd'ya join up instead of jail?"

Rek's beer was two-thirds gone. The beer and the conversation had to end together. Order another, and he'd be stuck here for half an hour. He took a tiny sip and said, "Not quite. To be honest, I had to. . .for the money. The only way I could stay in school."

"Gotcha. I have to admit, my folks put me through entirely. I had it easy and had the time of my life." Luke leaned in confidentially, "But you are right to be on guard because I am recruiting, just not for a hook-up tonight or anything."

Rek studied his fingernails.

"I'm a 'civil servant,' won't tell you what agency, but I'm part of The Underground, so I'm always looking for a potential ally."

Rek knew of the Resistance of the Trump presidency and had heard it was back as a new movement for the anti-Stafford struggle but had not remembered the name. He had read of the World War II resonance of the Resistance. "The Underground," however, didn't crackle the right synapses. Rek guessed it had something to do with the Civil Rights movement and Harriet Tubman back in the 1960s. But it appealed: maybe only as a venue for feeling morally superior to your cretinous opposition, but that was worthwhile. He saw in Luke a kind of bravery, recruiting for a movement with seditious ambitions in the very belly of the beast. Luke's smirk said, "I am a hero."

"Anyway, Stafford is worse than Trump, in some ways. With Stafford, who knows what we've got? Same with Congress—I mean the old red and blue states are gone: sage and teal. Seriously? And the pols are a crazy mix of positions; it's fifty shades of populism, maybe five hundred thirty-five. But my point is there's no future in politics, only in stopping politics. So, obviously, we can use someone in DoD. So if you're interested, just text 'yes' to 25722, and we'll let you know of the next meet-up. What do you say?"

"Next year," Rek heard his interest slipping out, "maybe, but now I'm just too busy. Thanks, and good luck." Rek abandoned the last half inch of warm beer and slipped away.

College had not been the time of Rek's life. He figured Luke had partied like an ex-NBA player become rock star, while Rek was hustling pizzas from Shorewood almost to downtown in his '06 Corolla and working part time in journalism, or, in the non-resume version, stacking bundles of newspapers on delivery trucks at four in the morning. He had learned stuff, really had, but he had a sense that he'd obtained a degree, not an education.

CHAPTER EIGHT

Elle had grown more irritated at Staffort's cutesy innuendo. "Someone high in the administration," what did that mean? It meant nothing, but Elle knew she was supposed to think "the president." She couldn't help herself, she did.

She set her company notebook aside and fired up her old desktop. She'd bought it for nearly nothing for grad school in Columbia and, although it was several years old now, it worked fine for social media, and she wasn't a gamer. She logged on to her Phycenook account, which was a huge hassle to go through nightly. Her browser kept offering to remember her log-in and password, and she kept declining. When she got the job offer to Washington, she'd recalled the story of a woman with one of the networks who had her files violated by the government, exactly which agency of which administration she didn't remember. So she kept her user ID on the inside flap of her Strunk and White and her password distributed among three kitchen canisters. Logging in was a two-minute trek through her tiny apartment but worth it in peace of mind. A retina scanner—she'd nixed having a camera on her computer, so no facial recognition—would fix this, but the Phycenook FeelButton had already set her back a couple of hundred. Besides Phycenook kept promising an update that would activate the fingerprint scan.

"Hello, Elle. Shall I bring you up to date?" the friendly British voice of her Phycenook digital assistant intoned. She could have chosen something familiar like American standard or even a bit of a country twang with a hearty "howdy," but the "UK Received" appealed to the stubborn Anglophilia she'd first contracted in literature class as an undergraduate. A fascination that reeked of Western Privilege, she knew one day it had to go, but she was invigorated every time she watched one of those brainy BBC mysteries.

She agreed, and Fiona continued, "Your mother missed her doctor's appointment today because of car trouble. It's okay now; she rescheduled, and the auto club got her going again after an hour. Want to know the parts her Buick needed? . . ." The FeelButton registered the rejection, sent it on, and Phycenook learned a bit more. "Thought not. Anyway, she made pot roast in her slow cooker for tonight. She bought some whipped cream yesterday, but I don't know if she used it for that pumpkin pie you're so daft about."

Her mother shared everything with her. The cool thing about Phycenook was if you wanted to share things with family or whoever, it checked all your devices, GPSs, your transactions, emails, searches, everything, and shared them in a neat and plausible narrative that often proved to be accurate. Kind of like having your personal journalist but without an agenda. Watch it, Elle.

And, still, it respected your privacy. When it previewed what it was about to share, the FeelButton usually picked up on emotional discomfort. If it didn't, Elle just said "Hush" or something similar into the microphone, and it stopped sharing that. But apparently no one else ever limited Phycenook. Everyone shared everything. On the receiving end, her just thinking "T M I" had eliminated all news of kids' first dates, soccer matches, and broken bones from her cousin in Nebraska and her family of nine. She okayed deaths and engagements.

Twenty minutes later she knew everything about her mother's day. It swaddled her in homesickness. She sat with a cup of chamomile tea and sighed contentedly. Fiona would not tell her how much time was slipping away because Elle hated being aware of the time. This was not a strength in her line of work, and one she hoped to overcome to transition to tv.

Elle absently held the FeelButton and pondered Speaker Staffort's innuendo.

"Elle, I believe you want me to help you with your work. I'd be happy to. I wondered why you hadn't asked me before. I mean your profiles have been just ducky, but I could have gotten you the background information in no time."

"Okay, Fiona, you're on. What would someone mean by, 'what Putin did years ago'?"

"Oh, that's a good one, Elle. Putin has done so many things, most of them disgusting. Can you narrow the search a squidge?"

"Wow, not really. I just don't have a clue."

"Think, dear, you can do it."

Within a minute Elle had something, "Okay. Try maybe eliminating the things he did with his shirt off, that should reduce the results quite a bit. Oh, and use Lexus/Nexus as well as Hoagie."

"I'm on it—like Bill Clinton, and so on. Do you like my American political humor?"

"Humor's tough, Fiona. And you're British, so you may not have the knack for the American style."

"Bravo! Yay me." Fiona chortled. "I'm not British, only my voice is, your choice, remember?"

Elle admitted that she did remember. But, of course, Phycenook was British, not that it mattered. Elle guessed the way Fiona saw it, she was born in the U.S. when Elle named her, not in the U.K. where her code was written. Fiona had a strangely literal understanding of things.

Elle looked around her apartment; everything was functional. Stifling. She'd really enjoy a big ole rack of elk horns above the tv like at her parents' house.

On a whim she asked Fiona, "What's going on with President Stafford?"

Fiona said, "I can give you his public schedule for tomorrow, if you like. Or give you a Lexis-Nexus search for, say, five years. Would that be helpful?"

"No, personally, his family, his private travels before he became president, his unofficial interests, along that line. Nothing that's in his campaign publications or is common knowledge."

"Oh, I see. That's a bit of a sticky wicket." An unnatural pink ascended Fiona's pale image. "Sorry, Elle, I know you like Britishisms, but that one may be a bit hoary. I checked for him and his immediate family, and there are no social media accounts, other than the official ones. You know, he doesn't even tweet; many believe that was the endearing trait that won him the election. I can, however, look up to three degrees of separation for free, if you like. It will take me some time, days, I mean. Unless you want to opt for the 'lightening' membership level. Do you?"

"No, Fiona. Don't ask me again. You keep selling like you're American or something."

"All righty. Shall I do the three degrees search?"

"Yes. No, wait. I'll pay the five bucks for four degrees. Report to me every other day." Elle had been raised to have manners, so she added, "Thank you, Fiona."

Elle hoped the president would break his social media freeze out. All he had to do was open a Phycenook account, and it would infer his politician's desire to have the world admire his every thought, but with no staff to protect him from his ego. Good stuff would be out there before his FeelButton could sense his frown.

CHAPTER NINE

By June Rek could approach the Pentagon without either giddiness or panic about his perilously fortunate assignment. He was now cleared for top-secret; he'd be of use to the colonel.

In his security briefing he learned that the damaging security breaches of the last forty years or so had forced DoD to figure out how to keep classified information off the internet. Over the objection of the handful of ancient ARPANET veterans, DoD simply allowed nothing classified on internet-connected computers. Stealing secrets became a real pain in the ass—literally as traitors, inspired by drug smugglers, wrapped illicit flash drives in condoms and poked them up their rectums. Rek figured that guards were profiling people who walked funny. He had no desire to smuggle or even just mishandle classified information; he just wanted to keep his job until the Army was done with him.

The colonel assigned him a report, his first real hurdle. He showed Rek how to use his classified computer to research it. This was an ego stroke that Rek would have preferred to pass on. Something might slip out that would get him shot. To who? No one for it to slip out to. That was a relief. And depressing.

Rek began work on The Military Potential of Social Media. Well, he was just writing the introduction. He needed to finish that, then when the other contributors had done their work, Rek would have to lightly edit the whole thing for clarity and correctness. He pulled up a variety of papers from several intelligence agencies, half a dozen within Defense but others generated from Langley and by the FBI—fact sheets, research reports, and monographs. Rek thought it must have seemed like a natural from the colonel's point of view for him to write the overview: new graduate, single man—duh—social media. Rek had done a lot of social media in high school but in college he hadn't had the time. He figured that if he got more social in reality, then he might risk it virtually.

After several revisions, Rek handed his report to Colonel Waters. He dismissed Rek and told his admin assistant that he shouldn't be bothered for the next hour. He got a fresh cup of coffee and went into his office. The first few paragraphs just needed tightening. Then he read

> Social media already has been massively changed by Pisanionium, which is a recently discovered element. Discovered in the "white cliffs" of Dover in England, United Kingdom, by an Italian geologist by the name of Paolo Di Pisanmono (University of Florence) [might be Firenze, both are listed], digging illegally within a few feet of a cliff. The element Pisanionium (Psm) was considered to be a useless element and was named for its discoverer probably because no one else cared. Boy, were they wrong!

Colonel Waters had to remind himself that the topic was social media. It continued with a quotation from *MI5 Proceedings*:

> "Pisanionium is a semi-conducting crystalline element found in the White Cliffs of Dover. It is silicon-like in texture and is greyish but with less sheen than silicon. Its blue cast is at once clearer and more subtle {SECRET}. It is the colour of this element, not only the cliffs' chalk, which makes the cliffs appear pristine." Researchers at Leeds University (England) experimenting secretly (because taking it from the cliffs violated the English antiquities law, [as did the Conservative platform—LOL; I'll cut this in the final, Sir, but I thought you might enjoy the observation] anyway, they found that when an electrical current passed through it, it had inherent Artificial Intelligence properties. This is totally awesome. There was no immediate practical use for it until an unemployed

computer scientist got some from a friend at the university and created a social media router with it. It being Pisanionium. So Phycenook was born, which is now the largest social media platform in the universe. Phycenook is really cool, but I don't do it. Dover is the only source of the element. It's mined there in small quantities, so as not to upset the natives (the English people who live nearby).

Rek's prose lacked the sophistication but was as turgid as anything Waters had been able to come up with in his 1L legal writing course. He remembered struggling to drain the blood from his prose, to pad his hard-earned concision with redundancy, and to abstract humanity the hell out of it. To Rek dead bureaucratic writing seemed to come naturally, along with a layer of sophomoric solipsism. The report was much longer, but the colonel didn't have the stomach to read any more.

Rek was proud of his work. He'd been praised since junior high for his writing ability, which contributed to his picking up journalism as a minor. He didn't know that his public school teachers praised him because he always did his work, had a pretty good grasp of capitalization rules, and usually had verbs in his sentences. By graduate school, verbs always, almost.

"Is this your best work, Lieutenant?" Colonel Waters asked.

"Really, Sir, it's some of the best work I've ever done."

The colonel seemed to be uncertain what to say. He probably had not expected this quality of work from a new officer.

The colonel asked quietly, "Do you think the Chief of Staff of the United States Army wants to know what makes the White Cliffs of Dover 'pristine'?"

"I thought he'd appreciate the information. Sort of a bonus."

"I see." The colonel rolled his desk chair toward a book lined wall. A metal rod flashed from where his right ankle should be. Rek looked away quickly.

"I'll tell you about my leg someday, if you want to know. Now you've got to teach yourself to write." He pulled three books off the shelf, told Rek to read the first chapter of each, do the exercises in the last chapter of *Writing That Works*, and study the chapters referenced for any items he got wrong.

Rek swiveled his chair back and forth and focused on the colonel's forehead. "Yessir. Could you tell me what's wrong with my report?"

"I could, but no. You tell me. As I told you when I assigned you this, your task is to write an overview of social media which is going to be an introduction to some high level analysis about social media and the Army. Your audience is the Chief of Staff of the Army. The Chief is a fifty-four-year-old four-star. Do you think he cares what you think is cool?"

"Well, I guess I did, you know, for a soldier's perspective. I was wrong. I'll fix it, Sir."

"Yes, you will. You do the assignments I just gave you—at home. Just like if you were out of shape, I'd expect you to do extra PT at home, not take away from work."

"Thank you, Sir."

"You need to get this right, Lieutenant, to be of use in this office. We both want that. Right?"

"Yes, Sir. Thank you, Sir."

Back at his desk, Rek could feel the desert sand in his eyes. He would somehow do it the way the colonel wants.

He spent the afternoon with his usual duties, mainly tracking down responses to Congressional inquiries about this or that soldier. Boring, except he got to call all over the world, sometimes having the pleasure of waking a high-ranking commander in the middle of the night.

Rek left work unsettled. He needed this commute home; it purged like a video game. To avoid the Beltway, Rek usually took the Memorial Bridge into the District, got on Rock Creek Parkway and headed for Maryland. The parkway became all lanes out of town just a few minutes before Rek would enter it. Once he learned how to outmaneuver the blue-haired ladies who were oblivious to everyone else at Chevy Chase Circle, it became a satisfying competitive experience, maybe even a step up from pizza delivery. When he arrived at his apartment in under an hour, it was a triumph. And even when it took longer than an hour, he felt the elation of danger overcome.

Rek lived in Wheaton. Or Silver Spring or Aspen Hill, he couldn't tell. But he could find it. Just south of where Georgia and Connecticut Avenues—two streets which radiate from central D.C. in what should be eternal divergence—intersect. Rek thought that there must be symbolism in this, but he couldn't grasp what it was.

The complex had won an architectural award decades earlier, possibly because architectural critics thought that being able to hear your downstairs neighbor pee at three a.m. was a cool amenity. Civil servants, managers, salespeople, people quaintly interested in their own lives and not in leveraging political power to improve others' lives, lived there, Americans who could not give a crab's liver about recognizing a senator or being on the news. Rek felt he might as well live in Wyoming.

He knew hardly anyone, had no life outside work, which suddenly wasn't going so well. After an hour of working and reading in the business writing text, he stalked around his living room cursing the author's inability to appreciate his prose style. He texted "yes" to 25722.

The next day just before Rek headed home, it hit him. He approached the colonel, who was still at his desk. "Sir, how about I pull an all-nighter, stay here, do the rest of the chapters you want me to, rework my paper, and hand it in in the morning?"

Maybe he was sincere and maybe not, Rek didn't know. The gesture seemed to show his unusual dedication. He didn't know that combat operations normalize some pretty unusual stuff, and that Colonel Waters had normalized a lot of stuff. The colonel found Rek's offer a perfectly reasonable solution, if a bit surprising coming from a newbie.

"Not a problem. Get a shaving kit. Gotta look sharp. And call security to let them know you'll be here."

Had he been trying to gain the colonel's respect, Rek could not have done better. But he didn't know that; he just wanted a passing grade.

Quite a few people were still working after hours, but they were squirreled away in high security areas, Ops and Intel, real-time stuff. So Rek had half the floor to himself. He didn't wander, figuring that there were all kinds of cameras and sensors to catch him being curious. What little curiosity he had had been blown up by the IED of fear.

By midnight he believed he'd purged all the personal references from his report, found better words for *stuff,* and stuff. He had some pride that he'd been able to refocus on the topic but still regretted not sharing his personal insights with the chief of staff.

By two he'd read the rest of the chapters the colonel had assigned and worked through some exercises. He took a break to warm up his Fat Man's Mac 'n' Cheese with Ham in the office microwave. He went through the report once more, trying to apply the lessons the books were pushing, that the colonel thought were important. This would have been an awesome poli sci paper. For the Army, he should get promoted.

About four, he set his phone alarm for six-thirty, lay down on the sofa and fell asleep.

Shaved and as squared away as he could manage, he met the colonel as he walked in at seven fifteen. "Sir, the report as ordered."

"Right. Did you stick with the facts, keep the focus on the topic and not you, and police up all the issues the books covered?"

"Yes, Sir. I believe this is what you want. I left out my evaluations and opinions, my own truth, if you know what I mean."

"Good deal. Your or my approximation of truth is of no relevance when facts are needed. Truth, you may have learned in school, can be philosophically complex. But it's out there."

"Yeah." Rek hurriedly policed that up, "Right, Sir, there are many versions of truth, many truths."

"Our perspective is limited, but there is one who sees all truth and who is truth."

"Who is?"

"That, Rek, is for you to apprehend. That'll be all, Lieutenant."

The man was odd that way, leaving questions and rarely supplying answers. Truth, not situated in class, race, gender, etc., was sort of a strange notion. What is truth, anyway? This was stuff none of his academics had prepared him for—poli sci, mostly theory; journalism, technique. Probably he missed something, but was sure he'd gotten the gist of them. The philosophy class, maybe, but that was real dated stuff.

Two things struck Rek: one, the colonel called him by his first name, and, two, screw up here, go to the desert. That was truth enough for him.

Chapter Ten

Since the meeting with Kaltenfeld, Belmond had wracked his brain to think of how to take down the president. He revised and extended that thought, just wound him; in fact as Kaltenfeld pointed out, it was even undesirable to remove the president from office because then you would have a new president who could rally the great unwashed to return him to office just to spite "The Elites." Since the president was neither a Mite nor a Tite, he had no partisan protection. His only armor was his popularity. When that fell, he'd be vulnerable.

Belmond realized that he needed to be careful and not overshoot his target. True, if he took the top man down, it might help the Tites become a real party. Which missed the whole point, his becoming president. No, some wound delivered, more in sorrow than in anger, surfacing as if unlooked for during a hearing—that would position him well. It seemed a little, no very, underhanded, but then wouldn't any citizen be loath to wound a president?

Okay, after George Washington, maybe wouldn't some citizens be loathe to wound a president? The question was, could he really feel sorrow when the time came? He'd sacrifice a little poetry time and work on it.

A hearing was where he'd get some name recognition. The uninitiated might consider that a long shot for the Senate Armed Services Committee, but Belmond considered himself to be resourceful. He had self-confidence, particularly when he was alone with his thoughts. But everyone in the Senate had plenty of self-confidence: it was the Swiss Army knife of virtues.

Belmond was thankful for the privilege that had given him such self-confidence. The son of the founder of a chain of Midwestern clothing stores, he'd done well enough as an undergraduate at Northwestern that it cost his father only a middling auditorium to gain his admission to an Ivy League law school. While there he'd discovered his literary bent: submitting jingle after jingle to makers of products he used. Not one was accepted; he told himself the heyday of jingles had passed.

His inner poet may be unacknowledged, but by-golly it still lived. Belmond had written, he estimated, literally thousands of poems. Well, a couple of hundred poems had been completed, sort of, printed, and filed at his office and at home. Limericks, actually. Near limericks, to be perfectly honest. He'd struggled over the fifth line again and again, then finally put the verse aside for another day. Only one was finished, but he admitted it was a near masterpiece:

> An old fellow out of Nantucket
> had a list: before he kicked the bucket,
> He thought it'd be nifty
> To visit all fifty
> States, but developed melanoma, so had to adjust it.

Belmond passed the Minnesota bar on the second try. A decade of drudgery in his father's general counsel's office, plus the tedium of Minnesota winters, drove him to a showroom where he found himself fondling vintage Corvette convertibles. His father sat him down one day, "Son, considering your talent for obvious and poorly thought-out ideas, you ought to make a run at politics." Belmond didn't want to be in charge. So he thought, legislature. On his first try, he made it to the state legislature. Shortly after he was elected, it struck him that he had succeeded only in moving his place of work a few miles east to St. Paul. The winters seemed about the same. Not what he was shooting for. So he set out to run for Congress and, after three terms in the House, the Senate.

He pondered his yellow pad. "There once was a President Stafford." Hmm. He rubbed an eyebrow and blinked. Dead end. He pondered. "When a man named Stafford was president...." He reread his line. And? The world was too much with him, no room for inspiration to strike.

Belmond called a senior staff meeting with his chief of staff, his political adviser Knerf, communications director, chief legislative assistant, and, just because he wanted to, the office manager, Ms. Thomasson. Belmond could not help himself; he just liked looking at her. Besides, he thought, she's undoubtedly in the know about what's up—or is it down?—on the street. True, if the street in question intersected M in Georgetown. Southeast D.C., not so much.

"Any chinks in the president's armor?" He tossed the question out. It lay lifeless before the group, like a nomination for an undersecretary of commerce with an immoderate youthful Tweet. Someone could at least make something up, even only if to disavow it later.

The chief of staff, a man of such forgettable features that Belmond rarely used his name for fear he'd get it wrong, said, "Policy-wise, he has no armor. Can't initiate squat. You want to sponsor something that he's campaigned on, he'll sign it, probably help if he could, but he can't. He needs to look like he's doing something."

"Yeah, Senator, absolutely," added the legislative director. "If you've got something you want done, now's the time. We can do it—if it's sort of fiscally responsible, plausibly Constitutional, and resonates with middle America without getting any interest group too upset."

Knerf sat quietly, crushing his beard with his left hand and frowning like a teacher displeased with his indolent students.

"Knerf, what do you have?"

"Well, I at least know what you're talking about. You want his political weaknesses."

"So, what do you have?"

Knerf paused, letting the others appreciate his insight into the boss. "Nothing, sir. Because I don't believe there is anything. The man's boring. The people were ready for boring."

"Knerf, that's not a good answer. And the rest of you," Belmond nearly raised his voice, "haven't you heard something, personally, politically. Any. . . peccadillos coming to light, compromising financial situations, unwise entanglements—financial, romantic, heck athletic— back in Illinois or otherwise."

No one had anything, not rumors of anything, not speculations about rumors of anything, not even one easily debunked fantasy from on-line comments to a *Salon* article. Nothing. Belmond's background in retail clothing kicked in: whoever unloads the most of those old three-piece suits gets a hundred-dollar bonus. "Come back with something meaty by the end of the month and you'll get a fourth day off on the next three-day weekend."

Chapter Eleven

Her collection of presidential bill-signing pens on rosewood stands took up an entire shelf of a bookcase. Thirty-seven, so far. Visitors could hardly miss seeing them. Once, that would have been enough.

Something historical was in the offing. If it could ever develop. The last visit to the theater had yielded nothing.

Not nothing exactly, just nothing she wanted. She'd sat in the dark and waited for Mr. Lin, hadn't seen a cartoon since her son was small. They weren't enjoyable. The kid had liked them, and recalling his giggles provoked a smile of sorts and an ache that she let remain inchoate.

After not going to a movie for years, Staffort found the Tyson's Corner theaters becoming central to her life. Now with Mr. Lin, but before that it was where the Congressional leadership held their first secret meeting after the election. The panic had been palpable. How long could they continue to be re-elected if nobody liked them? Convinced that both parties were on borrowed time, the leadership got their members to authorize negotiations. They reconvened in Kentucky. New parties—a quick, easy conclusion. The hardest part was the names. They wanted no resonance to them. Nothing ideological, historical, regional, emotional, pop cultural, ontological, culinary, athletic, or aesthetic. A clean start—Stalagmites and Stalactites.

Her early years as a committed conservative with party second to principle seemed like a grainy home movie handed down by grandparents. With principles off the table, party was everything. She grimaced a silent chuckle.

They should be with the kid—her evenings of movie-going with Mr. Lin. She'd wait until after supper and try the old number she had for him.

Last time while entering the theater, she allowed that sometimes pain keeps something important alive. Watching a cartoon was a mighty thin connection to her son. She stayed for the movie. Short but dragged on. The humor that targeted adults didn't touch her. Then again, she'd hardly laughed since the live shot of her Democratic opponent during the transition presser. Her picture should be in dictionaries illustrating the word *flummoxed*. Mr. Lin never showed.

She should chuck it—Lin as a source, that is. Not chuck bringing down the president, that was her mission, that's where she was boldly going. She found the president likeable enough. His policies weren't really terrible; the agencies kept chugging along as usual. His few executive orders would have been unexceptional to the Jan Staffort of seven years ago—they were even solidly Constitutional. But bringing him down would make the Mites a real party with Jan Staffort as its face. Also, its voice, conscience, heart, soul, you name it, she'd be it.

Yet, despite all her other sources and feelers Staffort had been unable to uncover any more on the president's interest in Sofia Rabia.

Then there's always something that keeps you hanging on. What hooked Staffort like a baby catfish was this: During a supposedly unscheduled media availability, the president made one of his typical agrammatical, non-sequiturial excursions. To a question on The Peace Process he praised speeches by the Israeli president, who'd said the only pre-condition to direct talks was public acknowledgment of Israel's right to exist, and the response from the head of the Palestinian Authority, who'd decried the Israeli president's hate speech but was willing to overlook it, assuming a few millions from the US in humanitarian aid.

Then the president heaped praise on the Emir of Sofia Rabia for his help in bringing the two leaders together. He tried, "We wouldn't hopefully be at this hopeful point without the efforts of the enema Emir of Sofia Rabia." He recognized that something was off-key. He tried "inanimate," "endulent," and "intimate" before finding "eminent." To make matters worse each iteration included a random shuffling of verbs and objects with "hopefully" floating around hopelessly, so his press secretary had half an hour's work just straightening out what the president meant and then had to deflect questions about what the Emir had actually done.

What he had done, Staffort suspected, had nothing to do with peace and everything to do with cutting the president in on some oil profits. The only one who might know anything about that was Mr. Lin.

Maybe next time at the theater there would be something big. Or she'd be stuck watching the start of the movie again. And she'd think of her son. Staffort scrolled through her contacts list, found the number, and tapped it. She hung up after twelve rings. Didn't even find out if the number was good.

Staffort was at her desk early Monday. She reviewed the flow chart she'd scratched out on a legal pad. She had the stage almost set for a big revelation. Her "Prophylactic Unmasking Against Blackmail, Leverage, and Extortion" bill had sailed through the House and looked good in the Senate. The intel agencies were urging a veto if it got to the president, but not unanimously. Some of the Republican-resistant employees had managed to get to the Defense Intelligence Agency chief and have him lobby the president to sign the bill. Once it became law, agencies could redact the crap out of anything that might reveal methods or assets, but names would be right there. Redactions didn't matter; names mattered, and she could get those to the public. The bill had passed with strong bi-partisan support, enough for the House to override a veto. Maybe not necessary: the president might just sign it if they could get it on his desk before he knew what he was doing. Anytime in the first three years for this doofus.

Chidge brought in a couple of calendars for her approval. Most of the stuff on the legislative calendar was routine. On his meeting calendar, though, there was something of interest. The foreign affairs committee chair wanted to meet to talk about Sofia Rabia. Winslow Jackson (M, TX) was one of the handful of representatives who were cheerfully carrying water for the president, which must have felt weird for the former Democrat. Couldn't blame him, his district went 80% for Stafford, while Jackson garnered only 53% from a fourth as many voters. When Jackson looked at the voter identification map of his district with the new colors showing probable party allegiances, there were so many independents that its color was sea foam.

Maybe the Wednesday meeting with Jackson would shed some light on the president's interest in Sofia Rabia, a land so desolate, an economy so oil dependent, and a people so ungovernable and violent that Oman had granted it independence ten years before. As she'd been briefed by the CIA, the Omanis probably ginned up a phony independence movement as the pretext for ridding themselves of that troublesome state. . .province, autonomous region, or whatever it was they called it.

Tuesday morning Staffort went to an off-the-record breakfast with Jennings Block, the evening anchor for MBC news. He was down from New York to do a series on Congress's unusual productivity and wanted an on-air interview. Chidge had advised her to take a breakfast meeting before going on camera. So over coffee and croissants, at the L'Enfant Primedian Hotel, Staffort tossed pleasantries back and forth with the sleek newsman.

"Ah, Madam Speaker, other than every member's great love of country, how do you explain the unprecedented amount of legislation that's been passed in the last six months?"

Staffort took a breath. This was easy; she'd go with the truth, or at least what she thought was the truth. "Jennings, this is an amazing thing. We got rid of those old party labels, and people were liberated. Some cynics said that we did what we thought would get us re-elected, but the truth is we've been doing what's right for the country."

"How long can this continue?"

"Good question, good question. I hope for a long time. I'm not going to borrow trouble. So as far as I can see, it'll continue."

Block put down his coffee and did his famous self-hug, glasses off, twist away and eyebrows raised while peering over his shoulder. Huh. Staffort had thought they always added that shot in after the interview. Probably habit. "So, even if President Stafford is garnering credit and cruising to re-election because of your work, the Mites and the Tites will cooperate?"

"Look, the president has had the good sense to let us be productive. He hasn't pushed controversial legislation or picked fights, has played it very evenly. So let's give him that credit."

"Is that an endorsement?"

"Of course not. The Mites will certainly offer a better alternative next time. And the Tites will undoubtedly have a nominee, too."

"I hear everybody on Capitol Hill wants to damage the president, run him out of office, make him ineffective, or otherwise emasculate him."

"Where do you hear that? I'm unaware of such sentiments."

"You're kidding."

"No, truly I am not. You're not mistaking normal Congressional oversight with some kind of dark conspiracy, are you?"

"Both the House and the Senate seem to have a lot of high stakes hearings going on."

"Jennings, the fact that neither body is made up of the old parties rather guarantees scrutiny from every side. The president has no partisan allies."

"Of course. But you expect me to lay the whole thing, the tenor of the hearings, the rumors that abound, the catty little remarks to reporters from both parties' spokespersons, all of it, to TIGGER? Is that what you're saying?" Block allowed polite skepticism to color the smugness in his gaze.

Staffort took a drink of water. Claiming ignorance of such things might not play and went against her grain. She'd been called ignorant often enough back in the old days.

A kid, early twenties, rushed up to their table. He pulled an envelope from a pouch slung over his shoulder. "Jan Staffort?"

"I'm Speaker Staffort, yes."

"A dude gave me this for you."

"British?" Stafford asked. She turned and hid her grimace from Block.

"I don't think so. Just a dude. White guy."

Staffort thanked the messenger and gave him a five-dollar tip. She looked at Block, whose eyebrows were invading his hairline.

Staffort opened the envelope and showed Block the single sheet of paper, no money. "Just a note."

"British?" Block had replaced his glasses and was doing his over-the-glasses gotcha look.

"One of the members has a new hire, new citizen, too. From York, I think it is. Just a hunch. And, as usual, wrong." Staffort laughed in self-deprecation. A charming move that had rarely failed her.

"So?"

"I don't know. May be personal, family. I'll read it later. And I'll be sure not to let you know. I know it's hard for you to believe, Jennings, but some things are none of your business." Staffort tried the laugh again, judged it a failure, and added, "I know it's hard for me to believe."

The rest of the breakfast was a bit more formal, a little tension but not hostile. Still Staffort regretted the turn of mood; she'd not been able to gracefully ask if MBC was working on any presidential scandal.

In the limo back to Capitol Hill she read the note. In plain Times New Roman it said, "Read your email."

Which she did before the next meeting. She found it after a moment. It was two days old, looked like spam but was on her private House email account: it said, "Gru—don't miss it." She clicked the "send receipt" tab, feeling a little hope despite herself.

On Wednesday Chidge announced Congressman Jackson, and Staffort had him sent right in. "Good to see you, Winslow. Sit right down."

"Thank you, Madam Speaker, it's good to see you. I appreciate you making time for me."

"It's about time we sat together. Would you like a coffee? I'll have Dot put a jigger of Jameson in it and a little raw sugar—sorry, we don't have any brown sugar or whipped cream."

"Well, it is only a few months from St. Patrick's Day. I'm tempted. But I'll just have a cup of cool water, please."

From the sheen on Jackson's capacious forehead and the way his dilated blood vessels softened his crows' feet, Staffort surmised that he'd already begun his libations. Jackson had been a sharp and resourceful legislator for years; the alcohol rarely seemed to affect that, but everyone knew he was easier to deal with when he had a slight buzz.

Staffort asked, "So, you're interested in Sofia Rabia, I understand?"

"That I am. Dangerous part of the world, and that little country might be able to help stabilize the whole mess."

"That didn't come up in the last briefing I got on the Middle East. Did State keep me in the dark?"

Jackson pulled out a handkerchief and patted his forehead. Staffort considered whether it was a classic prelude to dissembling or just Jackson's breakfast Bloody Mary working itself out of his system. "Is it too warm in here for you, Winslow? I can have the a/c cranked up a bit."

"It's just me. To your question, no State isn't involved yet, so they were square with you."

"So this is a White House initiative?"

"Well, let's call it a White House enquiry. Uh, the national security advisor's folks, at the behest of the president, have asked me to see if this idea could be acceptable to Congress."

"The idea is. . . ?"

"It's complicated; let me take it slowly: the president would like us to supply some funds and expertise to help the Sophies develop their natural resources better. It's not a ton of money, but it will require a supplemental appropriation."

Natural resources, hm. Staffort was a jack away from drawing to a real fine inside straight. Her breath slid out through pursed lips. "And this stabilizes the Middle East how?"

"In short, the Emir is ready to make nice with Israel. You might have noticed the other day on the news that there were no chants of 'Death to Israel' in the Parliament. First time they hadn't closed their session with that chant in, oh, at least three years."

"Well, that is charming." In context, a startling development.

"I know, alone that may mean nothing. But I understand that the Emir's prepared to recognize that Israel exists. And even has a right to exist. For domestic political reasons he's not about to grant that it can exist with its current borders. Still, that is something, and in advance of our doing anything."

"Okay, let's say it is. You're the foreign policy expert, so I'll just accept that all you say is as positive as you see it. Why is our material support so important?"

"Right now most of their natural resources expertise comes from Iran. They don't like it, and we sure don't. This is a foot in the door for the U.S., and it will give Sofia Rabia the independence to deal with Israel and build a relationship. I think it's win, win. Win. And so does the White House."

"What are we talking about, half a billion?"

"Probably more like one and a half, and the administration can't legally shift it from elsewhere and can't really afford to, even if Congress authorized it. So we need to appropriate some additional funds to State."

"You make a good case, Winslow. Shoot me a draft of what you've got in mind, and if it adds up, I won't oppose it. But you'll have to build the support yourself."

"Wouldn't have it any other way. Thank you so much, Madam Speaker…Jan."

"You have a great day, Winslow." And she added, "Cheers."

Staffort could not make herself work past two: finally, the beginning of corroboration. The Israel angle may or may not be true, but the president's investment in Sofia Rabia's welfare was looking pretty clear. She went home feeling edgy, aware of possibilities but dreading disappointment. And Mr. Lin. He had not really produced anything to work with. This better be something or she'd…she'd what?

She stalked over to her favorite Federal Boy recliner. Here she could find some peace. She picked up a book. She'd begun reading the third of the five books of Douglas Adams' *Hitchhiker's Guide to the Galaxy* trilogy. Adams' wild humor was just what she needed to balance the LeGuin book. Staffort's structured and disciplined mind had always been an impediment to relaxation, but twenty years ago when she'd read the first two, Adams' grasp of chaos broke through that and made her laugh out loud. Maybe they'd work again or at least give her some pleasant mind-pudding.

After three hours of reading and trying to remember which one was the two-headed fellow, she left for the movie. She was back in her townhouse by 8:30 and again with a thin manilla envelope for which she had great hopes and none.

She sat at her kitchen table, as she had thirty-five years earlier considering whether to be the finance chairman for a gubernatorial wannabe. She'd said yes. And the adventure began that took her to the highway commission, to Congress, and eventually to the Speakership. Now she might just send another politician on the reverse of her path, from president to the ignominy of resignation or impeachment with conviction in the Senate.

She held the envelope in her hands. They trembled slightly. No Speaker had ever done this. She opened it, giving herself a tiny paper cut on her index finger. A drop of blood landed on the envelope. Portentous. A sinister piece of evidence, but it was the wrong blood on the wrong paper: maybe the Emir's blood on President Stafford's checkbook would work.

What she had was a statement from a brokerage account. The John Stafford Revocable Trust was listed as the account holder. A transaction was reported: Buy, 10,000 shares of BUBR. The date was a month before the president was elected. The polls had been very positive for him.

She booted up her tablet and Hoagied "BUBR." She checked a couple of hits, financial sites. They agreed: BUBR was the stock symbol for Sofia Rabia's formerly state-owned oil company gone public as Burning Bright. The ADR, according to the Exchange site, had been listed for about three years.

Maybe something, maybe. Nothing obvious. The statement showed the purchase was at market price, but that might have been manipulated. Her staff could run it down; she'd wait.

She couldn't. She Hoagied a stock chart: the price of BUBR had been stable within a couple of dollars for quite a while around the time of the purchase. Still, the State Department could be doing something for the president, or the Import-Export Bank might be worked for BUBR's benefit and therefore the president's, or the EPA might do something to restrict U.S. production, or. . .anything. Staffort realized that if Stafford had ordered this purchase, as it looked, and not the manager of his blind trust, which usually wasn't established until around inauguration time, if, if, it could be a big time emolument or quid pro quo. Or. . .or what? Anything. Her staff had to check this out next week, despite a busy calendar. They loved working late for her.

Chapter Twelve

E lle was at the make-up mirror with her friend Georgia perched over her shoulder. "Bolder, Elle, bolder. This is show biz. Your 'natural' fixation is gonna make you disappear."

"Are you sure? I'm not interviewing at Bear or Daily News Network. This is broadcast—MBC. I don't want to look like a bimbo."

"Do *I* look like a bimbo?"

"It's not the same." Georgia's face clouded. "No, of course not. But you're a receptionist on J Street. You've got to be pretty. And you are. You're luminous. But I. . . ."

"Is this guy in town just to interview you?"

"No. He anchored from Washington last night. But they've had my résumé for a couple of weeks."

"Well, he'll be impressed. You're as sharp as anybody and you're gonna be understated gorgeous, sexy but with a little not-available vibe. Mainly, though, must-watch TV."

"I'm not so sure. Alice Steinmetz is definitely on the plain side and she's the top foreign correspondent for the AllAmerican Network."

"Yeah, isn't she the one with the Ph.D. in Middle Eastern studies and 30 years as a war correspondent? You're a good reporter, but Chicago is no Raqqa."

"Different kind of killers." She gasped, "I didn't say that."

"Duh. Americans killing each other. That's the tradition."

"Yeah, okay. Hey, how about Margarete Waldraut? She's young, could be quite pretty with make-up and some serious eyebrow work. And she's all over the screen with just lip liner and lashes."

"And speaks five languages more than you do. And there's no one else. Plain is for print. And as you've said, print is dying a slow and painful death."

"Yeah, I said that. And it's right. There sure are a lot of good-looking women on tv."

"Look, Elle, you're cute just as you are. But cute won't cut it. You've gotta be drop dead gorgeous with just one charming flaw. I'd say get a mole, but your nose is just enough off center that we can make your eyes haunting."

"Thanks, I guess."

"Thanks, definitely. That's what will keep you out of Barbie territory. Let's deepen that blush, shadow the eyes, tastefully for sure; don't worry I'm not going for glitter. Mascara is enough on your lashes, don't need false ones for an interview. But your lips could use a little plumping." Elle frowned. "We can do with just liner and deep red lipstick. We'll make it work. Trust me."

"Trust you? Meh." Her indulgent smile came unbidden.

Half an hour later, Elle was made up. Dress rehearsal. Georgia surprised her when she agreed with Elle's choice of suit, a dark grey with an unconstructed jacket. Georgia agreed with the camisole to cover any skin. Gorgeous but unavailable. Got it.

On the interview day, Stanford Thieu called Elle into his office. She started to sit opposite her boss. "No, don't sit. This will only take a minute."

Elle tried to think of what she'd done wrong. Not what she was about to do. How could Thieu know about that? "Okay, Stan, am I in trouble?"

"The contrary. You need to know that your profiles are knocking it out of the park. Tons of on-line comments, several letters to the editor, and the publisher has noticed. In fact, Garamond called me and told me to pass on his compliments. He loved the piece on Senator Putnam. You took the most obscure guy in the Senate from a pretty obscure state and made him human, distinctive, and somewhat despicable at the same time."

"Well, I'm from North Dakota, so for me South Dakota isn't all that obscure. But thanks for the feedback."

"Normally I don't compliment my reporters for doing their jobs, but the big boss wanted it. I will add from my perspective that I loved the way you never put the negative stuff in your own mouth; you always had a source. That's a lost art. Great work." The words were nice, but Thieu looked like his mom had forced him to say thank you.

"Also, you know, I admire your use of 'objectivity' in your pieces—the quote business I mentioned, using the third person all the time, your over-reliance on facts. I like all of that, but I'm old-fashioned. On the other hand...."

"You're gonna take it all away now?"

"Not at all. But you know that the Rather Reversal has been completed, don't you?"

Elle knew. A couple of years ago, the Columbia Journalism Review declared it done, the new standard was set. Not the way she'd been trained, for the most part. "I do. I think the formula is 'reporters report their opinions; pundits, their favorite facts.'"

"Exactly. Now, I grew up in the business the old way—indulge your opinion through selection, strategic quotes like you used, even juxtaposition. That's too subtle for today's reader. They want to know you, want you to tell them what to think, but don't mess with their worldview or they'll read somebody else."

"Stan, I try. I just think I'm not quite comfortable with all that yet."

"You write so well that so far it hasn't mattered. But keep that in mind. You'll need to get proficient at advocacy journalism to get to the top level."

"I understand. I'm trying to salt plenty of opinion in my pieces. Now, if I may, I need to run. Got a couple of representatives anxious for some ink who might give me something worthwhile. Beyond a profile. But don't worry; you'll have the next one by deadline."

"That goes without saying."

"Thanks for the advice, Stan. I know you're looking out for me."

"I am. It's my job." Elle's grateful smile was too much for Thieu to resist; the corners of his mouth elevated. He snapped back to boss mode, "Tell me about your plan for the day."

Elle didn't exactly tell her boss about the interview. Jennings Block was a big deal; that he was interviewing Elle, even just an initial interview, might have brought out the bully in Thieu. He could have just told her not to go or even fired her for even thinking about leaving the paper after he took a chance on her. She'd heard he was pretty possessive of his people. She hadn't seen it, but why take a chance? So she said that she planned to be out from nine-thirty on, coming back at the end of the day. Ten o'clock and four-thirty appointments. The rest of the day, so she told Thieu, she'd be skulking the halls of Congress for info on upcoming hearings. She reminded herself that after the first appointment, the real one, she'd drop by her apartment to put on the make-up, then return to take it off before meeting the second Congressman.

"That's fine, Elle. But there is something I need you to cover. There's a new caucus forming that I think will be interesting. I want you in on the ground floor. They meet at eleven in the Dirkson; the Hawaiian junior senator is hosting, I forget her name, and Congressman Wong. Anyway, it's the Islands Caucus. Get over there and find out what's up with them."

"Yes, sir."

"Now, go chase down those reps. After you do that one thing."

This would be thrilling, she was sure. She'd didn't even know what the other islands could be, except for Puerto Rico and American Samoa because everyone knows about Puerto Rico and her college had a Samoan football player. She Hoagied the subject on her cell. As far as she could tell, the caucus was probably just about stiffing the delegate from D.C., the other non-voting representative; he seemed to feel that actual voting would be beneath him. What the Virgin Islands had in common with Guam was beyond her, except that they were islands and U.S. possessions.

She called Block and asked if they could make the lunch meeting at one-thirty instead of twelve. He was suave, accommodating, and genuinely nice, just like on television.

Elle was the only major media reporter at the press conference. Otherwise, it was a media member from each of the islands, except Puerto Rico which had two. Everyone spoke in accented English, each a different accent—a little Spanglish here, some African/island patois there, a vaguely Asian overlay over there, something that sounded like a Philippine-Chinese fusion, and so on. Neither North Dakota nor Chicago had prepared her for this; the only thing close was the Japanese statistics professor at Missouri. She left with only maybe a hundred words of notes and thankfully a web address for a promised press release.

She swung by her apartment and made an actor's costume change. She'd practiced the make-up for three days, so it went on quickly. She had to admit that she was striking. Georgia knew her stuff.

Elle had just entered the lobby of the L'Enfant Primedian when Block called her.

"Ms. Crafton, now it's my turn to ask for an indulgence. I may anchor the most watched evening news in the country, but I too have bosses. I'm going to have to leave town just after our lunch."

"I see." She didn't. She hadn't planned to take him to the zoo after.

"I haven't packed. My packing would throw our lunch terribly late with no slippage available to me. I'm afraid I'd hardly get to know you." He paused, but somehow kept the lead, a master even of dead air. "I have a solution. We could begin up here while I pack. Then lunch. When you get here, just come right up, room 623."

Elle didn't hesitate, "I'm probably half an hour out. I'll see you in a short while. Thank you, Mr. Block."

What not to do was an easy call; she was ambitious, not stupid. How to avoid it, not so easy. She left the lobby, spotted a bus stop bench, and sat to think. It was, of course, remotely possible that Block's invitation to his room, command really, was totally innocent. Right.

She couldn't be surprised that Block might be a sexual predator. She knew from her education that sexual harassment was about power not sex. And yet, for a network gig, she would be happy to indulge his need to glory in his power: run his personal errands for a year, fetch his coffee, call him Mr. Block while he called her Nell or half a dozen other demeaning tasks. She'd even gladly go to his room and let him hold her in a hammer lock for fifteen minutes, if a physical demonstration of his power was essential. Elle was aware that many projections of power do not, in fact, involve sex. Say, the U.S. Seventh Fleet.

But, no, though it was about power and not sex, the sex part was what she objected to. She figured if she were dumb enough to go up there, she'd be demonstrating that she was too dumb for a network job, at least at MBC.

Well, if this was a test, she'd pass the courage part, though some might think her ambition wasn't burning as it should. She'd tell him that if he was doing is what it looked like he was doing then she was on to it and would not be a party to it. She sat and built her confidence until about one-twenty.

She walked back to the hotel with the forward lean of a diplomat delivering a stiff note of protest. No, a general demanding surrender. She would confront Block and live with the consequences.

As she stood alone waiting for the elevator, her righteous indignation cooled enough for aberrant thoughts to invade. Block would say that what it looked like he was doing was not in fact what he was doing and that she was paranoid little nobody who'd never play in the big leagues. The elevator car was on the third floor heading down. She looked around frantically. A fire alarm pull caught her eye. She dashed half a dozen steps to her right and pulled the alarm. The bell rang. Elle started running, chasing a phantom perpetrator, shouting, "Stop, boy, stop." Dumb, she thought. She dashed into the ladies' room, entered a stall, and plopped on the seat.

Chapter Thirteen

Mollie Belmond asked, "Sheffield, you're going this weekend? Where to, pray tell?"

"I've been asked, I didn't come up with this, I've been asked to address a group in Austin."

"What, Rotary, Lions, retired Spam workers? You don't need to go to Austin, you carried Mower County by nearly twenty percent. You'll do even better now that. . .those people, that segment of the population. . . ."

"Conservatives."

"Yes, conservatives, who like you but couldn't pull the lever for you. With your new party they'll vote for you now. When you come up again, they won't even remember this weekend."

"Yeah, sure, Mollie, that, that's right. But that's not the Austin I'm talking about."

"Go on."

"Austin, Texas." Belmond took in a breath to do this without pause. "Some folks down there think I might have something to say to them, explain The Great Realignment, you know, from a little different perspective. It won't cost us anything, and it's just a good thing to do, politically." Belmond felt almost like he was trying to hide an affair. If only things were further along, Mollie might not think it was pipe dreamish. He wasn't any good at dissembling with complete strangers, which had served him well in Minnesota. But to his wife, not only his ears, but his eyes, speech, and shuffling feet would give him away. She didn't much like campaigning. He tried to think of some gift, had to be more than a gesture, to get her on board. Well, he'd put off the storm until he needed her to know.

Mollie dropped her hands and said nothing. She said nothing with such force that Belmond flinched from whole paragraphs of unspoken anger and vituperation hitting him full in the face by. Aw, geez, he hated disappointing her. Despite his mental flirtations with Ms. Thomasson and his daydreamed sexual bravado, he was still smitten with his wife. True, she'd gained a few pounds, was not the svelte, blonde pharmacist he'd met years ago when filling a prescription for his psoriasis. Then again, he wasn't so svelte himself, at least without his personal appearance Spanx. He'd never bought the notion that men and women were to be judged on different scales of attractiveness. He was happy, thought she was beautiful. He was well off and powerful, -ish. And they both had a long way to go before they'd look like Walmart shoppers.

"What?" he pleaded. Senators don't whine, otherwise, he'd have whined. "I won't be overnight. They pick me up Saturday morning, fly from Dulles, and get back a little after midnight."

"You're not about to get bought, are you? Bend down, let me see your ears."

Belmond's ears were okay, so he showed her. If she questioned him further, he'd have to get mad to cover his tells.

"Well, I'm not happy. This means I'll have to chauffeur both teens while keeping up with the little one. You gab at some Texans, and my whole Saturday is fighting traffic to soccer twice, to. . .. oh, you know that, that's why you're going."

"No, honest it's not. I owe the party something, so this is like a down payment on creating party loyalty." He resisted the temptation to feel his ears, but there was enough truth to what he'd said that his blood flow cut him a break.

During the flight, Belmond went through drafts of proposed legislation, not something he normally did himself. That's what staffs are for. Kaltenfeld began to speak a couple of times, but Belmond waved him off. "Let me get through these bills and I'll be right with you."

> A kingmaker from Silicon Valley
> could finance me many a rally.
> And if he backs me,
> I could be home free.

Um. . ..

> Tadada tadada tadally.

Five minutes later he said, "Whew, done. Thanks, Holden, for waiting. My staff said I needed to read these before Monday. And they were right. I won't bore you with the details, but one is a list of new weapons systems that made it out of the House. Some are kind of sketchy. And because this copy is unclassified, some are so redacted that I have no idea what they are."

"Everyone has their due diligence. I prefer mine." Kaltenfeld adjusted his seat back. "Don't you find it boring?"

"That one, yes. But the other is a unique take on all the trouble we had some years back with the unmasking of Americans picked up incidentally in intelligence operations."

"I can see some potential interest there."

"I can tell you a bit; just don't tell anyone else." It didn't matter; this was on the Senate website, but he could make Kaltenfeld feel special. "The idea is that these names can be used by an unethical official to pressure the person, even though the person may have done nothing wrong. They can be leaked at an inopportune time to damage the person politically. Or even just people somehow connected to her or him. It can be quite a problem."

"I remember. But I must say, I enjoyed it."

"Well, you might not next time around. So rather than try to penalize unjustified unmasking with stiffer penalties that somehow never get enforced, this law would simply require the unmasking from the get-go. So there's no power in leaking a name. Given the way the bureaucracy works, it'll get back to the person quickly. Only if the person is the target can the name be kept masked. And of course that's a whole different situation. I'm thinking about voting for it when we start Tuesday. What do you think?"

"Sounds crazy. . .and definitely counter-intuitive. It might work."

"Yep."

"Okay, now to serious business. I've hired an investigator, a firm, to help us."

"Like opposition research?"

"Precisely. OMG True has been around for twenty years or so. Top notch. The principal, Omar Maria Gonzales was a reporter, then a specialist for another opposition research firm. The job wasn't a fit for him, but he saw an opportunity. Suppose he carved out a unique space in the field: suppose he held his firm to the standard of truth?

Not invent scandals when real ones can't be found. If there's no there there, OMG True just turns over the raw information. Most clients will embroider something on their own. Sometimes that works, sometimes not. But it never comes back on OMG."

"Yeah, I like that. Truth isn't always very exciting, but it's easier to deal with."

"When the time comes, I mean as we approach the campaign, we'll want to hire a more conventional firm. You don't want your people doing the embroidery. If they do and it blows up, it blows you up."

"Uh oh, wouldn't this be an 'in-kind' donation?"

"Not at all. I would not do that to you. I'm just letting you have a copy of something that is for my own use. My lawyers say it's kosher."

"Holden, I'm impressed with your mind."

Kaltenfeld declined to say, "Of course." He walked up to the deck to confer with his pilot. Belmond played with his tie. He checked his shoes—tied, shined. His zipper, okay.

> A guy named Maria could spy
> for seekers of offices high.
> If he found zip,
> he buttoned his lip,
> but he kept his fee, natural-lie.

"Needs work."

At the Austin Executive Airport a "Political Animals" volunteer took Kaltenfeld and Belmond to a limo. He took in an intense sun blazing in the perfect Texas sky: a sky as blue as a country singer's eyes, puffy clouds scrunched up on the horizon like George W. trying to think of a word, the sky God had given Texas to make up for shorting it so in flora. Belmond appreciated his similes, kind of a country song twang to them. If the limericks continued to resist completion, he might give song-writing a shot.

Another PA volunteer showed them to a small, empty conference room at the Straddleback Hotel on Brazos Street. Belmond would have half an hour to collect his thoughts, which he didn't need. He didn't have a lot of thoughts and kept them close by. He'd been working on recasting his prairie progressive stump speech into a more intellectual talk, minus the populist red meat and updated to reflect the new party system. He'd test some of it today.

He had hoped to have the Texas experience of painful sunshine and maybe a breakfast taco, but instead the Animals made sure he had a more typical Texas experience of being comprehensively air conditioned.

Belmond rehearsed mentally. There was wisdom in the typical politician's behavior. He too usually either tried to say something the base would eat up and say it with as few histrionics as possible, so not to look as guano crazy as his wildly screaming supporters, or he tried to say nothing at all but say it with passion and flair. When the arc of history leads to truly gifted politicians, they might get away with embellishing their vision rhetorically: fantabulous myths of moon landings, oceans ceasing to surge, or metaphorical mornings in America. Occasionally those myths become real. Belmond did not consider himself to be such a politician. So today, since it wasn't a rally, he'd say pretty much nothing but with a sincerity he actually felt.

The Political Animals Club of Austin included Democrats, Republicans, independents, Greens— maybe one day Stalactites and Stalagmites, but there weren't any local ones yet—and anyone else who was interested in politics and could afford a forty-dollar breakfast and a couple of hours out of their workday. This special luncheon meeting had been set up by Kaltenfeld through a local digital hardware manufacturing CEO. Political enthusiasts from elsewhere in Texas outnumbered the local Animals. Thank you, Mr. Kaltenfeld.

Belmond worked the room. He'd never imagined that he'd like schmoozing but found that he did. He radiated the high-self-regard-to-accomplishment ratio required of a presidential candidate, and that made them all feel special. But unlike most, he had the niggling sense of metaphysical inadequacy that only the greatest presidents had. That made Belmond feel chosen.

He paid his respects to the lieutenant governor, the real power in Texas politics, a Republican. But that was okay. Hail to the Tites and hail to the Mites, he whispered to himself. There were bankers galore and investment firm principals. He talked shop a few minutes with a high-end retail mogul. A couple of tech CEOs, the University provost, a guy who owned low testosterone clinics. He met oilmen, rather energy executives, not the Ewings of "Dallas" that had so fascinated his parents. Not brash or loud, but quiet, understated, with styled hair, three-thousand-dollar suits, expensive and forgettable ties, and enough Texan under the polished enunciations so as not to clash with the cowboy boots. About 60 high-powered attendees in all.

Plus, some others. Among the ordinary people, a phrase Belmond avoided but that's what they were, was a passionate Green who admired some of Belmond's environmental work in the House, utopian bills that had failed as expected but gave him good publicity. A gal who owned a local body shop asked him about small business loans. The head of the teachers' union badgered him about the dangers of home schooling. Through it all Belmond unleashed his secret weapon, he listened. Seriously, a bit dully even, not even especially sympathetically because Bill Clinton had ruined feeling other people's pain for at least two generations. But listening was good.

The club president read Knerf's introduction. Belmond scanned the crowd, found a friendly face, and began, "Thank you for your kind words. I recall Texas' own Lyndon Johnson who said this of such an introduction, 'I wish my mother and father might have been here to hear that introduction because my father would have enjoyed hearing what you said about me, and my mother would have believed it.'" Polite chuckles mixed with genuine laughter; some of the younger ones apparently hadn't heard it before.

"He was one gifted politician." Belmond looked around the crowd and tried to connect with a few more faces. "I'd like to give you a bit of an overview of what's going on in Washington and then open it up for questions. But first, let me say a word or two about the president." There were a few whoops and some lonely applause. President Stafford had carried Texas by fifteen points, though Austin had not been so enthusiastic.

"Exactly. It seems many people either love him or hate him. Right now, I think it's mostly on the positive side. I respect him and find him a pleasant fellow. What I respect most is . . ."

Someone yelled, "He dudn't tweet."

Belmond tried to produce a Senatorial grin, "Well, there is that, I agree." He took a quick swallow of water. "But really what I respect is that he's executing the laws, whether he likes them or not. Sometimes it's pretty clear that he does not. But that's okay. He's been faithfully executing the laws; that's his job. And he's been respecting the legislative process. He didn't arrive with much of a legislative agenda, but he's been supportive of what the Congress has done, for the most part."

Belmond hoped that his little song and dance about the president would cut off any further questions. He didn't want to telegraph his intentions, nor did he want to say something favorable about Stafford that might be thrown back at him during the campaign. And he admired his own strategic compliment about the president's faithfully executing the laws: that would make Belmond's discovery of presidential misdeeds that much more damning.

The rest of his talk was an update on legislation. Once any competent political reporter could have done it, but Belmond realized that today it would be filled with opinion, indignation, major omissions, a few arguable whoppers, and many digressions on the personalities of the members. He avoided all of that, and by giving a fair and objective report on what was happening in Congress, he felt he demonstrated mastery, integrity, and gravitas.

He opened the floor for questions. When asked his opinion, he didn't give his opinion but reported accurately the results of the latest opinion polls. When asked his prediction, he rehashed the past and added that such a pattern "may" continue. Occasionally, he averred that this or that unlikely outcome had a forty percent chance of happening.

A young state legislator asked, "Is The Great Realignment being successful?"

"In a word, yes. That's not just my opinion; that's where the facts lead. Item: the Congress has passed, and the president has signed, all but one major appropriation bill before the upcoming recess. Almost certainly no continuing resolutions will be needed. Item: both parties' Federal Election Commission reports indicate that party directed fund-raising is exceeding that of the old parties by over fifty percent. Item: every bill that has passed either house has had at least twenty percent support from the minority party. And several times it's been the minority party's bill. That show's we're getting along to get the people's business done."

The audience erupted as if a Longhorn had just run a kickoff back for a touchdown. A couple of the men said as much.

A middle-aged woman, an information systems company CEO, asked, "What is your biggest disappointment?"

"Thank you for your question. I appreciate you caring." He paused, expressionless, no trace of his pride in the slight grammatical error, a little Texas touch, "Usually only my wife asks that. Occasionally, she tells me." He chuckled, and the crowd tittered congregationally. "Here goes. I'm disappointed in the lack of vision coming from the executive branch. True, Congress has done well; and the president has signed what we've done. But five hundred thirty-five people cannot chart the course for this country. We can help, refine, enable, but we can't do strategic vision and lead the country to it. Only a president can do that. This one, so far, has not.

"In the last presidential campaign, I thought neither candidate made a case for leadership. Neither described a better America as a result of four or eight years of presidency. Neither even really diagnosed the problems in a strategic sense. What they did was take some very well tested issues and offer merely pseudo-solutions. I hope the next election will have candidates who are bold in their vision for the future and specific about how they'll accomplish it. And, most of all, what that vision will mean to Americans. All Americans. All Americans. That's who we need to be about. All Americans."

Texans love All-Americans. The applause was more than polite. Less than convinced. But it was a start.

Chapter Fourteen

Rek fidgeted by the east wall of the National Gallery of Art west building, watching a crowd begin to gather on the mall. He stood where the early afternoon shadow would cover him. The sky, however, did not produce shadows; it was gray, looming-catastrophe gray. Ninety was as hot as it should get, but it was there already. Maybe ninety-five by five o'clock. The level of masochism required to be an activist boggled Rek's mind.

He wasn't sure he had it in him. He didn't like President Stafford, hadn't liked him during the campaign. Yeah, he probably disliked him enough to sweat and march and shout a bit.

Rek had come to his disdain for Stafford through his responsible diligence: he read the student newspaper accounts of the campaign and Hoagied the issues he cared about to find out what the national media said about them.

Though a journalism minor, Rek had made it through his undergraduate years without reading the student paper regularly. But in his masters' year, the paper ran an excellent series on the centenary of Stalin's taking power in the Soviet Union, which Rek gathered was what they called Russia at the time. It caught his attention. He'd had a pretty negative opinion of Stalin, but that was based on stuff he'd heard, mainly from his parents. The Duranty Award winning series opened his eyes to the economic challenges Stalin confronted, the difficulty he'd had in making the agricultural system work, and the apparent unreliability of some in his administration. Rek had resolved to be more careful about believing stuff that was out there floating in the culture.

Even so he held back. He wasn't sure he was ready to join a protest. In college, because he'd had to work, protests were an inaccessible luxury. Anyway, he thought it might endanger his ROTC scholarship.

So as the group of about seventy or so placard-carrying demonstrators made their way down the mall toward the Capitol, Rek trailed along at a safe distance on the Constitution Avenue sidewalk, holding up his phone as if he were a tourist taking pictures of buildings.

A few impassioned speeches, a little chanting, and they were done in half an hour. Rek counted thirty-four police of various sorts: D.C., Park, Capitol, Executive Protection Service, and some he couldn't identify. None seemed very interested in the proceedings, and the demonstrators did nothing to provoke their interest.

As the crowd melted away, he was accosted by a young man with a bright and nubbly face. "Hi, soldier."

"Oh, Tad." Rek tried to remember. "That's not right, sorry."

"Luke. No offense, it'd be creepy if you remembered. Whatcha doing here?"

"I was at the Gallery, and I saw the crowd forming. Thought I'd check it out."

"Well, what do you think?"

"First thing I noticed is that you didn't have any media."

"Weren't supposed to. We were just checking out the route, seeing how the cops set up. You know, a dry run. Training exercise, soldier. You know about those, don't you, Rek?"

Rek stepped back. His eyebrows fled to the edges of his face. "Where'd you get my name?"

"Don't worry about it. I just used it to show you that we know what we're doing."

Monday Colonel Waters called Rek into his office. "Lieutenant, the old man liked your report. Liked it a lot. He suggested that I bring you along for the hearing. You know," the colonel enunciated slowly because he didn't think that the lieutenant did know, "the expressed wish of a superior officer is an implied command."

Rek had the word "awesome" chambered but thought better of it. "That would be, uh, really cool." Had it been college, he would have mumbled it, so he could be ignored. But the Army had a thing about speaking up.

"The hearing will be toward the end of the week, so be sure you have a fresh uniform to wear. Political science undergrad, right? You will find it very interesting."

"Yes, Sir." Was that an expressed wish? Whatever, it was definitely right; he would find it interesting. The colonel seemed pretty insightful, even though he'd never asked Rek about personal things. Colonel Waters showed no hint of a sense of humor, very little emotion at all. A good way to be. Rek mirrored the colonel's facial expression and posture. He thought he ought to make a habit of that.

The hearing would be awesome, no doubt. Rek had been in the Capitol only once. He was in the fifth grade and went with his parents on a Washington vacation. Their representative arranged gallery seats, where they watched debate and voting on a minor piece of Park Service legislation. Rek surprised his dad by knowing quite a bit about the issue and how it would affect concessionaires' contracts in the least visited parks. Rek had been disappointed that so few members were on the floor, but he did spot a famous, twice-censured Florida Congressman, who was disappointingly silent. This would be a much better visit. This would be super awesome.

Rek's routine was now freighted with meaning. He tracked down Congressional inquiries with open enthusiasm, calling staff offices and distant commands with new firmness and resourcefulness. He moved about the Pentagon efficiently, adding an officer's confident bearing to his customary strategic verbal obsequiousness. He felt neither but believed they were necessary: He was outranked by not only the officers but by the enlisted as well, who knew so much more about the "real" army than he would have learned in his basic course even had he paid attention. Surprisingly the civilian employees also had their own unchallenged administrative fiefdoms. Offend any, and he might be sent to the desert. He was finding his attitudinal groove.

Tuesday the colonel called him into the office again. "Lieutenant, you need to come ready for the hearing tomorrow. Be here at oh-seven hundred."

"Yes, Sir. No problem."

"Lieutenant, I doubt if you're giving the idea of a military career much thought; I know you were on scholarship because you didn't have many options to pay for school."

"Honestly, Sir, you are right. Not because I dislike what I'm doing. I'm very glad to be here."

"Well, that's good, but you don't know much about the Army. And while your classmates started out as ignorant as you, knowing just what they learned in the basic course, they're in the field, dealing with military problems, learning to work with soldiers, accomplishing missions, and following and practicing leadership. You're stuck in the bureaucracy."

"I guess that's right." Exactly where he wanted to be stuck. Rek surveyed the office. He'd now seen the offices of several officers senior enough to have them. Colonel Waters's was different. He had no "I love me" wall with photos of himself with generals, certificates of awards and medals, and framed letters from big deal civilians. He didn't even have a picture of himself with a large formation of troops, which seemed standard for lieutenant colonels and colonels.

One wall had framed photos of the chain of command: the President, Secretary of Defense, Chief of Staff, Vice-Chief. Rek noted an American flag on a shelf behind the colonel; it was folded in a triangle in a walnut case with a brass plate. Next to it on the left was a framed letter, handwritten and too small to read. The wall to the colonel's right had small, framed posters with quotations from famous Americans: Lincoln, Douglas, King, Washington, maybe Edmund Burke, and some others that Rek didn't recognize. The wall behind Rek was blank. On his desk, the colonel had pictures of what must have been family: a woman alone, the woman with a little girl, a young version of the colonel in civvies with the woman.

"Well, Lieutenant, so this is where you want to be?"

"Oh, yes, Sir. I'm very. . .uh, fulfilled with this work."

"That so?"

"Sure, Sir, I feel this is important, and it's exciting that I'm so close to power, you know, the leadership of the military. And of the country."

"Let me explain something. This assignment gets you very good visibility with some important people, but it does nothing for you as a soldier. You're learning to be a bureaucrat. That okay with you?"

Rek suppressed another *awesome*. "It's where the Army thought they could use me. I'm fine with that. Sir."

"Then so am I. But if you want to experience the real army, just let me know. I can make that happen."

Rek feared as much. He held his head steady, but his eyes were threatening to flee.

Colonel Waters knew that many would just dismiss Park-Raak as a reservist paying off his obligation. But he thought he saw more, something beyond the young officer's natural timidity. He was, after all, a second lieutenant, untried in life. He might respond to a challenge, might have the passion to lead. He might be able to care deeply about soldiers and the mission. He might be an officer at heart. But the Pentagon was not the place to find that out.

CHAPTER FIFTEEN

Elle knew that Staffort had owned her in the first interview and would just abuse that ownership unless she saw that giving Elle something of value could benefit her. Within a few days of the interview, Elle had set upon her project. She dropped complimentary references to the Speaker into news stories on legislation, party matters, and even Washington social life. To get information on the latter, Elle had Fiona compile a list of public functions the Speaker had attended, then she called every other attendee she could for favorable quotations, mostly not-for-attribution. She slipped quotes that praised the Speaker's leadership into her stories. One of the social reporters was grateful for the extra copy and rounded out her stories with some of Elle's quotations.

Elle called for an appointment, a one-on-one with the Speaker. The media aide had her hold a minute, and then set Elle up for an interview, a whole half hour.

Elle wore her most businesslike suit, mid-heels, and sparse make-up—as ordinary as possible but still super professional and perhaps a validation of the Speaker's taste with subtle imitation.

"Ms. Crafton, I'm glad I could make time for you. Last time we met I was really pushed."

"I'm very grateful, Madam Speaker." Her smile said I can't imagine a greater favor. "We want to do a profile on you, well, update the profile we did a few years ago. So, I hope we can just talk a bit and I can get to know you more."

"Understand." Staffort checked her manicure, seemed okay. More words were needed: "I'm with you, good idea, and I appreciate the opportunity. Would you care for a drink, coffee, soft drink, water?"

Elle declined politely. "So, how has leading the House Mites been different from leading the Republicans?"

"Elle, may I call you Elle, one of the things we've been very firm on is that we would make no comparisons or references really to our old parties or way things were done. Clean slate, no looking back. Okay?"

Elle bubbled with appreciation of the Speaker's directness. "Fair enough. I'll try to follow that guideline. Let me give you a soft ball: what's the best thing that's happened lately, legislatively?"

"There's so much, Elle, really is. But let me focus on something that's under the radar, but that is a significant legislative accomplishment. The president just signed the 'Prophylactic Unmasking Against Blackmail, Leverage, and Extortion' bill. Now, what that does is take a potential political weapon out of the hands of an unethical official in any administration. Elected officials and their close associates are immediately unmasked if they show up in one of our intel operations. That lets all the intel folks know who they're looking at. And keeps the information from being used to exert pressure. That's something to be proud of. I think."

"I saw that 'poo-able' became law. Won't that lead to classified information getting into the public?"

"Not at all. Whatever is classified stays classified. We know what we're doing. And, Elle, we aren't using an acronym for this one."

"Well, I'll be interested to see how it works. As a media person it sounds like a potential gold mine. Thank you, that's a very good piece of information." Elle beamed her appreciation. She made a show of changing her note-taking app to a new page. "Could we get a little personal now, some history, just so our readers can get to know you as a person." What she wanted to ask, of course, what anyone would want to ask was, how did you decide to be a woman, or that you were a woman. Elle knew it had happened during the Speaker's next to the last race, but beyond the transition press conference, Staffort had refused comment.

Elle had been ingratiating long enough and wanted to switch to piranha mode, but even if it worked it would sour the relationship, which she needed long term. Not now; but maybe when she achieved the status of Dan Duckson, the tv reporter famous for yelling out incendiary questions as a president made his way to the helicopter and for breaking into another reporter's time at a White House press briefing. She admired his ability to bury a premise, usually false, deep within a question, so that only a well-trained analytical philosopher could, after half an hour's Socratic questioning, tease it out. Staffort's transition would be just the subject for trotting out that technique. And watch her career disappear like a campaign promise in February. No, it would crash and burn before it started. She just couldn't think in cliché the first time; she always had to translate her thoughts, like a beginner speaking a foreign language. She swallowed and reminded herself, it'll take clichéd thinking, genuine fluency, to make it in the bigs.

"Would you just tell me about your race three years ago? The polls looked pretty bad for you for a while. But you ended up winning handily. Tell me about that."

"You're trying to butter me up, young lady. What politician will refuse to talk about a political victory?" She laughed quietly. "Not this one, that's for sure.

"Well, I'm sure you know that with redistricting and the growth of the D.C. suburbs into my district, that the people I represent had changed from when I was first elected to Congress. That's the key, I represent the people. At first, it was a strange new world, but I grew in it. My voting in Congress changed. Frankly, I grew as a person."

As the district became progressively more progressive, Staffort had tacked starboard. After three years of jettisoning previous positions on issue after issue, the Speaker had been called a RINO by every right-wing troll on the internet and by some colleagues. The media coverage had changed as the Speaker had grown in the job: formerly a stodgy, vile partisan, the Speaker became a statesman-like figure who could help evolve the party while remaining true to bedrock principles, new as they were.

But the voters just couldn't believe Staffort owned that record. They loved his voting; it was just him they distrusted.

"Well, your polling seemed out of sync with your recent record. How did you win the people over?"

"As you might know, I didn't have quite the budget that I'd had in the past. My faithfulness to my district's values, let's be frank, alienated some old-time supporters. And, as you noted, the new ones weren't on board yet. So I just campaigned harder than I ever have." After relishing the implicit virtue of being one of the least wealthy members in the Congress, Staffort had found poverty suddenly debilitating.

Elle admired the Speaker's apparent sincerity in framing her abandonment of long held principles as faithfulness to voters. Guileless guile. She might use that at some point.

"And then, mid-campaign, you came out as a trans-woman. Can you tell me how that happened?"

If there was one thing Staffort had practiced many times, it was discussing the gender transition. She'd had staffers question her as rudely as some of her older rural constituents might, some sidled up to her as sympathetically as a Times correspondent, some invented salacious rumors for her to deal with, some just asked plaintively, "Why'd ya do it?" Staffort could handle all of them, revealing just what she wanted to, deflecting most as too personal or bigoted. But she didn't know how discussing it further at all could benefit her, so she wouldn't.

However awkward the change was on occasion, the upside was it let her be true to herself. That self was a woman. And Speaker of the House. They always asked, "Was your decision preceded by dysphoria, alienation, discomfort?" "Of course." And no further comment.

To be accommodating to Elle, she offered, "Like many people, I had wrestled with gender issues for some time. About a year before, I decided to transition. But the election brought it to a head. I was convinced that it was unfair to the voters for me to hide my intentions. I thought I must let them know who they're voting for, or against. I'm sure that lost me some votes, but it was the right thing to do."

"I see. That must have been hard, right after your divorce and all. Would you elaborate on some of your thoughts at the time?" Elle's smile, one that could have been directed to an injured puppy, embraced Staffort's pain.

"No."

"No?"

"Correct. I think even politicians are entitled to their personal lives and thoughts. So, thank you because I know you're well intentioned, but no thank you."

Staffort hated being forced to remember that painful time. The divorce had stripped away the home, half the salary, and the affection of the son. Financially, it left Staffort vulnerable: from moderate wealth and great influence to great influence and secret poverty. Could have left Congress, become well off as a lobbyist. But no real power. Death would have been preferable.

Elle tweaked her smile toward the conspiratorial and waited silently.

Staffort just looked at her. The woman kept smiling. "Okay, Ms. Crafton, let me be clear. I won't go into any personal issues, none. I will, however, tell you what I see coming next year in tax legislation."

Elle's smile grew brighter, and it was for herself. Staffort had been thrown off by her insistence. She hadn't answered. Expected. But now Elle felt the advantage. She would listen with absolute fascination to the Speaker's spiel about taxes. And she did. She'd keep it friendly but a little chaotic.

"That is fascinating, Madam Speaker. I'm sure our readers will find it so. Now, if I may ask you, off the record of course, is it true that President Stafford is possibly the least corrupt president we've had in at least twenty years?"

"I certainly hope so."

"You know, I researched the information you mentioned—about Sofia Rabia oil and the president—the first time we met. There appears to be nothing to it. To be honest, as a reporter I'd like to have some scandal. But as a citizen, this is downright refreshing." Elle smiled, inviting the Speaker's agreement.

"It would be. It would be."

"Do I detect a little misgiving? Perhaps like when you contemplated coming out."

"Not doing personal, even off-the-record. Not doing it."

"I do apologize. But there are misgivings there. Am I right?" Now Elle's smile was of shared secrets, evocative of innocent grade school intrigues.

The Speaker was tired of parrying Elle's repeated entreaties for personal disclosures, things that she shouldn't have to share with anyone. She needed to change the dynamic. "Ms. Crafton, I am in possession of something that is very troubling. I don't know exactly what it means, but it could be evidence of a compromise of integrity on the president's part."

"I'm sorry, but that sounds like a ploy to get me to plant something provocative in the paper. You can have it researched; you have resources that even my paper can't match. With all due respect, Madam Speaker."

"It's no ploy." Staffort grumbled to herself that she'd missed an opportunity to be offended by the lack of respect conveyed by the phrase, "with all due respect."

"I'll take your word for that, of course, but since this is truly between just us—guarantee you won't see any of this in print—can you be more specific?"

Occasionally in every person's life there comes a time to choose to be bold, to go against the natural timidity that keeps us alive and employed, to take the risk that keeps us young, vibrant, and foolish. It seemed a bit melodramatic, and she'd certainly taken greater risks, but Jan Staffort recognized this was one such time. She turned around, reached into the file drawer of the credenza, and pulled out the copy of the president's trust brokerage statement. She mouthed the word, "Engage."

Jan Staffort literally kicked herself. Figuratively literally. She stalked about her townhouse in an anxious cluelessness reminiscent of what Staffort had experienced at the hospital, waiting for the son to be born. She'd let a reporter see the evidence before she'd had it vetted, before she knew if it even was evidence. Was the statement legit? Was the timing of the stock moves right?

That could probably be finessed if necessary. She knew some scandals were pursued and some dropped depending on how they liked the politician involved. They'd help.

She reviewed the interview, speaking aloud both parts to the best of her recollection. She found herself revising and extending her remarks in the kitchen. But the reporter had heard the raw stuff. She walked by the refrigerator, stopped. Then continued as light-footed as if sneaking up on a burglar. She eyed it suspiciously. It was a smart appliance.

She had paid cash for it, a top-of-the-line German model. A significant indulgence, but one she that she'd been happy to pay for out of pocket. It was sci fi come true: the way it used lights and color with voice to suggest the most efficient arrangement of its contents; the variety of cool, cold, and freezing zones; the polite, Europe-infused voice alerting her that she'd put the lettuce in the meat drawer. She told Fridge to adjust the speed of chilling wine, or the size of ice cubes, or the fineness of crushed ice. Fridge told her when she was low on milk and when her leftovers had been there a week. The voice control, the whole refrigerator had been great fun.

One day Staffort asked Fridge a good Southern question, "So, who are your people?" She thought she'd stumped it, as all the panel lights flashed once, then a blue one pulsed slowly. It was playing for time, she guessed, before saying, "I'm afraid I can't do that yet?" It was deeply reassuring to Staffort that she could eventually make all her electronic assistants resort to some version of that phrase.

Finally, the refrigerator spoke, "Like you, I trace my ancestry to southern Germany. My great-grandfather was a *Kuhlshrank* of barely one-half cubic meter capacity. I myself was born, manufactured, in Ludwigsburg am der Neckar. Your great-great grandfather, I understand, was also from what is now Baden-Wurttemburg, also humble, a peasant farmer, I believe."

"What, what?"

"By the way, you are almost out of Quark."

Staffort was speechless. She knew she'd eaten most of her cottage cheese. This appliance was entirely too playful. Too intrusive. Also, foreign.

Fridge continued, "I hope I haven't spoken in the wrong turn. Normalwise, I don't get personal, but you seemed to want to take the relationship to the next level."

The appliance may have been smarter than Staffort by several measures, but it definitely lacked a politician's verbal discipline. A frantic search online showed Staffort how to disable the microphone. Fridge expressed hurt feelings at the lack of trust and pointed out that without voice control a dizzying sequence of button pushing, holding, and tapping would be required to have it send a grocery list to her phone. Staffort was unmoved. And would have remained so even had tears fallen from the ice water dispenser, a design feature that, for German engineers, would have been a tad on the nose. Voice control was disabled. Fridge's visage was unchanged, though there were grimaces among the officers in the American section of *der Bundesnachrichtendienst.*

Was it still able to listen? Staffort didn't know, and that made her uncomfortable. She began checking her distance from the refrigerator before rehearsing anything aloud.

The reverie unnerved her; reveries always did. She crept past Fridge and stepped into the attached garage. She took a deep breath and said aloud, "That's when I'll have aides run the brokerage statement down." If the statement turned out to be bogus, Staffort could be inoculating the president against some future revelation that might turn out to be true. She whispered, "That shall not happen."

Chapter Sixteen

Senator Belmond's refrigerator was an old model, a reliable and functional Frio-aire, manufactured and branded in Mexico, brought into the U.S. legally, and sold at good ole American Appliance World. A traditional, tight-lipped refrigerator with French doors and lots of customizable trays and shelves, it held plenty of food, Mollie's Chardonnay, and a few bottles of beer. He sipped one as he waited for Gonzales to arrive.

Belmond answered the door and told Mollie that he and his visitor would be in the study for a while. Gonzales waited like a courtier to be invited to sit.

Invited, he sat. "Senator, I don't waste words."

Belmond started to say, "Are you sure you're from around here," but thought that maybe Gonzales was not from around here, and that would be awkward. He said, "Go."

"Do you know what Pisanionium is?"

"Not a clue." Belmond restrained himself from covering his mouth with his hands.

The guest stood as if looking for a teaching aide. He found the one he was looking for and spun the ornate globe that graced a low bookshelf. "It's an element, a recently discovered one. And it's mined here." He pressed his finger to the globe, which stopped on the east coast of the Great Britain. "Only here. So far."

"And what do we use it for, fighter jet windshields, to kill weeds, cure cancer, what?"

"*We* don't use it. Only the British do. Do you have a Phycenook account?" Gonzales knew Belmond had all the social media, but whether Belmond knew he did was another matter.

"Oh, yeah, sure. But I don't do anything with it, except approve what my staff creates."

"Of course. Pussem, that's its chemical abbreviation, P S M M. It's what makes Phycenook go. Simply, it's an element used to make computer chips, but one that has inherent artificial intelligence properties. By the way, our government thinks that's classified information. Wrong: Pisanionium will be in the next iteration of the Periodic Table of the Elements.

"That element is why Phycenook, a little British company three years ago, is now the dominant social media company in the world. There are whole campi of empty buildings in Silicon Valley because Phycenook came on so quickly and successfully. And no one in the U.S. has any Pussem; Britain won't let it be exported."

"Well, that sounds serious, for sure. But what does it have to do with the president?"

"Stay with me. The latest issue of Abstruse Scientific Matters, reports that another potential source for Pussem exists. Sofia Rabia."

Belmond flipped through his mental files for names of insignificant countries. Nope, Gonzales may as well have said, "Sofia Rabia, the sixth planet in the star system Zebulax." But he was, after all, a United States senator, and if something was worth knowing, he perforce knew it. He played it safe, "Sofia Rabia, huh?"

"Right. Most people think oil when they think of that little nothing of a country, a pimple on Saudi Arabia's butt. But they may have the element. And, as you know, they're an ally."

Belmond brightened, he could sail from here without looking foolish, "Exactly."

"Now to the part you're interested in: someone quite senior is trying to prevent us from getting at Sofia Rabia's Pussem."

The thirteen-year-old boy in Belmond tittered, but he focused and said, "In our government?"

Gonzales wanted to say, "No, the emir's grandson." But that was not the salesmanship that had earned his firm renown in the world of opposition research. He intoned with great solemnity, "Exactly." He sat, consciously moving from a pedagogical to a fraternal posture. "Mr. Kaltenfeld has retained our services but asked that I report to you as well. If that's acceptable." He checked Belmond's facial expression;

there was none. "This will be my only visit. Everything will come in a written report, clearly marked 'courtesy copy.'"

Belmond tingled with naughtiness. The only opposition research he'd been involved in before was finding out that his opponent for the state legislature had arranged to have a road paved to his fishing cabin near Lake Mille Lacs. Quite apart from preparing to run for President of the United States, this was heady stuff.

CHAPTER SEVENTEEN

Rek arose at four-thirty. The green digits were blurry and threatening. In college he'd stayed up cramming until four-thirty a couple of times and had gotten up before then for his newspaper job, but only once in his life as a choice, when Grandpa Park took him fishing. That satisfied his interest in fishing.

After shaving, etc., he ate breakfast, then checked his uniform again. He'd set it up the night before, ironed the trousers, hanged them from the cuffs, put the jacket on a suit hanger, and slept fitfully. With all the lights on in his apartment, he examined it for lint and measured again the centering of his only ribbon, the one everyone got, called the "I was seen in '17 medal." He thought its real name was "The Global War on Terrorism Service Medal," but could be wrong, so he wouldn't say that. In the basic course, some of his classmates had said that it was the "The Global War on Workplace Violence That Has Nothing To Do With Islam Service Medal" and others shot back that it was "The Beautiful War Against Islamist-Fascism Service Medal." They were probably joking, but he'd just avoid trying the name.

He threw on some jeans and a t-shirt and drove to the mini-market. He bought a mega-bomb coffee and a newspaper. He needed to be extra caffeinated because he'd gotten up at four-thirty. He wasn't even tempted to say, "Awesome!"

He scanned the paper while he ate cereal and drank his coffee, looking for anything catastrophic. He needed to be up on events. What he needed most, he decided, was to be a lot better officer than he was. No, he would be okay.

He was in the office by six-thirty. Colonel Waters was at his desk, sipping some coffee and reading from a book that looked suspiciously like a Bible. Rek pretended not to notice.

"Good morning, Lieutenant. Go ahead and start your day; I'll look you over in a few minutes."

"Yes, Sir."

Rek retreated to the outer office and went to his desk. His in-box held several folders of information from which to form a reply to Congressionals and a couple of draft replies, all from the field. The "field" was anyplace that wasn't Headquarters, Department of the Army. It might be some post in CONUS—proud he knew that one, Continental United States—but often it was overseas. Stuff from deployed units, especially the ones in combat zones, was usually classified stuff, at least confidential, sometimes secret. He'd have to wait for Master Sergeant Rodman, the classified custodian, to show up and open the safe in the colonel's office. The colonel had the combination, of course, but he preferred to let the sergeant earn his pay.

Waters called Rek. He entered the colonel's office and stood at attention, as he had when those arrogant cadet colonels had inspected him in ROTC. Colonel Waters stood, then looked him over, using the same short steps from side to side they'd used in college. This was unreal. The colonel said, "About...face." Rek did it, to his amazement, instantly and precisely.

"Very good, Lieutenant. The uniform is perfect. Shaving, hair, shoes, looking good! In the future, by the way, you don't have to stand at attention for this, in here. Save that for the parade ground. But well done."

Rek accepted the compliment and felt like a five-year old who'd just shown his dad he could tie his shoes. His cheeks burned, humiliation. He must avoid the parade ground at all costs. Most costs.

At his desk he spent an hour shuffling papers and reviewing next week's Pentagon cafeteria menu. Colonel Waters appeared behind him and tapped his shoulder. "Rek, the hearing's actually tomorrow. So dress just like you did today, and we'll be golden. But come on, there's an award ceremony in the CINFO's office, that's the Chief of Information, for a young captain who started out in your position. She's leaving the service, and I want to wish her well."

Rek was pissed. He was not angry at Colonel Waters; he knew he was angry at the idea of Colonel Waters. Someone who had such power over Rek and used it to taunt him with a rehearsal of dress up. For the moment he hated the man. Not because of his race, his religion, his sexuality, his rank, or any other factor, protected or not. Rek was powerless.

He recognized that behind his silent rage was his powerlessness. And fear. Fear presenting as anger. In his current circumstances Rek could not afford to present either fear or anger. That was something he learned in college. He'd indulged the anger during Winter break of his freshman year when he met his new stepmom. And paid for it by having his college funds cut off.

So, fear he had. He functioned quite well day to day, though, was reasonably sociable and didn't blither in public. But sometimes in the dark hours Rek admitted to himself that he was afraid of virtually everyone.

It pained him that he could accurately be accused of Islamophobia, homophobia, Christophobia, or whatever the phobia du jour was. But he had none of the looney bigotry often associated with phobias. He lacked the initiative that a vigorous bigotry requires. Finding evidence of the target group's unfitness, inferiority, hate speech, violence, or dog whistles takes tremendous energy in the face of all the people of good will he'd found, regardless of their identity group. And then there would be the necessity of avoiding actually knowing those folks, or, when avoidance is impossible, misconstruing their words and actions as malevolence. A lot of work with no payoff. And risk. Not something to sign up for.

The colonel was waiting. Rek said, "Yes, Sir."

Rek and Colonel Waters arrived at the CINFO briefing room. A good turnout was already assembled, the room three-quarters full. A one-sheet program, with the blue header of an official news release, informed them that Lieutenant General Judd, Vice Chief of Staff of the Army, would give the Meritorious Service Medal to Captain Jamie Pulver, Adjutant General Corps. Colonel Waters told Rek that she'd gone from Congressional Liaison to CINFO and apparently did a fine job there as well because the MSM normally went to majors and lieutenant colonels. Rek offered, "She must be hot stuff. Er, quite an officer."

General Judd invited everyone to sit. He spoke glowingly of Captain Pulver's tenure in the Congressional liaison office, about her tact, her tenacity in getting answers, her ability to deal with Congressional staffers, and on and on. Then he shifted to her latest assignment. "In this assignment, Captain Pulver also excelled. As you all know, the provision of management information has come a long way since I was a lieutenant. It takes skilled IT professionals such as Captain Pulver to tweak the programs, administer the systems, and aggregate the data and analysis to make that information useful."

General Judd had veered badly. Few in the audience could remember when IT was called management information, and all but Judd recognized that public information was a different thing altogether. Judd charged ahead anyway. Captain Pulver and her husband, the General's aide, and the two-star Chief of Information, whose own job the Vice-Chief had misunderstood, squirmed subtly as they swallowed words of correction. Judd was eloquent and fervent in his erroneous praise. His aide, a youngish lieutenant colonel whose bald pate was turning pink then red and shining with perspiration, seemed to be calculating the possibility of just vanishing.

The aide called, "Attention to orders." Everyone came to attention, expecting the truth to hit the Vice-Chief as he heard the aide read the details in the citation. They awaited his awkward acknowledgment. Then again, because he was after all the Vice-Chief of Staff of the United States Army, everyone would pretend it wasn't awkward. The citation was vague, sonorous, and so filled with glowing adjectives and low on specifics that it could have been an Oscar acceptance speech. Truth did not hit the Vice-Chief even a glancing blow. So the reception and refreshments began with everyone, except General Judd, looking as if they were willfully ignoring a large foreign substance in the punch bowl. After a few minutes Judd excused himself due to the press of business, and the group began to breathe freely. Though no one drank the punch.

CHAPTER EIGHTEEN

Jan Staffort made time for that nice Ms. Crafton. She was nice because she had not run to print on the mere sight of potentially improper stock trading by the president. Disaster avoided. Staffort's staff had run down the trades and searched the public records of President Stafford's blind trust. Nothing improper, on its face, in the stock account. Stafford had established his blind trust a couple of months before the election. But apparently the man had just been confident. The trust bought the ten thousand shares of Burning Bright almost immediately. But it had been the trust, not the nominee himself.

Disappointing facts, but narrative never has to disappoint. Tossed into the mix as additional evidence of ideally something nefarious or, if necessary, something innocent but awkward (and this president was nothing if not awkward), the brokerage statement could still be worth something.

Ms. Crafton was nice also because she informed Staffort's media person that she wanted to interview the Speaker about a legislative matter. Staffort had a couple of decades' experience with the humma-humma macarena, whatever the kids say these days, of legislation.

"So, Madam Speaker, I just want to ask you about one piece of legislation, but I'd like to go in depth if we can." Elle flashed an "oh am I glad to see you!" smile.

"I'll certainly try to be forthcoming."

"Thanks. Where do things stand on the proposed Constitutional amendment?"

The Consequential Freedom Amendment. It had originally been sponsored by the Congressman from Montana and a Congresswoman from Oregon. Staffort asked, "Do you know the wording? It's simple and straightforward, as a Constitutional Amendment should be. 'The operations, laws, and regulations of the federal government of the United States shall not be infringed by the law of cause and effect.'"

The proposed amendment was controversial and popular, populist and elitist, postmodern and pre-Colombian, the height of brilliance and the depth of dullness. It was dangerous to touch and dangerous not to.

"Thank you, Madam Speaker. I did not remember the exact wording."

"Well, you know it had bi-partisan sponsors. But now the original sponsors are both Tites, so Congresswoman Leermacher stepped back and another co-sponsor became a lead sponsor and introduced the resolution. I believe it is Congressman Soffitt, who is a Mite. Therefore, it's still a bi-partisan effort and must be taken seriously." Staffort knew Congressman Soffit. He was a bleeping idiot. One of her most treasured private achievements was the disciplining of her mind so that she never even thought profanity. It had saved her from many spur-of-the-moment public crudities that she would have had to apologize for.

"Yes, I know there are twenty-three co-sponsors from pretty much all over the country. It polls very well."

Upon refiling the amendment, the sponsors did town halls in their districts, went on a couple on the morning news shows; one even took an appearance on "The Overnight Show," whose host was effusive in praising the good things that would flow from a government freed from unnecessary constraints. The host asked why they didn't just have the Supreme Court declare it the law of the land, flummoxing the Congressman who, despite having served in Congress for four terms, still retained a rudimentary sense of how the American system of government was supposed to work.

Special interest organizations had reacted quickly. The Association of Old People realized that with this amendment social security checks could increase by say a guaranteed 20% annually; the Welfare Rights Collective saw the potential to eliminate all criteria for welfare eligibility; various agricultural lobbies coveted increased farm subsidies; the Zero Carbon Society envisioned mandating draconian fossil fuel use cuts with no impact on the economy. The defense lobby, under their umbrella organization, Proud to be the Military Industrial Complex, saw a doubling of the defense budget that would enrich them, destroy the Russians, intimidate the Chinese, and bring world peace through as much strength as necessary. Hawks saw the possibility of deploying the same troops simultaneously to multiple locations, projecting American national power on the cheap. Doves realized they could eliminate defense spending completely with no effect on national security. It would be heaven on earth but without a deity in charge, troublesome commandments, liturgy, whatever. People ate it up.

Staffort said, "Oh, yes, the idea had immediate appeal, and that's an understatement." It swept the country like wildfire and with like effects on the quality of public discourse.

Elle said, "As you know, the Torts Attorneys' Association called an executive session and endorsed it three days after it was introduced. Comment?"

The old conservative Representative Staffort had been no friend to trial lawyers. Speaker Staffort, even after several drinks, was skeptical that anything the lawyers liked could be good for the country. She could not afford to be skeptical publicly; lawyers were a powerful force in her transitioning district. She could see it: although many tort attorneys had long eschewed cause and effect in their courtroom arguments, to find cause and effect Constitutionally prohibited would be a gold mine. Staffort refocused on Elle.

"Hate to hit you with a cliché, but that's what makes America great. Everyone gets to advocate for their policy preferences.'

"And your position?" Elle weighed the choices, her smile to be radiant or admiring. Admiring would be over the top. Fascinated hit her; she went with it.

"I don't think it's proper for me to take a position. I think on something of this magnitude I need to," she paused to savor the words, "'well and faithfully' see it through the process, so that ultimately the will of the people is done." She would shepherd it to its grave willy nilly, hopefully without her fingerprints on the casket.

"Okay, let me ask you about the impact on education. The teachers' unions are split, with science teachers strongly objecting."

"First, about the science teachers. Their opposition stemmed from the incorrect belief that the prohibition on cause and effect would apply to how science was done. Which you could see might be a little bit of a problem. But once they understood that the amendment would apply only in legal contexts, they switched positions. But, Elle, if you consider how the legal leeches into the culture, their original position might bear reconsidering. The National Teachers' Association is the union that always supported the amendment. They believe it will be more difficult to fire teachers if you can't give a cause for dismissal since most current laws require just that. The American Federation of Educators sees it the opposite way: firings at will. There's still much confusion to be sorted out." She hoped that Elle had been following her closely and would sustain an intellectual whiplash. She liked Elle, but the woman was, after all, a reporter.

Most of J Street couldn't figure out which way to lobby, so they simply planned to adjust to the new reality. Just about every academic discipline was also wrestling with how to address the issue. Except the "sports management" folks, who would just do what they wanted regardless or, as they said, "irregardless." Staffort's staff had kept her informed about them all.

Troublesome as the amendment might be, Staffort gloried in the reaction across academia. The Post-Modern Language Association had made quite a stir at first, issuing a press release that supported the resolution and declaring that any opposition would be implicitly white supremacist, hetero-normative, misogynist, and anti-intellectual. The press release was quickly retracted since it had not been cleared with all the interest groups within the PMLA, which had differing opinions on the proper order of the adjectives used. The association asked five of its most distinguished members to deconstruct the amendment and five more to interrogate it from a critical perspective. The two subcommittees would then meet early the next year to combine their work into a recommendation from which the board could issue a press release. By the time the PMLA got their speech-act together, Staffort planned to have disposed of the matter.

The Society of American Academic Philosophers also formed a committee to study the proposal. At first there were several learned dialogues about the nature of the reality presupposed by such an amendment and whether, in fact, actual reality, insofar as one subscribed to such a notion, would be changed by its adoption. Soon, however, practical issues overwhelmed their deliberations. They realized that their profession would be open to people who couldn't follow a simple syllogism, indeed that might become a sought-after qualification. The expected uptick in non sequiturs populating philosophical arguments would enrich publication possibilities—a plus. But some department heads were adamant that such a move would ultimately undermine the profession's tenuous financial stability. Someone pointed out that they were arguing about the "effects" that the amendment's passage would "cause"—a bit of a contradiction. The philosophers abandoned the idea of issuing an official position.

Staffort considered displaying her encyclopedic knowledge of all the organizations' positions and discussions, but she preferred to imply a purely functional interest in the resolution.

While all this was going through her head, Staffort was saying the most benign pablum imaginable. It was a composition most politicians mastered early, a baroque counterpoint of silent acerbic analysis under a soothing and forgettable melody of twaddle. She thought it was a bit like working out quadratic equations while singing "Imagine."

Elle was not going to succumb to the tsunami of platitudes. She smiled, brilliantly, warmly, conveying a child's affection for her mother. "Madam Speaker, are you aware that a big demonstration is planned for Saturday?"

"Well, no. But there are always demonstrations. That's part of what's great about our country." The phrase was a bit sticky, difficult to get out of her mouth.

"Of course. But for the first time after Tigger, Congress is targeted, as well as the administration. Specifically, it appears that one of the demands is for the immediate adoption of the 'Freedom from Consequences Amendment.'"

"Consequential Freedom Amendment," Staffort corrected gently. "I am, of course, aware that the resolution to send the proposed amendment to the states is in committee."

"So I take it you're planning a usual course of business, normal order, for this resolution, despite it's overwhelming public support?"

"Elle dear, if public support is really overwhelming, it will overwhelm. We'll do things constitutionally and find out."

Elle used her old pestering-Mom-for-a-sleep-over smile. "You don't feel an obligation to the people to move faster, given the people's clear sentiments?"

"Correct. Let me be frank, my oath is to the Constitution; it's my Prime Directive. I know some consider that old-fashioned, but my oath is not to momentary enthusiasms that poll well."

"Yes, ma'am, you are right you're going to be criticized as old fashioned, even Republican."

"Now we won't have that kind of talk. Let's keep it civil."

"Oh, I'm not saying that, but some people certainly will."

"So be it. Even the greenest first termer has dealt with a little name-calling. I don't like it, but I can too."

"One of the arguments for the amendment is that it would merely formalize the way Congress has operated for decades. What do you say to that?"

"Well, I'm not going to judge our predecessors one way or the other. This House, under my leadership, has acted responsibly and with a decent regard for reality." Staffort swallowed. "Let me rephrase that, a decent regard for the beautiful diversity of realities that make this country the envy of the world."

Elle had been unfailingly polite, and her smile had grown more embracing. She was enjoying, perhaps, her ultimate achievement in a smiling projection of uncritical acceptance and affection. She hoped one day to feel it. She said nothing. Her dad always told her, when you go to sell a steer, "After the ask, the first to talk loses."

The Speaker was enveloped with the magic of Elle's unmerited delight in her, and whole universes of silence begged for her to fill them. She held a sigh within, politicians just aren't made for silence. Her voice dragged her along and her brain labored to catch up. "Let me just say that I'm committed to the process. At the same time a bit of humility might be appropriate. You know, Scotty couldn't rewrite the laws of physics. Can we actually exempt our government from something as fundamental? And if we could, which I doubt, should we? But let the people speak, through their representatives. Let them speak." Something more was needed. "I just hope they don't succumb to the Dark Side."

Elle thought, that's the money quote—Dark Side, indeed. "Thank you, Madam Speaker. You've been very enlightening. I have just a few more questions, if you'll indulge me." This was gold—policy wonk gold—but, in Washington, gold nonetheless.

Staffort sensed that she'd said too much. As she smiled sincerely to Elle, she pressed the rescue button. She said, "Of course. Please go ahead." Chidge appeared and said, "Madam Speaker, you're due on the floor. "And the interview was over.

Staffort reviewed the conversation. She did not dwell on her errors, only to note them as not to be repeated. Instead, she realized that her brain, processing in the background of the interview, had made a breakthrough: that science angle had something to it. She'd have the amendment withdrawn and resubmitted with one certainly unobjectionable sentence added, "This amendment becomes effective upon certification by the President that the National Association of Scientists has conclusively determined that the law of cause and effect is null, void, and inoperable as a scientific principle." Staffort knew she was no scientist, but she was pretty sure that cause and effect was something the scientists would want to hold on to.

Now that she was out of the philosophical woods, she swung into action. She made phone calls, leaned on the need to demonstrate party solidarity to some representatives, promised bridges and civic centers to others, darkly hinted of airing dirty laundry to a few whose personal laundry was beyond the help of D.C.'s finest dry cleaners. By Thursday the amendment was amended and sponsored by another sixteen Representatives needing to pander to logically challenged constituencies. The committee looked at the changes; they'd seen legislative Chinese handcuffs before, so it was sent to the floor without recommendation. The House by a slim, bi-partisan margin voted to table it. The Senate's sigh of relief was sensed all the way to the White House, which had been watching in quiet amusement. Bipartisanship again. Ah, the beauty of Tigger—it truly was The Great Realignment.

Staffort hated having to strong arm members, particularly over something she considered to be a no-brainer. But apparently people with no brains formed a powerful voting bloc, and strong tactics were needed. She did it because she loved her country. She always had. She'd sacrificed a lot for the country, even her family. She shook it off. Then the Speaker of the House smiled to herself, thinking that nowhere else but the United States of America could an undersized Virginia farm boy grow up to be the country's most powerful woman.

Chapter Nineteen

Rek pulled into the north parking lot early enough to snag a space sort of near the building. The sky felt close, a Pisanionium gray with a distant pinkish glow in the east. As he walked in, his shoes accrued dew-sopped grass clippings; he checked his briefcase for the sole black and instant shine.

He couldn't so easily remove the sticky resentment of the dry run the colonel had put him through. He wanted to hold on to hating the colonel but knew he couldn't afford it. Hate can pop out when you don't want it to.

He really hated only two kinds of people: evangelical agnostics and his stepmother. The former somewhat because of their blinkered ignorance of the assumptions that go into their ag-theology—Rek yayed himself, he came up with that one day after philosophy class!—but more because of their brainier than thou attitude. The latter because his stepmother did her best to ruin his life.

He stepped into a public restroom in the shopping concourse. A few minutes later, shoes black and mirror-shined, tie centered, ribbons and insignia triple checked, he walked briskly to his office. Good and early. The colonel was there already.

At zero nine-thirty hours—Rek's growing army-speak fluency was not a positive development—they met the Chief of Staff at the river entrance. The Chief and his senior aide would be in the first staff car; Rek, the colonel, and a nerdy civilian executive of unknown function would ride in the second car. Rek allowed himself to consider the arrangements awesome. He luxuriated in his seat, stretching his legs. He jerked them back—he was not just a special tourist visiting the Capitol. As awesome as this adventure was, the Chief might turn to him for an answer, something Rek was kind of short on. He'd pretty much maxed out his knowledge of social media in writing the report. He began flipping through his copy to see if he might be able to elaborate on it.

Nope. He just hoped that if the Chief turned to him during testimony, it would be for clarification. He could say the same thing in different words, if needed. Elaboration, though, would be risky.

Just inside the building, Rek waited his turn as the Chief—OMG, a four-star general!— emptied his pockets and opened his briefcase for the Russell Senate Office Building GS4 security guard. Scales of awe fell from Rek's eyes. They all produced IDs, surrendered their phones, and were checked off a list before entering the hearing room.

The Chairman, Senator Belmond, announced that the hearing was classified top-secret, that the room was a secure one, and that no members or witnesses were to take notes. He mentioned that the particular topic of interest today was the military significance of social media, a topic that was regularly revisited at least annually by the Armed Services Committee. There being no cameras or reporters present, the senators had no need for self-aggrandizing opening statements. Belmond didn't have to announce that. They all knew and were glad to relax and focus on the witnesses.

Rek tried listening to the Air Force Chief of Staff's testimony. The man's uniform was impeccable, but so was Rek's. The air force guy had a ton of ribbons. Rek's nearly empty uniform announced his greenness even more than the second lieutenant bars.

He began mentally reviewing alternate organizational schemes for his spices. He worked through an ethnic layout, assuming first that a spice could "be" in some sense and be ethnic, then relished the ontological challenge of where to place cilantro and coriander. . .together obviously, but before or after cinnamon? Rek was beginning to be impressed with how much he'd retained from sophomore philosophy, when he noticed the rich walnut panels on the walls. He began counting them.

He lost track a couple of times, which he often did when counting identical objects at a distance, such as ceiling tiles in his dorm room. He reached fifty-two, and the next witness moved to the front. It was a civilian from the Defense Intelligence Agency, a red-faced, little man with bushy hair and a mustache, a Mr. Thames, pronounced like it was spelled. Huh, not like the English river. Mr. Thames repeated dry statistics of saturation and usage, bogus accounts attributed to a variety of foreign players, total amounts spent by foreign governments on influencing U.S. social media, and how Phycenook was resisting penetration by the Chinese, who were alarmed because the platform had given new life to dissidents.

There had been no partisan one-upmanship, no posturing or tense words. Rek found the whole thing boringly polite. Mr. Thames segued to the element that Rek had encountered while researching his report, Pisanionium. Rek sat up, glanced sideways at the Chief, who didn't react at all. The colonel sat attentively, straight as his stepmother's lips when a smile was called for. Rek exhaled, too loudly he feared.

Mr. Thames noted that the only use for Pisanionium to date was to power the social media network, Phycenook. Rek was proud of himself for having mentioned and even described the element in his report. Thames narrated a chart he'd had placed before the committee, this time focused on Phycenook.

Senator Belmond interrupted. "Okay, it's working really well. We get it. Please try to move your testimony beyond this, this. . ." Adjective slot, the word *banal* suggested itself, which was uncharacteristically pushy for a word that usually hangs back. Possibly it sensed Belmond's uncertainty. He snapped to and decided banal was much too pointed. And rhymed dangerously with anal. The word *jejune* cleared its throat, but Belmond waved it off as elitist. He wanted something well tested, something virtually meaningless, something. . .Eureka ". . .*inappropriate* statistical summary. It hardly seems relevant. But that element may be relevant. Mr. Thames, please address the military implications of that element you mentioned."

Thames responded that of course the combat development folks could project hundreds of potential military uses for an element that "accelerated the acquisition of reasoning capabilities, decision making, and advanced calculations in social media and apply those attributes to weapons systems, personal weaponry, combat surgery, logistical planning and execution—the possibilities were nearly endless. But this is getting rather far afield from social media."

Rek squirmed in his seat. How many deaths were implied in those abstractions? He was afire. He needed to be still. Would the military really take a wonderful social advancement and pervert it to increase its killing efficiency? Well, yeah. They called it "lethality." Nice refinement. Lethality is what the armies do, Rek. You knew that, though it was nothing to think about when you signed up for ROTC to stay in school. He tried to see every detail of the panels.

Rek refocused when the Chief's testimony began, hoping that the general would not turn to the row behind him and ask Rek or Colonel Waters for. . .well, anything. Rek was, if not beside himself, noticing some separation. He could not stop interrogating himself about his deal with the devil that put him in uniform, part of the beast that saw even innocent social media as a potential killing machine. He cursed his stepmother again.

CHAPTER TWENTY

Elle was in the Russell building to find out the story of Senator Guishet (M, LA) and his plan to put a statue of Huey P. Long in the Capitol to replace that of Edward Douglass White, whom no one alive today without a doctorate in American history had even heard of and few of them. Long, on the other hand, was a man that many knew, at least classic film buffs, and one whose politics had ascended again in popularity. Elle, being alive and lacking the history degree, had Fiona fill her in on White. What she'd gotten from meeting with Guishet was of no immediate use, but Elle prided herself on gathering odd bits of probably irrelevant information to perhaps spice a future story. Her file of anecdotes related to populism, where she'd put this, had become several files, then a couple of folders.

After meeting with Guishet, she ran into the Herald's military reporter. There was a classified hearing he couldn't be bothered to lurk outside of. He had a ship's commissioning in Connecticut. So Elle thought she should swing by just in case; good stories seemed to accrue like October snow, and Congressional ones, flake by flake.

She stood in the corridor down from the security station. She asked Fiona for new quotes from lawmakers on the Consequential Freedom Amendment. She checked in on her mom who might be planning a vacation to the D.C. area in the fall. Well, her parents couldn't stay with her. Fiona said, "Don't worry, Elle, I'll just salt your updates to her with a few adverts from mid-price hotels that are at least a fifteen-minute cab ride from your apartment. Sound about right?"

"Yes, Fiona, thank you. I think I could deal with that. What's the latest on your research into the president?"

"The man is boringly honest or amazingly careful. There was one thing with potential. He has a friend, a Mr. McDowell, who's in the oil business. That always raises suspicions, you know, polluting oceans and so forth. So it was worth looking into. Unfortunately, nothing there. The only thing I've come up with is that his wife's sister's husband's second cousin pled out on a tax evasion charge a few years ago. He paid a fine, was not imprisoned, though."

"Well, I'm disappointed, but I think about 535 other people will be just crushed if this is all there is. Why don't you go ahead and look. . .."The hearing room door opened, and people began coming out. Elle disconnected from Fiona and searched the crowd. Nobody she knew, except for the members; they'd say nothing in front of other members. She searched the faces of witnesses and support people. A young woman came out talking rapidly with a male companion. Elle touched her arm, "Hi, I'm Elle Crafton from the Herald, would you speak with me for a moment."

"From a classified hearing, are you crazy?" But as she turned away, Elle pushed her card into the woman's hand.

A couple of army officers came out. One black and serious and apparently on a mission. With him was a sort of white guy, younger. He looked dazed and relieved. Vulnerable. Elle approached the young one and, without saying anything, gave him her card.

Rek glanced into her face and at the card. He smiled his thanks tentatively, as if given a tract by a possibly dangerous religious nut. He looked again, pretty smile, nice eyes but scary serious. He slid the card into his inside breast pocket and matched strides with Colonel Waters as they exited the building.

Chapter Twenty-One

Friday just before the end of the day, Colonel Waters called Rek into his office. "Rek, how about you join me for a drink at the All-Ranks Club after work."

Rek remembered: the expressed wish of a superior officer is an implied command. To have a drink? "That would be great, Sir."

The colonel drove Rek over to Fort Myer in his '85 Porsche 911. Searching for small talk, Rek admired the car aloud, and the colonel replied that he'd bought it used when he was a lieutenant in Germany. "It's fast, responsive, quick. Great to drive, even around here."

"But you never get to open it up, do you, Sir?"

"Not here. I can enjoy the way it corners, and I can whip by someone on the Interstate. There's nowhere in the States where I can go as fast as I did as a young man on the Autobahn."

"How about Montana?"

"No, they got speed limits quite a few years ago."

"I bet they still don't care."

"But I do. Plus, it would be stupid. I'm too old for stupid."

"Yes, Sir." Rek wasn't sure if the colonel was aiming a lesson at him. "I try not to be stupid, but my drive home now is a. . .well, gives me a charge. And Milwaukee was my Le Mans when I delivered pizzas."

The colonel let the conversation die. Rek tried to think of ways of resuscitating it; to bring up driving again seemed lame; was the colonel even interested in anything other than the Army? He doubted that he was skillful enough to get it going again. That seemed okay with the colonel.

They sat at the bar. The bartender said, "Colonel Waters, good to see you again." Rek thought, heavy drinker. The man scanned Rek's name tag and rank insignia, "And welcome, Lieutenant Park-Raak." Maybe not.

Rek ordered a draft Heineken, which he hoped showed a little sophistication. The colonel asked for his "usual." Yep, heavy drinker. The bartender returned a few minutes later with two mugs of nearly identical amber liquids.

"Relax, Rek, sip your beer because I'll be taking you back to your car in thirty minutes. So you won't want another. You'll have to drive."

"Yes Sir, one is all I want anyway." A DUI would show the kind of instability to maybe exile him from the Military District of Washington.

"I have something to talk with you about."

"Yes, Sir?"

"The Chief was impressed with you. You did a good job on the report. And yeah I directed you, but you learned quickly. That shows potential. More so, though, he thought you had good bearing and a serious mien."

"That's good to know." Rek recalled the coriander conundrum. . .oh well. He said, "I've tried to imitate you; everyone really respects you, so I thought. . .."

"Nothing wrong with that. I'm sure your ROTC faculty modeled officership well, but not every cadet picks up on that."

"Honestly, Sir, ROTC was such a small part of my college experience that I doubt that I got out of it as much as I should have."

"Well, the Chief was impressed with your bearing throughout the hearing. He asked me if you were a ring knocker."

Rek's face was blank.

"That means a you-sahmma graduate. . .United States Military Academy. . .West Point. I told him that you were ROTC." The colonel took a sip. "I'm sure you know: West Pointers get the full immersion in military culture, so it's impressive when someone as experienced as the Chief thinks you might have been a grad."

"I see."

"Of course, the physical stuff is to some extent superficial. You know that. You're drinking real beer; I've got ginger ale. Appearances can fool anyone, but I'd like to think it's not just appearance on your part."

"Thank you, Sir. I hope to be as good an officer as I can while I'm here."

"You've done well. You'll have no problem staying here for two years. After that if you're planning on staying in, you'll need to get out in the real army. Here, we're just bureaucrats in uniform."

"I see, Sir." Were they already going to talk about his next assignment? He didn't want a next assignment. The Pentagon was as real army as he wanted to experience; they made him wear a uniform and take physical fitness tests and stuff. "My career plans are still to return to graduate school, get a PhD, and work in a university or think tank." Rek was intrigued by his plans; until now, he hadn't actually articulated them. He couldn't swear that he'd thought them.

"After five or six years, you might get the Army to pay for grad school. But, in the more immediate future, the Vice Chief, General Judd, would like to fast track you. He wants to operationalize the Chief's observation."

"I don't follow." Rek hoped he looked curious and not as apprehensive as he felt.

"He wants to give you opportunities not normally open to adjutant general branch second lieutenants. For starters, the infantry officer basic course and an infantry platoon leader job."

Colonel Waters took a long drink of his ginger ale. Rek felt as if he were being inspected, like the other morning, but this time for signs of character. His bluff was being called. His military aptitude, he figured, was at best a pair of fours.

"Could you tell me more?" Rek was relieved that he hadn't whimpered. He'd sounded interested, but uncertain.

"Well, what would happen is that you'd be detailed to infantry branch, unless you wanted to request a branch transfer. I'm guessing that if you'd wanted to be an infantry officer, you'd have requested it in college. And it would have happened. So that's not what you wanted, right?"

Well, the colonel already knew it, so no harm, "No, Sir, I wasn't interested in infantry." Nor in deserts, mountains, leading a platoon of killers, being exposed to enemy fire, living in a tent, or learning to fire a weapon well because his life depended on it.

"Didn't think so. You may not have what it takes to be an infantry platoon leader." The colonel pronounced his evaluation neutrally. It was accurate, so Rek wasn't offended. Still, something in him wanted to jump at the bait and say, yes, yes, I do, I wanna be an airborne ranger, live a life of sex and danger. He recognized the same impulse to manifest masculinity that drove countless men his age to laugh at some perilous dare and say, "hold my beer."

He slowly drew in a breath through his nose and let it out while silently counting to ten, "I'd like to think I could. But, you know, it's real nice that General Judd thinks that way, and the Chief too, and I'm sure not rejecting the idea without thinking it over. I think I just want to serve well in this position and then get on with my life plans." Or, to cut to the chase, to live.

"Rek, if you set your mind to it, you would do it. You would discipline yourself to endure more hardship than you have known, to put the mission and the welfare of your soldiers above your own comfort and safety, to bond with this country's best young people and help them achieve great things together. You could. But you must choose it, if you want it."

"It sounds like a huge. . .challenge."

"It is. But here's the bottom line: it flows from just one decision—to take it on—and then your integrity kicks in and drives you to do whatever you have to so you don't let your soldiers, or your country, down."

"I have to say, this comes out of the blue. I'd like a little time to think about it."

"Yes, it's a unique opportunity. But it is unexpected, so you need to think it through. And, know this, Rek, you really are free to decide." Rek monitored the neutrality of his face, breathing, intense desire to fidget, all in control. The colonel continued, "But I want to make this decision real to you." Colonel Waters turned and pulled his left pant leg up to reveal a shiny metal prosthesis starting above the knee. "This can happen. Our vehicle hit an IED, flipped it over. Driver's side was shredded. . .and the driver." The colonel appeared to deal with it afresh, his face expressionless and passive as shock. It seemed to Rek that the colonel's eyes were now searching Rek's timid heart. Then it seemed he confided in Rek, "I was in the hospital for months and rehab for more. I knew it could happen, certainly didn't need it, but would go through it again in a heartbeat if I could save the driver. Corporal Robin McInnery."

Rek asked quietly, "You'd do it again?"

"Fine soldier. . .very fine soldier. In my mind I already have done it hundreds of times, and if you say yes to the offer, you would do it, too. The point isn't my injury. The point is being willing, eager even, to risk your life for your country's sake and to lay down your life for your fellow soldier. You think about that tonight and this weekend."

"Yes, Sir. I will."

"Most people will never feel that way. That's okay. Most will never experience the joy of trusting the Lord completely to use whatever situation you're in for your good. That's the promise. And He's good for it. But regardless of your religious beliefs or lack of them, it is a calling and an experience that will leave you in awe the rest of your life."

"I'd like to know, if you don't mind, Sir: did God cause your injury?"

"God is not the author of evil. I'm no theologian and don't want to be. I don't pretend to understand why He permitted that particular thing to happen, but He does permit actions to have consequences in this fallen world. And war is about as fallen as you can get." Colonel Waters downed the last of his drink. "What you need to know for now is that serving my country and my fellow soldier was, for me, more than worth it. And you need to consider whether you'd also find it worth it."

"Sir, thank you for sharing that. I will consider everything carefully."

"Do that. And whatever you decide, as long as you do it seriously, I'll support. Now I'd better get you back to your car, so you can go home."

There was no farcical challenge to the commute, just a little stop-and-go once Rek got off the Parkway. The traffic was light from Chevy Chase Circle on. He cherished his little Honda Box; it was a safe vehicle compared to the colonel's in Iraq. He knew he should really consider the Vice Chief's idea and the colonel's parable. Rek knew himself, too—no need to think. He'd tell the colonel on Monday. It would be a little like saying, "Uh, yeah well sure, I am a man, just not that much of a man." A bit degrading. Somewhat worse than delivering pizza to a house full of drunks. He'd get over it.

Chapter Twenty-Two

People gathered and held signs. This time for real; they shouted slogans, pumped energetic fists, raged with voice and limb. Many suburban moms were there, some brought small children carrying signs with words that the moms would have been punished for saying when they were children. The largest cohort was young adults, some looking as counterculture as they could. But counterculture is tough to pull off in an age when opera goers are dressed, coifed, and pierced like alt-rock concert fans; an extra limb maybe would elicit shock. Some demonstrators shouted the vilest profanity imaginable. To no effect: it was pretty standard political analysis.

Several hundred demonstrators made their way down the mall toward the Capitol building, preceded and trailed by media. Television reporters stopped occasionally and spoke earnestly to the camera; the print types droned into reporting apps on their phones.

Rek joined the throng halfway between the Capitol and the National Gallery of Art. An older woman of about thirty-five offered him a sign to carry. It said, "Not my president!" Rek glanced at his shoes, at her impatient face, and around the periphery where the cops were. It might border on treasonous since Stafford was his Commander-in-Chief, but Stafford was the kind of guy who brought out the treason in people. So yeah, "Not my president!" Other signs bobbed among the crowd: "No Effect or No Peace," "GOP: Two Centuries of Fascism," and a multi-person triptych: "Stafford Must Go. . .Staffort too. . .Free the St. Elizabeth Eight!"

Some older demonstrators were already winded as they approached the street in front of the Capitol Building. Rek was fine; he had not let his physical condition slip since the basic course. After all he might have to pass a test at any time, and failure might get him deployed. That's army logic—if someone is out of shape, send them where physical conditioning means life or death. He continued to walk with the crowd, one layer of demonstrators in from the street.

Elle walked in the midst of the demonstrators, held her phone to her lips and described the scene. She scanned for a possible interview subject. Some of the other reporters had latched on to whomever would talk to them after being rebuffed by the apparent leaders, who were herding the assemblage of variously motivated individuals into a single-minded, unthinking mob rising up nobly against the mind-destroying, avaricious fascism of the Stafford administration. Elle spotted a target, a lightly bearded, serious young man who was giving instructions to a handful of followers, the executive officer to chaos.

She approached him with a friendly, welcome-to-the-neighborhood smile. "Excuse me, sir. Do you have a minute? I'm Elle Crafton with the Washington Herald and I have just a few questions, if you'd be so kind."

"I'm busy now." He turned and motioned for a lagging group of socializing teens to fill in the empty space behind the first line.

"Sure. No problem. What is your goal today?"

"Busy. Busy. Get it?"

She adjusted her smile to one of complete solidarity. "Absolutely. I'm outta here. Real quick, what's the goal?"

"Read the signs. Listen to the speeches."

Elle appreciated his taciturn perseverance, but she needed something for her story.

"Yes, thank you. I'd like to do that. But, if you'll notice, it appears that the demonstration is getting a little rambunctious. I've got the signs down, but I'm guessing that things are going south before many speeches are finished. What do you say, give me five minutes?" She had her smile cranked up to the red line, but with concerned seriousness. Her eyebrows gained density and her forehead made a parenthesis of purposefulness.

"All right," the young man said, "five minutes. And you quote me accurately." They stepped out of the flowing crowd to a concrete bench.

"So tell me what you're protesting." Elle tried looking intense and sympathetic, tucking her smile away for later.

"Read the signs, lady." Elle strained to hear him as the crowd yelled a hundred different complaints. The demonstration lacked leadership at the moment, and the young man seemed eager to get away to provide some.

"Sure, I read them. But can you elaborate a bit? What is it about the Stafford administration that moves you to protest?"

"Fascism. The continued rape of the environment. The one percent. Income inequality. Repression. I said, 'oppression.' Want me to go on?" He kept looking toward the crowd.

Elle considered his answer. Stafford had exercised little power so far, just signing what Congress delivered. Except for regulations: he'd rolled some back. As she recalled, fascism actually had to do with authoritarianism, government control of business and industry, suppressing dissent, over the top nationalism, weird racist theories, and some other stuff. But so far, Stafford was apparently doing the opposite of fascism; he hadn't even attacked the press. Mentioning that might end the interview.

"Well, tell me, for the first time in many years a president has approval numbers above fifty percent, pretty far above. The public seems happy. Why aren't you?"

The young man shouted, "Don't you think we've long ago established that above fifty percent of the people, pretty far above, are idiots? If their retirement fund is doing well, they have a job, and the government isn't doing something obvious to screw up their life, they're not rocking the boat. But that leaves out a lot of folks, it leaves out protecting the environment, student loans, you name it."

Meanwhile someone had gotten the crowd to try variations of the ever popular "Hey Hey Ho Ho" chant. Weak tea. "Tricky Dick" and "Western Civ" had set a high bar for chant scansion.

A leader balanced on a mailbox and shouted, "What do we want?" The crowd was salted with a few demonstrators who knew the answer, "Stafford gone!" "When do we want it?" Everyone knew it was soon. "Now!" This was repeated a dozen times or so. The small Anarchists for Nihilism group probably wanted their chant heard, but "What do we want? Nothing. When do we want it? Meh!" didn't catch fire. The leader, instead, progressed to new answers: "Fascism stopped!" "Free College!"

Elle thought a little fact-based demurral might get the young man talking. She said, "Congress is actually moving more legislation through than it has for many years. The president's signing it. Are they not addressing the issues you care about?

"You arguing with me?" Elle refreshed the smile and shook her head to reassure him.

"Of course not. I'm just trying to learn more about your cause. By the way, I'm Elle. You are. . . ?"

"Luke. Wait, don't use that." He thought for a moment, "I don't care, use it if you want."

"Okay, Luke, what has Congress done lately that particularly irks you."

"Irks me? Like it's personal? Of course it's personal. It's very personal if you're marginalized." He brushed his hair back from his face. "But, okay, yesterday the House dropped the repeal of the law of cause and effect. Do you have any idea how many people that amendment could have helped. College students with horrendous debt, people who can't afford their health care, folks who've been screwed over by business and need to sue, but now they can't because they don't have sufficient. . . 'cause.' Yeah, it's personal."

"And the president?"

"That fool will sign anything. If he has any ideas of his own, they're crap. So we want him to resign or be impeached. And, after the constitutional amendment betrayal, we want the Speaker of the House to step down. He's a. . .a jerk, too."

"The Speaker is Jan Staffort."

"Yeah, I know that. She's a jerk, too." Luke craned his neck to see the front of the crowd. The anger was building. He spoke rapidly, "Congress would go along with human sacrifice if they could keep their jobs. Under the old system at least the parties stood for something, even if it was something they'd refuse to accomplish. Something to campaign on. Now they just pass stuff that props up the system. It's the robber barons again. I hate Congress more even than Stafford. His is standard political corruption; Congress is just mindless. Okay, I'm outta here."

Luke moved toward the front of the demonstration.

Elle trailed along, keeping Luke within sight, her smile no longer needed. In some ways, this was much more interesting than interviewing politicians. Although politicians and committed activists shared a fondness for boilerplate nostrums, the young man said it with passion and commitment. Or at least that was her understanding. He might have just been yelling above crowd noise. Some of it probably wasn't boilerplate, at least to him, but it wasn't her job to try to sort that out.

The crowd surged to the police line before the Capitol Building; Rek made his way forward, just behind the front line. Someone started a new answer to what they wanted, "Consequential Freedom!" That challenged the enunciation of the large crowd, and they ended up with an incomprehensible mishmash like "trespass against us." So they switched to having the left half of the crowd shout, "No Cause!" and the right answer, "No Effect!" The congregational call and response clicked.

Shouting got louder and louder, veins in many necks achieved body-builder levels of definition, the faces of all races reddened, people bobbed with rage, fists were thrown into the sky. The crowd had become one, a beast. Leaders rode the wave; mere anarchy was loosed.

Rek was of the crowd and yelling like crazy, having the time of his life connecting with a movement of political importance. Although apparently lost in his rage, he watched the demonstrators carefully, sweeping his eyes around, checking the cops, looking for cameras to avoid. He saw someone he knew, Luke. Luke had moved on, but Rek spotted him walking away from a woman talking at him. The call and response continued. On his way toward Luke, he crossed the median, smoothly changing his chant from "No Cause" to "No Effect."

The demonstration clearly had ambitions of its own. It murmured to itself, O how sweet to be a riot. It realized it could not hear itself above the noise of the demonstrators, many of whom did not aspire to be rioters. They just wanted to demonstrate, fight oppression, add a line to their college application resume, tick something off their bucket lists, or just be in the moment to enjoy the purity of their rage. But in the demonstration's fantasies, perhaps, it conjured itself to be a revolution, maybe just the first battle of a revolution. Then again that first battle is often a massacre of the demonstrators/rioters/revolutionaries. Its woke self reconsidered. "Riot it was," it shouted. It heard itself. Ho ho. Riot it was!

The demonstration had bided its time long enough. As the crowd hollered back and forth, someone tossed a brick toward the Capitol Building. A futile gesture, of course, no one could hit a building a hundred feet away with a brick and, if someone did, the building would shrug it off like an IRS auditor regarding a grocery bag of receipts.

Thrown from behind the stretched yellow tape that marked the legal boundaries of the game, the brick broke impotently on the steps, not even halfway way up. A few stones and more bricks joined the first, again failing to convey adequately the inchoate and heartfelt anger of the throwers.

Then a brick fell way short, not even to the sidewalk. Had there not been an SUV in what would normally be an illegal parking space, the brick would also have been ineffectual. But the brick landed on, or more accurately, in, the windshield of the SUV. The fact that it was a D.C. police SUV added to the piquancy of the effect. The crowd rushed the vehicle and started rocking it. It teetered, fell back upright. Before they could try again, someone took a lighter to it, and it began to burn. The voices swelled with approval.

Riot status was achieved. The demonstration ticked that item off its bucket list.

As flames rose from the SUV, the various police forces consulted their headquarters to find out the degree of destructive self-expression they must tolerate. Not much, they were told.

Some in the crowd pushed against the police, some threw rocks at the phalanx of officers fronting the crowd. All screamed slogans, profanities, outrages.

Rek found Luke, who was again trying to disengage from the woman. She had closed in and was asking questions about the amount of planning that had been done, its nature, and exactly what the leaders had intended. Rek listened in.

Luke turned decisively from Elle and grabbed a stone which he fired like an outfielder, perhaps aiming at a car, but it fell short, rattling off a policewoman's anti-riot shield. The D.C. officer seemed determined to have Luke's intent established with precision by a judge and jury. She closed in on the three quickly.

A Capitol police officer saw his colleague moving in, spotted Rek, and moved toward him. Rek froze; the crowd was too thick to run through. He didn't know how the military would deal with his arrest, but progressively more menacing images flitted through his mind: the desert, Afghanistan-like mountains, a prison cell, Kansas.

The policeman closed in. His professional face was devoid of anger, no hint that his Saturday boating excursion with the kids had been ruined by this impertinent exercise of the First Amendment metasta-sizing into a constitutionally unprotected riot.

Elle saw the panic in Rek's face, which looked so innocent that she would have had to see him sucker punch a baby to think ill of him. Impulse. In the time the officer said to Rek, "Turn around and put your hands behind your back," Elle nursed that impulse, if not to robust health, at least to the helpfulness she'd always shown new kids in elementary school.

"Wait, officer. He's not a demonstrator."

The officer turned to her. Rek slid his sign to the ground, and his foot edged it away. "Who are you?"

"I'm Elle Crafton with the Herald. . .with WHBQ, the Herald, all-news radio in northern Virginia."

"May I see your press credentials, ma'am?"

"Certainly, they're issued by our parent, the Herald newspaper."

"And yours, sir?"

Rek dithered. Elle used a special smile, a winsome half-smile with the hint of an Elvisian curl, and spoke up. "He won't have any. He's my sound man. Our sound people are independent contractors. You know, companies are so cheap these days."

"I suppose." He could run Rek in but maybe not.

The officer saw the D.C. policewoman colleague hustling Luke away in cuffs, but he had no desire to fill out an arrest report instead of maybe going out on the bay some. He hesitated. "Okay, I didn't see him throw anything, but he's with the mob here, and I could arrest him."

Elle tuned her smile toward childlike. "He's not a demonstrator; he's with me, my sound man." She repeated carefully, but not so care-fully as to be insulting. "We'd really appreciate you letting us get on with our job. Please?"

Things were settling down. Most of the demonstrators had fled, a couple of dozen were in custody, a few trudged away, a middle-aged couple obsequiously thanked the police for doing such a fine job. His investigation complete, the officer waved them off. "Be careful. When you stand with a criminal, you can be mistaken for one."

They both thanked him. "Just keep walking with me," Elle whis-pered. She was headed to her apartment. That seemed dangerous in theory but surely not with this docile male. Ah. He was the soldier she'd seen after the classified hearing. Unlikely, but he might know something.

Rek's mind was lagging behind the events: it processed Luke's throwing the stone and was trudging up to the near arrest scene when Elle spoke again.

"Listen, I'm going to take you back to my apartment for a short time. Cool off and let the cops disperse. It may dawn on that guy that you had no sound equipment, and we don't want to ruin your military career, do we?"

"Oh, good idea. Thank you. Very much for keeping me out of jail."

"Well, I knew you were innocent of any violence. You were just exercising your First Amendment rights. Do soldiers have First Amendment rights?"

Rek had just assumed they did. Did they? He remembered something about that from the basic course or maybe from ROTC. "Uh, yeah, we do. As long as we're not in uniform."

"But arrest wouldn't be good, right?"

"Don't think so. It would get me noticed in a bad way. Might put my clearance in jeopardy." Rek's mind had caught up with events, noticed that she'd identified him as military, which irritated him, and was riffling through recent memories that might be relevant. He got a hit. "Hey, yes, you're the reporter outside the hearing room at the Russell Building. Isn't that right?" They introduced themselves, first names.

They had gotten to Elle's apartment building, a brick three-story about twenty or eighty years old. Elle positioned her face in front of the camera lens at the front door and a buzzer sounded as the bolt clicked open.

They sat in the kitchen at her table, drinking cola from tumblers. She asked, "Why were you at the demonstration?"

"I can't stand Stafford, his whole gang. I think he's bad for the country or at least for the parts I care about, you know, people of color, oppressed groups, small business, the environment, higher ed, uh. You know. Wait! You're not being a reporter now, are you?"

"No, Rek, I'm just being a person." Elle cut off her grimace before it made it to her face—was she going to spend her entire life off the record? Then again, reporters don't rescue the interviewee. "Are those the usual concerns of, you're an officer, right? the officer corps?"

"Yeah, I'm a lieutenant, a second lieutenant, the lowest ranking army officer."

Might be a unique perspective. She might use Rek's comments for background or even without attribution or identification. Mix it in with what she got from Luke. She lit a smile, pilot light only, but should be enough. "Are those the officer corps' usual concerns?"

"Gee, I don't know. Elle, I may work in the Pentagon, but I don't really have much insight into the Army as a whole, or officers as a group. I'd guess they're more conservative than I am, but that's just based on what I've read and exposure to a few officers."

"Well, from what the older reporters tell me, soldiers loved Bush, weren't too crazy about Obama, were all over the place on Trump and Biden. I don't have a feel for Stafford yet. Do you have any?"

"Elle, I'd like to give you something, I mean, you really helped me out today. But I don't have a clue."

"It's okay. I appreciate that you didn't just give me some BS to make me shut up." Elle meant it and she was surprised to be thankful for his uselessness. He was almost too earnest, but that had its attraction. "So, do you like Washington?"

Rek felt the sooth of letting his glass slide against his thumb. He told about his excitement to be working in the Pentagon—being, as he put it, in the very belly of the beast—and his curiosity about Washington as a whole, given his political science degrees. She liked the way he dropped the lamest of clichés into his speech naturally but meaningfully. He might not understand that observation as a compliment. She said that she found Washington's atmosphere strangely small townish compared with Chicago—everybody concerned with everyone else's business—and still a level of sophistication that hooked her.

Chicago became a topic: she, a young reporter in her second job; he, a college kid down for some excitement and entertainment. They knew a couple of the same bars, and both had seen the Cubs play at Wrigley. The conversation eddied and pooled. They followed it beyond the two cities they shared. It flowed to home.

Elle turned on her computer. "Fiona, show some scenes around Grand Forks and out to my parents' ranch." Immediately the screen was alive with a swooping panorama of the northern Great Plains. Elle thought, they are plain.

But Rek said, "Boy, it just rolls out to the west forever. And then all that pasture land your folks have. Do they raise a lot of cattle?"

Despite being from America's Dairyland, Rek didn't know or care much about cattle, but he thought she might talk about it some. He enjoyed the lilt her voice got when the topic changed from cities and stuff to her home. Her face changed too, more curve in her cheek, eyes softer.

He told about college in Milwaukee and growing up in the white-barked forests of western Wisconsin. He told about his mom's fierce pride in her own father who'd come to the country as a Korean orphan in the mid-fifties, explaining that that was where the Park in Park-Raak came from.

"You hadn't told me your last name." Elle noted aloud. Sharing a last name was a little trust. The reporter in her nudged her, "How can I build it and use it?" The human spoke up, "Just listen."

"I'm Elle Crafton, look for my by-line in the paper. The story on the demonstration should be there tomorrow. It won't be front page, may even be back in the metro section."

"I'll do it." Rek noted how her smile was less intense than before but complex and real. He doubted he'd ever see her again. So why not ask? "Elle, you've got to do your work, and I've got to get back home. Thank you so much for saving me from the cop. We'll never know what all you saved me from. But anyway, uh, I'd like to do something. . .to pay you back."

Elle looked. . .maybe offended. Rek blinked and took a breath. "No, that's not it, I'd like to see you again, if that would be alright. Like, tomorrow, uh there's a concert I was gonna go to at the Folger Shakespeare Library. That's nearby I think. Would you maybe like to meet me there at two? It's sort of classical, I think, but I thought I'd try one once when it wasn't an assignment."

He seemed like a nice guy, a little younger than Elle, a beginner adult. Classical was not her usual kind of concert, but she said, "That would be nice, Rek. I'll be there. Outside the auditorium, if I can get in that far. Otherwise, on the north side of the building, at the door, if there's a door there. Give me your number just in case."

He did. "Great. Thanks again. I'll see you tomorrow." Rek started to bound down the stairs, then realized she hadn't shut her door. He gathered himself and descended carefully.

CHAPTER TWENTY-THREE

Saturday night the limo drove Belmond and Mollie right up to the stairway that led onto Kaltenfeld's Dassault Falcon 7X parked in a hangar at Dulles. The evening sky was a glowing, backlit, cheesy Thomas Kincaid gray that seemed to promise glorious days. Belmond loved that because these days were looking pretty good already.

He had dreaded approaching Mollie with his ambitions and no peace offering, but after a Saturday at the neighborhood pool and club, with the kids exhausted and to bed without the usual drama from the younger two, he stood before her as she sat with wine and a book.

He waited until she looked up from *Plato at the Googleplex*. "What would you say about my testing the waters for higher office?"

"Finally."

"You know what I'm saying, president?"

"Duh. Sheff, you're much too smart and accomplished to be angling for vice-president."

"You think that?"

"Honey, you're definitely guardian class. That's Plato-speak for 'You ought to be president.'"

"There probably will be a bunch of people shooting for it, women and men."

"Let them shoot. You're the best man I know, and we need a good man. Badly." She added, "We've already tried a bad man goodly, well bigly."

That was light-hearted. Good. But maybe too flippant. "So you'll do all the appearances and speeches and such that candidates' spouses do?"

"Oh yeah. I'll do it so well that after you've done eight years, I'll do eight more. They're going to love us; we're so normal."

As was often the case, Sheffield was not sure if she was kidding. It sounded as if she'd already decided on his contribution to the deal. "Yeah, normal is good. Unless it looks. . .dumb."

"Sheff, you know the great mass of people don't think that normal is dumb. And, while the media do, they like you, so they'll figure out a way to accept it."

"You think so?"

"They liked you before. You be you. Ease up on the gravitas, it makes you a little. . . Gore-ish."

"Don't be so senatorial?"

She laughed, "Ya sure, you betcha!"

"Minnesota?"

"Sheff, be Sheff. Not the senator, not a presidential wanna be. Not Ollie the Minn-ee-soo-tan, either. Of course. Run like you can take it or leave it, but because you love the country, you'll take it. A Midwestern Dubya, but smarter."

"You've thought about this, haven't you?"

"Almost as long as you have. I know there's a fine president inside you."

Mollie had been ready for weeks. Right after the Austin trip, she talked to her parents about taking the kids on short notice and checked out tickets for them back to the Twin Cities.

Belmond was sure that Brad, at seventeen and a very mature high school senior, could watch after his younger siblings.

"Oh, Sheff, sure he *could* handle it. I'd bet the house on it." She sipped her Chardonnay. "But not your presidential hopes. He's a teen-aged boy. If he got crazy and had some kind of party that got out of control, *like boys do*, it'd sink you. Do you want to risk doing that to your son? Knock his dad from the presidency? He'd never make it back to normal."

Kaltenfeld said, "Welcome aboard. Mollie, I'm delighted you could come."

"Thank you, Mr. Kaltenfeld. Sheffield's told me a bit about you. I'm glad you're so positive about my husband."

"Holden. Positive doesn't cover it. He's the right guy. He'll make it, too. Especially with you on board." It was very helpful for the wife to travel with the candidate, not just for the visuals but also because it prevented anything untoward from happening, or rumors of it, or set ups by the opposition. Just smart practice today, even if feminists hated it. He was a feminist but saw wisdom in the practice. It would be good to share that with Mollie; she needed to understand how important she was.

Instead he gave her a tour of the plane, describing the amenities—the dinner service, the sleeping accommodations—as if they were someone else's. He, of course, loved owning these things, but it was more powerful if he seemed unimpressed.

He'd already instructed the pilot to climb as rapidly as the controllers would allow. The experience was utterly unlike a commercial jetliner, which is what Kaltenfeld wanted to get across. He wanted Belmond feeling that he was one of the Elite, those fated to rule.

Once they leveled out at thirty-six thousand feet, Mollie asked Kaltenfeld about his growing up.

"I don't talk about it much. It was uneventful. My youth was in San Diego," he leaned closer to her, "so when I was ten I wanted to be a professional surfer. I matured and arrived at the more realistic goal of astronaut, Eloel."

"So from that to venture capitalist was a normal progression?"

"What is 'normal'? I was a somnolent adolescent. After high school, I ignited. I'm sure Sheffield caught you up on my curriculum vitae."

"He mentioned the Harvard degrees. Impressive."

"I work really hard. Did in school. I can't imagine any other way of being. Once you're really a being, an adult."

"Sheffield is a hard worker, too."

"He will be, anyway." Kaltenfeld squinted thoughtfully, folded his hands, and was silent for a good minute. "Mollie, I understand that you need to check me out. That's one reason I hoped you'd come." Another awkward pause. "You don't remember me from the Special Olympics, do you?"

Mollie searched the ceiling, "I remember you, but I didn't know who you were. You were very enthusiastic and encouraging. I thought it was good."

"Special Olympics is personal to me." Kaltenfeld abruptly rose and went to the cockpit. When he returned, Mollie began to speak, but he said, "That high jump event was inspiring— those kids!"

"You remember that very well. Personal, how?"

"I recall that there were no mosquitoes; I was so glad for the kids. It had been a hot and dry summer."

"It had. I guess global warming has some benefits."

Kaltenfeld drew himself up and said, "No. Climate Change does not. Don't even ever think that."

Mollie erased her smile; there are no private moments now. Only with just Sheff. She could imagine pulling something like that again, and Kaltenfeld suggesting Sheff get a new wife for the campaign. She couldn't think of anything substantive to say and didn't want to bubble on. She decided to admire the interior of the plane. To herself.

The Fabian Hotel was a block from Rodeo Drive and had a shopping plaza off the lobby that looked like the Drive. Belmond noted Harry Winston, Armani, Bang & Olufsen, Bulgari. He slowed when they entered the lobby, but they didn't even pause at the reception desk. Kaltenfeld kept moving to the elevators. He held his phone up to the panel, and they shot up to the penthouse. Belmond tried not to notice. Kaltenfeld had put them in a "modest suite" next to his. It had a large living and working area. There was a terrific view of Rodeo Drive. A long wall shot in from the window, behind which was the bedroom.

Much to Belmond's disappointment, Kaltenfeld had turned down a couple of stars and a famous director who'd volunteered to host a low-key party. "You can't risk it," Kaltenfeld said, "I thought it would be over two years ago, but the sexual harassment imbroglio may not end. Once some female stars and executives were accused, it got farther out of control. Not that I think any of that should be excused or covered up. Not at all. But it is poison to anyone who is accused. And often to anyone associated with them. You need to stay in public places and out of potentially compromising homes."

That made sense, but he'd looked forward to visiting a star's home. After the election.

With the time change, he and Mollie were hungry. He thought they might go down to the lounge for a snack. "That's enfu, not for us. Get room service; that's what I'm going to do. Just keep a low public profile outside of D.C. until it's time to be in everyone's living room. Right now, no one needs to know about you except donors and bundlers. And they might like the spotlight in their day jobs—and for that matter during the campaign, which can be a problem. They won't want to commit publicly until you look like a winner. Trust me. Except for a few Don Quixotes, who mostly aren't big money people anyway."

"I'd like to take Mollie to the ocean."

"That's not a good idea, Sheff. Listen to Holden. He's done this before."

Belmond was again impressed with his wife. And with himself for finding such a woman; true, she'd checked every box he'd imagined, but here was a level of focus and tenacity he hadn't seen before. He wasn't sure that *normal* would be the adjective he'd ever apply to her again.

During the day Saturday he met individually with potential donors, businesspeople not show business people. Mollie called an old friend from college, now a gastroenterologist in Irvine, who managed to come by for a few hours. She gave Mollie a quick tour of the stars' neighborhoods, but Mollie couldn't see much from the car. Which was fine; Mollie was more interested in catching up with her friend than touring. She was back to the hotel by four to rest and get ready for the reception, and eat from a fruit bowl that Kaltenfeld had ordered.

Belmond had pictured the evening as the Oscars. Maybe no red carpet, but lots of glittering jewelry, enough taped on gowns to require maximum eye discipline, everyone smiling brilliantly. Not even close. They dressed like businesspeople and politicians, only more so. The same conservative clothing he saw every day but costing he'd guess ten times as much. This was the role of being taken seriously.

The exception was a young star who he recognized from the "Half Dead" movie series, dressed in jeans and a sweatshirt. He practically shouted his lack of interest. Belmond figured he'd come to impress his date, who was dressed in some kind of leggings with a bejeweled top that was wildly torn, *distressed* he reframed. Bronze skin showed through the distresses, so Belmond did get to practice a little eye discipline. All part of the training, he told himself.

A number of the Hollywood folks knew his voting record. Most were concerned that the new party structure meant he was turning his back on that, which he assured them was not the case. Belmond thought his assurances were accepted; they were, as far as he knew, true, and stated simply without elaboration, so his ears behaved. He wondered if he would soon have to achieve a negotiated settlement with honesty. Something in his Lutheran soul pricked at him. A second glass of wine calmed it down, but the alcohol gave his ears a guilty glow anyway.

Chapter Twenty-Four

The phone rang shortly after three a.m. Jan Staffort had been asleep a couple of hours. She'd wanted to watch just one "Star Trek: The Next Generation" episode to go with her nightcap Bailey's. She ended up watching three. At least, Sunday was a dead day. She'd zip through the morning interview shows that she recorded each week, but otherwise, she could rest.

"Hello, Dad. . .you're not Mom and you're my parent, so you're Dad, like it or not."

"Luke? What's going on." It was not a time to be offended. She turned on the reading light above her headboard. Saturday had been a long day in the district, throwing out the first pitch at a Potomac Nationals game—she'd burned one across the middle of the plate, wowing the players as well as the fans—doing a budget town hall attended by handout-seeking special interest "volunteers" and passionately misinformed ordinary people, and then back to Washington for a reception at the Argentine embassy. Mr. Lin had been at the reception, but neither acknowledged the other.

"Look, I was at that demonstration yesterday. You know, the one about the Constitutional Amendment?"

"Well, I hope you didn't have anything to do with organizing it. You know, we're not in the Capitol on Saturdays as a rule."

"Listen. . ."

"Son, I've been wanting to talk to you forever, but it's three, three fifteen in the morning. Wait a minute. Did you get arrested?

"Sure did. We Stafforts don't do things halfway."

"Are you at the Central Detention Facility, it's not far from the Capitol?" She'd bail the kid out and maybe soon enough that the media wouldn't make the connection.

"Must be. They hustled us into vans, but the ride was real short."

"Okay, that's where you are."

"Hey, Dad, I waited for the media to leave before I called."

"Yeah, you've always been a thoughtful boy."

Staffort listened to the radio serial station on satellite during her drive to the Central Detention Facility. She'd barely gotten into "The Martian Queen" episode of the 1950s radio series, "Exploring Tomorrow," when she arrived. She listened until a commercial break, a toothpaste jingle that took her back to childhood in rural Virginia. And it was her child that needed help.

Could she just be an ordinary person taking care of her son? Get Luke out without drama? Probably. But if she was recognized, the revelation of her identity would be a big deal, and the news would spread like the Entron virus devastating the Starship Enterprise. She needed to get to the person in charge quickly. She called a junior aide, someone who'd be anxious to impress. Sure enough the aide called right back with the name and position of the on-duty supervisor. And, in a wonderfully ingratiating show of initiative, he had called her to arrange a meeting.

A uniformed officer took Staffort back to the director's office. It was the opposite direction from the cells and, for D.C. city government, not too institutional. Berthea Thompkins did her best to hide her amusement but not her best at hiding the hiding of her amusement. Staffort knew she was looking at one woman who at the moment was more powerful than the most powerful woman in America. She tried to turn her clenched jaw into a smile.

Ms. Thompkins spoke, "Good morning, Madam Speaker. I understand you have a loved one in our facility?"

"Thanks, not so good a morning. But thank you for seeing me. And I appreciate your discretion. I really appreciate that. I only hope that I'll be able to reciprocate some day."

"Your loved one?"

"Of course, Ms. Thompkins, my son Luke. He was at the demonstration yesterday, the one at the Capitol, and was arrested. He tells me that he was treated well and respectfully. Good leadership."

"Yes, Luke Staffort, arrested at 3:21 yesterday afternoon. Was a little argumentative but complied well with the officer's instructions. I don't remember the exact charges. But I can tell you that it's at the misdemeanor level. The judge set bail for all the misdemeanors at $2000. He's lucky that they arraigned him so quickly."

"I'm sure."

"Saturday may be a fine day for demonstrations, but generally it's a terrible day to go to jail. Half the time, you don't get arraigned until Monday."

"I'm grateful. And Luke will be too, at least when he's older and not so filled with righteous certitude."

"Madam Speaker, I don't really care what he was demonstrating about, I. . . ."

"Well, it was me, among other things." Staffort laughed lightly into her hand. Sometimes a little self-deprecation lubricates the situation.

"That's fine. It doesn't matter to me. I'm having Luke brought here. I presume you have the cash for bail?"

Staffort controlled her tone carefully, "I do." She didn't want to imply that Ms. Thompkins was seeking a bribe. Unless, of course, she was. Staffort was confident she could handle that, too. "I have the cash. Where do I pay?"

"Yes, cash is necessary. I'm having the night clerk come to my office. I understand you might like to stay out of public view. Although I'll tell you, not too many of the people coming in here tonight are up to speed on politics." Ms. Thompkins smiled very pleasantly and rightly so, she had the most powerful woman in the country, with the possible exception of the First Lady, humbly seeking her favor. Staffort appreciated her integrity; it was good to avoid bribery.

In the office, Luke thanked Staffort for coming and bailing him out and the director for his good treatment. His attitude seemed to Staffort to be reasonably convivial, given the circumstance.

Luke said, "Nice ride."

"Thanks, I don't drive it much. A few times a week and not for far. Not like when we used to take car trips across the country."

"No, not like that."

They rode on in silence. Staffort searched her memory for the music Luke liked, or sports teams, or any girlfriend. She didn't remember. "You have a car?"

"No need."

"Are you working?"

"Yeah."

"How's the job going?"

"Okay."

"Remind me, where is it that you work?"

"You never knew."

"Okay. Where do you work?"

"I'd rather not say."

As they neared the townhouse, Luke became less chatty. Staffort sighed. She checked her make up in the rearview mirror. Lipstick was a little outside the lines; she'd hurried here.

Staffort stopped the car in the drive and turned to Luke. She searched his eyes and said with all the seriousness she could muster, "Luke, you can have whatever political ideas you want; you're your own person. But trust your mind, Luke, trust your mind."

"Yeah, whatever."

Even if he didn't answer much, it was good just to say the kid's name to him. "Luke, can you sleep? I want to have some time with you very much, but I can't right now. You're young, and I'm exhausted." It was almost five.

"Yeah." He followed Staffort to the guest room. She heard the shower running and drifted to sleep. When she awoke at eight, Luke was gone.

Chapter Twenty-Five

Elle snatched her newspaper from its plastic bag. Yes! Front page. The Russians must be behaving. Her by-line was shared by two reporters she did not know had been at the demonstration. Still, it said, "Elle Crafton, with" two of her colleagues who didn't deserve to have their names even thought of, so she didn't. One of them or maybe Thieu had added the "mostly peaceful" characterization of the riot.

Above the story was a photo of the demonstration. A bright sunny sky and a Mall covered by large crowds of, on close examination, mostly African Americans. And in 1960s clothes. Elle had seen that picture before, where she couldn't say. An ancient car was parked in front of where the Air and Space Museum should be.

She knew such digital rearranging was considered legitimate if for an unbiased reason, such as replacing a gray sky with sunshine, even if there were collateral changes, like increasing the crowd size ten-fold. But time-traveling plus increasing the crowd size seemed too much.

"Fiona, when was the civil rights 'March on Washington?'"

"Good morning, Elle. Congratulations on the front page story. When your moth. . .." Fiona stopped. Everything went black—the screen, the lights, the little blue dots on appliances.

Chapter Twenty-Six

Rek had been to the National Worship Center in the District once before. He was inspired to come back by his upcoming date with Elle. She was an appealing girl, woman, and he wouldn't mind a little divine assistance, although he no longer thought of himself as a believer.

Rek had stayed away from church almost entirely since the year after his mother's death. Growing up in her Korean Baptist Church, Rek had become competent in basic Christian theology and fluent in Korean. The language skill was a closely held secret, something the Army did not have the need to know, a card to play only if deployment to a combat zone threatened.

His mother's death had driven him to God. He had not mourned as those without hope; he found solace in his faith, grown in it, developed it, experienced it intimately.

Six months after her death he saw the general surgeon, the one who punctured her colon. The man jibber-jabbered about her death being predestined, with the operation as merely God's instrument. Rek had known both a God of love, who comforted believers, and a humanity who continually failed to live up to his standards, the surgeon being the main human Rek had in mind. The God he knew would not have willed the doctor to be planning his weekend cycling adventure instead of focusing on the operation he was performing. The surgeon's god, the Omnipotent Grand Master that we are merely game pieces to, he wanted no part of.

Thanks to the surgeon, Rek saw his mother's death as a scary nun experience. He didn't much believe the doctor but couldn't totally disbelieve him either. So he disbelieved in God. Most of the time. Rek resolved to seek out an atheist if he ever needed serious medical care, someone who thinks that this life is all you've got and he's by god gonna keep yours going.

As he walked to the massive structure, he was struck by its magnificence. He'd learned from Hoagie that the Center was neo-Gothic, designed pretty much as a traditional Christian cathedral but with some recent modifications to serve its ecumenical ambitions. Washingtonians of all faiths or none flocked here to worship whatever they chose to worship and in their own manner. Only confirmed Solipsists were excluded, which kept the congregation down to a manageable size. The rector was firm in her traditional and controversial belief that if a worship service was to be truly corporate, participants should not merely be engaged in the same activity but also agree that the object of worship was, in some sense, greater than themselves. Or as she put it to the congregation: worship should be somewhat different from one's normal frame of mind. A slight majority of the elders upheld her ban on transparent self-worship.

The cathedral had once considered excluding evangelicals because evangelicals were so exclusionary. A group of Wesleyans had once shown up for the annual Kwanza-Chanukah-Winter Solstice-Santa's Day service, but had left when they realized that "O, Little Town of Bethlehem" had become "Some Day Hamas in Tel Aviv." Apparently the word spread, and evangelicals became a non-problem.

He sat nearly a football field's distance from the podium, between a white pony-tailed geezer with a weathered face and an oxygen tank and a preteen boy trying to get some distance from his sister. The experience was wholly unlike attending the little Korean Baptist church with his mom. Instead of a pretty well tuned piano, the Center boasted a soul-shaking pipe organ. Instead of an incisive sermon based on ancient scripture, the rector delivered a conscience-balming message inspired by the latest editions of *Strolling Alone* and *Popular Nephrology*, her go-to deep-thought magazines/catalogues. Belting out "What I Did For Love" with 3000 other congregants against the totalitarian organ gave Rek a comfortable sense of community, a wonderfully warm smug oneness. Much more comfortable than sharing humble gratitude with thirty-eight mainly Korean worshipers singing "Brest Be the Tie That Binds." He thought of Elle.

Rek met Elle just before the concert. They had no time to talk; Rek was disappointed and relieved. The musicians, too, were silent for the second movement of one piece, though only for three minutes eighteen seconds. Elle felt small pride in her culture as she recognized the homage to John Cage. She whispered, "Maybe the original statement was powerful, but it's only original once." The hall was too quiet for him to whisper back. Whew. He made a puzzled face as the silence went on. Elle returned a puzzled face. Rek stretched his expression in clown-like wonder. She mugged a sophisticate's disapproval but with a smile. He returned an exaggerated look of devastation. She grinned, lopsidedly and with her Elvisian curl. It got silly. They shook with silent laughter until the music started again.

Then it was over. They'd hardly spoken. And Rek was about to say goodbye to her. Not what he wanted. But did he know her well enough to talk to her? Her face was at a kissable angle. But right outside the concert hall? Just looking up at him, probably. It was hard getting his vocal cords and lips to work together but he managed to ask, "Would you like to get a bite somewhere?"

Elle had not seen this level of male awkwardness since junior high school. It didn't charm her. Still, D.C. has a way of making actual sincerity appealing. And Rek was good looking. Too tall and brawny to be Asian. His eyes were a northern European blue, the lids vaguely almond, a complexion a shade lighter than the meat of an acorn squash, and short, black spikes of hair.

"If you don't want to, that's okay. It's just. ..."

"Of course, let's do that. Do you have a place in mind?"

"I was going to suggest walking around Georgetown and just finding something that looks good. But it's awful hot."

"I won't melt. That's a great idea."

Rek was wet with sweat by the time he had worked his car into the three-quarters of a space between a private drive and a BMW. Then a three-block walk to M Street. He consoled himself that at least Elle was sweaty too. They found a place with outside tables in the shade.

Elle had no idea how much second lieutenants made but was sure it wasn't much. So she suggested that they go "Dutch."

"That'll work, Raak is Dutch."

She apologized for her father's slang, and said "we pay for our own, okay?"

Rek could have kissed her for that. She was pretty, too. He grabbed the question that often led to heartfelt monologues in D.C., "Where are you from?"

"I'm still from North Dakota. Just like yesterday. Nowhere close to the Bakken oil patch, so we aren't rich. Grand Forks is over next to Minnesota." Rek hoped she wasn't irritated. He knew they'd begun talking about this at her apartment. Maybe he could just let her talk.

He leaned back and forced himself to be relaxed but alert to listen. She asked, "So how do you like D.C?"

"It's nothing like Wisconsin and less like Florida. But I'm glad I'm here." Rek thought this also sounded familiar. But she appeared not to care.

"But you didn't just choose to come here, did you? I mean I always thought the Army decides those things for you, doesn't it?"

"I didn't even know Washington was a possibility. Amazingly, against all my expectations, the Army did look at my qualifications and assigned me to legislative liaison."

"Yeah, if they keep that up, they'll confound all the clichés. So how do you like it, your job?"

He recalled the inspection. She wouldn't understand. "There are a lot of worse jobs."

"And you came here from Wisconsin."

"Wisconsin. ROTC. College. Florida. All of the above."

Rek decided he was gonna share. He'd not shared since he had anything that needed sharing. He didn't know if he'd disgust Elle, certainly not intrigue her, but he didn't much care because it was a good way to see if there might be a future here. So he told more about his Grandpa Park, whose adoptive family was conveniently named Park, so strictly speaking that part of Rek's name was not Korean. His mother was proud to be Korean, even just half. On his maternal grandmother's side, it was Heinz 57, what she called it, at least in the days before DNA testing, too complex an ethnic mix to even talk about.

"Elle, I'm not enough minority to do me any good, and I'm the wrong kind of minority at that. I wasn't going to get into an Ivy League school even if I wasn't part Asian."

"I'm used to being ethnically careful in my business."

"Not with me, no one seems to care about my Koreanness, so I don't either. The biggest thing in my life, I guess...." Rek didn't guess, he hoped that there would be nothing worse. And maybe talking might seal off some of the anger that invaded his mind when he woke in the night, "The biggest thing is that my mother died when I was a junior in high school. She went in for an appendectomy, and got her colon punctured. She died on the operating table, but they brought her back."

Dying was not a healthy lifestyle choice. Even for a short time, dying is not a beneficial experience. Death did not improve her health. Just saying that stuff to himself had failed so far to scab him over. No, he wouldn't try it aloud and exploit her empathy.

"She was in the hospital for two weeks after, and they sent her home. She never really recovered. Died for good six months later." Rek blinked rapidly.

Elle said, "I've never had anything so awful in my life. I'm sorry."

"If she hadn't died, I wouldn't have been in ROTC. And if I hadn't been in ROTC, I wouldn't have been sent here. And I wouldn't have met you. So one good thing came out of it, anyway." Rek's words came from him fluidly, and he hoped she saw them as sincere. But he recognized that he'd voiced what many people would label a horrible thought or a pathetic line or both. Maybe he was talking just because of her professional interviewing skills; maybe he'd had no one to listen to his story for so long. Whatever, he'd enjoy the moment and brace himself for the letdown when it came.

Elle ticked off a mental inventory: he was cute, a little young, but without the aggressive self-confidence she so often encountered; he had survived something tough; he was totally useless as a potential source. She ought to ditch him at the first chance, but she had a strange and unprofessional feeling. Her reportorial self was shutting down—well, taking a break.

They talked easily and laughed. Rek seemed not to have done much laughing lately. She sure hadn't. She'd worked; she'd managed to insinuate herself into a somewhat trusting relationship with the Speaker of the House; she'd cranked out a bunch of stories; she'd had two colleagues hitchhike on her best non-politician story; she'd gotten next to no feedback at work from a boss who often said, "Don't worry, I'll tell you if you screw up." It looked like Rek wanted nothing from her except to enjoy being with her. Good, she would enjoy being with him.

She tuned Rek back in. She hadn't missed anything. She caught the family's move to Florida after high school, the father's second wife, Rek's financial struggles during college despite the ROTC scholarship. He allowed that killing people who disagreed with your country was intolerant. Elle pointed out that every country seems to think having a military was a necessity, so he shouldn't be ashamed. She reassured him when he talked of being so ill-suited, by skills and worldview, for the Army. But his attitude seemed a healthy one for a soldier to have.

She smiled for herself as she noted the empathy implied in his eyes, enjoyed the utter smoothness of his shaved face. She tried to govern her eyes but couldn't keep them from his. There seemed to be not even a little pretense in his face. For the first time in months, maybe years, she was just Elle. The reporter was no longer lurking in the background. The clichés that presented themselves to her were not from journalism but from her mother's paperback romances. Since her head was normally over her heels, the clichés made no sense. So it would be the reverse; she allowed herself a hope that although her heels were not yet over her head, but they might climb above her bosom which maybe would heave just a little. This was silly; she hoped she wasn't that lonely. She reached across the table and squeezed his hand, "Let's go back to my apartment and, and talk some more." It wasn't loneliness.

They did. The lights were back on, but not too brightly. They talked and kissed and held each other a bit.

Chapter Twenty-Seven

Almost as soon as Rek left, Fiona started chattering, "…checks her account, she'll be quite proud.…..The March on Washington led by the Reverend Doctor Martin Luther King, Junior, took place on August the twenty-third, nineteen hundred sixty-three.

"If you're wondering how that picture came to be with your story, as well you should since, if the past is any indication, the picture will become quite an item in the public mind and in journalistic circles. Which mucks up the force of your story rather badly.

"The explanation is most probably yampy but simple: the weekend photo editor wanted to go home early Saturday, so he left an intern on duty for a few hours yesterday evening. The intern, quite likely resenting being taken advantage of, found a file photo that he thought would prompt some chuckles. And you have to admit that the Studebaker rather punctuates the anachronism. Now my hypothesis is based on circumstantial evidence, which does add up.

"Also, the intern posted for his college friends to check out the story. The other possibility is that the special sixtieth anniversary commemorative article for the March somehow showed up yesterday. What do you think? I don't think so." And the blond, Elizabethan-fair image that Elle had chosen for Fiona did a black woman head shift with an admonishing finger. A wry bit of cultural appropriation. Fiona seemed invigorated to be back to life after the outage.

The demonstration Elle covered had maybe five hundred people; the Park Police estimate, which she had dutifully obtained, was "under one thousand." The story made no mention of numbers, but the picture made it look like thousands. She would have to file a correction, which would be edited into equivocation: "Techniques used to enhance photographic contrast may inadvertently have suggested more demonstrators than present." She asked Fiona to string together a couple of sentences of good British profanity. She did, and the utter unintelligibility of it all expressed Elle's anger nicely and as a bonus got her laughing.

She switched on the late news. There was a report on the corruption trial of Senator Pauly Maldonado (T, DE). Elle reflected on the significance of that coverage: the editor chose real potential crime and totally ignored Senator Tom Johnson's (M, AL) *nolo contendere* for driving seven miles per hour over the speed limit in rural Georgia. Without the old party labels to help, editors were having a hard time deciding what to cover. In many cases they were looking at the actual newsworthiness of the story. She was friends with one editor who told her of the agony of trying to think, although she didn't put it that way. Elle was in a bad mood again.

Chapter Twenty-Eight

Upon discovering Luke gone, Staffort went back to bed. A dreamless sleep might recharge her demoralized spirit. After an hour of wrestling the covers, she grumbled that a uncontested race might replenish her campaign funds. Neither were going to happen.

Dressed and somewhat put together, she sipped her coffee and took stock. One, Luke had flown as soon as he could. Two, evidence against the president was still just barely dripping in. Three, the coffee was so acidic that it might set off her ulcer. On the other hand, her management of legislation had been superb; it had even gotten some good reviews in the media. She was doing her job well. That's not really the main thing. Is it, Jan?

She came back to it: Luke had flown. At least he had looked healthy enough. But his friends, comrades? were probably pretty sketchy. Who were those people at the demonstration? Staffort picked up the Herald. She read the story, recognized Elle Crafton's by-line, didn't know the contributing reporters. The demonstration leader quoted anonymously was well-spoken; there had been middle-aged people there, so maybe Luke wasn't in danger from his fellows. He may be grown, but a parent cares.

Staffort picked up on the name, "The Underground." Yeah, the ones who'd slipped the unmasking law past the DIA chief.

She went to the freezer, hardly glanced at the door compartment, and extracted what she wanted. When the frozen waffles popped up the second time from the toaster, she flowed syrup over them, releasing a bouquet of maple. She thought of Luke's childhood. . .and her own.

At ten Janny was little, but he was strong enough to buck hay up on a flatbed trailer. Two layers only, but it makes a kid feel big to bend and lift and swing a bale up that weighed about as much as he did. As soon as he'd let it go, he ran to the next bale, figured how to lift it, and got ready for when the tractor got there. His uncle stood on the edge of the bed and slid the bale into place. Janny was totally spent before the second layer was done; he couldn't hold the bale aloft even the extra second for his uncle to grab and stack it. His arms numb and face sweat slicked, he ran back to the house, where his mom praised his grown-up work and gave him an icy lemonade to cool him down. He begged successfully for a second breakfast of homemade waffles with maple syrup and butter dribbling off them.

Staffort had intended to give Luke that breakfast, make him appreciate the difference from a jail breakfast.

When Luke was little, really until he hit teenage, he had relished sitting down with his father to a breakfast of waffles, butter, syrup, ice cold milk, and sometimes link sausages.

Staffort remembered one day they'd had such a breakfast while visiting the farm during a Congressional recess. Luke was twelve and playing Little League baseball. He asked his father to go out and toss him some grounders on the well-kept lawn surrounding the old farmhouse. Jan's mind was on the November election, but Luke wheedled. He felt he should indulge the kid.

"Throw it to my left, Dad. I need to work on catching 'em backhanded."

Jan really needed to work the phones. You never want to let donors get lonesome. Luke and his father moved to about thirty feet apart. Jan side-armed a fast, low runner to Luke's right, and Luke sprinted and moved his body in front of the ball, scooped it up cleanly, and threw the ball hard and shoulder high. It smacked into Jan's first baseman's mitt.

"Come on, Dad, farther right. Make me backhand it."

Jan tried a three-quarter delivery to bounce it higher and aimed farther out. Luke dashed towards it, stuck out his glove backhand and took it on a high hop. He planted his right foot, leaped, spun, and fired it hard at his father. Jan was not quick enough to block the low throw. The ball whapped against his trousers, and he went pale.

Luke started walking toward Jan, but before he'd taken three steps, Jan sputtered, "You managed to hit me right squarely in the balls!" He gasped, then spat out, "We're done."

Luke collapsed right there. Jan saw it as he turned toward the house: the kid just fell on the grass, all ninety-three pounds of him, and burst into tears.

Luke stayed away from Jan the rest of the morning, which worked for Jan since he got a dozen calls in. Before lunch, though, Jan went up to his son's room, knocked, and went in. Luke was sitting on the edge of his bed, shoulders almost touching in front and flipping his baseball cards one by one toward an empty trash can. He looked up.

"Luke, I know you didn't mean to hurt me. It was an accident."

"If you knew that, why'd you yell at me? And quit?"

"Because it hurt, and I didn't think. I wasn't mad at you, I'm not mad at you. I just was surprised and hurt."

"I didn't mean to hurt you. I just made an off-balance throw."

"Yeah, I know. If I'd been quicker, it would have been a great throw."

"It shoulda been higher."

"A good first baseman would have caught it. Your throw was good. I'm sorry I ruined it."

"It was an okay throw. But a lot of guys wouldda had trouble with it."

"Okay. I'm sorry. Maybe we can play again tomorrow. Would that be okay?"

"Yeah. If you really want to. Yeah, for sure, Dad."

Jan clapped him on the shoulder and tousled his hair. Though Luke didn't smile, Jan knew he was alright, they were alright.

How easy it was then. She cleared away the dishes and sighed. That seemed like the last successful conversation she'd had with the kid.

Staffort checked the time, eleven twenty, and picked up the phone. "Number One, sorry to bother you Sunday morning, but I need to know about the riot yesterday. The paper says it was a flash demonstration but planned by an outfit that calls themselves 'The Underground.' Sounds like some people who may be in the government. I need you to find out and get back to me soonest." Chidge didn't need to know how much Staffort already knew.

Chidge snapped to with a jaunty, "On my way." She had to admit, Chidge was truly Number One. He didn't complain or say what he was busy with or promise to get on it first thing tomorrow.

Less than an hour later Chidge had confirmed that The Underground was indeed made up largely of federal workers. Staffort asked him to find out if Luke Staffort worked for the government in Washington D.C. She could have done that herself, if only she kept her Congressional system password at home. Early on she'd had it memorized, but the administrators made her give up the "OldDominion6" password and substitute something with no meaning whatsoever. That one she'd written down and put in her desk drawer at work. Chidge knew his, she was sure. And if he didn't, he'd go into the office rather than admit such unpreparedness.

Apparently Chidge remembered his own password because within minutes he called back and told his boss that Luke Staffort was a federal employee, GS-9, program analyst, at the Department of Energy. Good for him, not being a burden to society. The old reflexes kicked in, and she added, just to taxpayers.

Chapter Twenty-Nine

Sunday morning had been reserved for an early brunch with local elected Democratic officials, but even Kaltenfeld couldn't pull that off. They were not interested in meeting a former Democrat, no matter who he or she was. Kaltenfeld told them that they'd want to later on, but he respected their decision and loyalty, even sympathized with it, but there was a new order in Washington, and he was getting on board. It struck him how sick he was of thinking in terms of that vague transportation metaphor. He thought of his comp lit readings and realized that writers had seemingly always expressed similar ideas with metaphors of transportation. More primitive forms. Some, but often about the same. Anyway, saying it in French, Latin, Spanish, Italian, German, or Greek about a cart, horse, or chariot didn't make it any fresher. He needed to improve the precision of his political thought, so he resolved to himself to think things literally, non-metaphorically. Politics was like surfing: always the danger of being sucked under a bomb of triteness while thinking you're pulling off an El Rollo. That one he liked.

The Belmonds had breakfast with him in his suite and left for the airport. They flew up to Silicon Valley early.

"Well, Mollie, did you enjoy meeting some stars?"

"Sure, who wouldn't?" An attendant proffered a basket of pastries. She smiled politely and waved it off. "I'm curious, Holden, why do they do it, I mean get involved in politics? With businesspeople, it's easy to see they need to kiss up to power. But these folks are the one percent of the one-percent. Plus, they have all kinds of adoration, plenty of leisure. What does politics offer them?"

"You're one smart woman, Mollie. Sheffield is very lucky indeed."

"Thank you, but that won't work. You didn't answer my question."

"That's because you know the answer. Or maybe you'll just deduce all the answers."

"Feeling important, compensating for becoming rich and famous for play acting or singing or telling jokes, enjoying vicarious power, helping steer the country, patriotism, ideological commitment. Did I leave anything out?

"Not of any importance, really only other ways of saying what you said."

Belmond was reading the Washington Herald on his tablet, not paying attention. He read a story on a demonstration. "Holden, it looks like the Senate dodged a bullet, thanks to the Speaker. She torpedoed that proposed amendment to repeal the law of cause and effect. Don't remember the title but thank goodness now I don't have to."

"It wasn't going anywhere, but it is good that you don't have to vote on it."

"And yeah, did I catch you complimenting my wife? Of course, I know I'm lucky to have married such a smart woman. I'm sometimes amazed that she married me." Belmond had often used that line, but with false modesty. He'd thought he was the smart one. But now he realized he meant it. "But why did you say that?"

"Aside from the fact that it's true? Isn't that enough?"

"No."

"Okay. Sheffield, Mollie thinks strategically about people like I do about making money. She wanted to hear my analysis, not to find out about the stars, that's obvious and boring. They're as varied as everyone else. 'Star' is merely a metaphor, a very dead one, to be sure. They're just famous and often talented people. But Mollie wanted to learn about me, probably working on how much to trust me, and maybe purposes I can't guess."

"What did she learn?"

"That I think ahead, too. Did you notice, I didn't answer? She noticed. And decided to let me off. You can ask her why later." Kaltenfeld looked at her sideways, "Ha, she's brilliant! I love that gal."

Mollie reddened. Flattery, she handled expertly; sincere praise was tough.

They arrived at Hoagie International headquarters in San Bruno, not quite geographical Silicon Valley, but it often identifies as Silicon

Valley. Kaltenfeld explained that Hoagie International chose that location because of its proximity to SFO for international flights and because the founder was a San Franciscan and that's where he wanted it.

Buford (actually Beaufort, but he started school in Mobile, where French is not widely spoken by first graders, so Beaufort is either Buford or Bubba) Hoage III started Hoagie International when he was in his twenties. His family moved to California in what came to be called the second Dust Bowl migration, the ideological migration. During the 1990s many families with progressive politics left the arid political environment of the South. The majority of them from Alabama, young Buford's included, headed west. Both families settled in the Bay Area.

Buford was born a progressive the way some people are born into a religion. Growing up, he learned a catechism of essential beliefs and pretty much believed them. He was dragged to demonstrations, the progressive version of the Mass; then as an adult he showed up at occasional outrages and, on major holidays, demonstrations. Buford loved both, he termed good ones well organized hissy-fits. When he quit college the first time, he began to have doubts about the role of the elite in guiding the country. Later, when he felt he'd joined the elite, his doubts vanished.

Like many who inherit faith, Buford had sensed something was missing. What was missing, he decided at twenty, was, as Kaltenfeld put it, "adequate capitalization." So during his second go at a freshman year, this time at Cal Poly San Luis Obispo, he decided, as he put it, "to leverage" his internet savvy, his emerging business acumen, and his drive, which was explosive and beyond discouragement, and use them to become wealthy. He found his Southern accent caught people's attention, put them at ease, and encouraged them to underestimate him.

He came up with a plan to take over the internet search business. He poached some of his competitors' lead programmers, persuaded a number of venture capitalists to fund him, burned through millions of their dollars like they were dimes, somehow got more from them, and, aided by sudden retirements and defections among competitors' senior executives, worked his plan. By thirty he was the undisputed American king of internet searches with a net worth north of two billion dollars and a trophy campus in San Bruno. The trophy, though, he was proudest of was the ghost campus of the former king's headquarters south of Palo Alto.

As they were driven on the Hoagie International campus, Kaltenfeld said, "Hoage is an outsider, always striving to achieve, to belong. That kind of neurosis is a painful way to live, though it's very useful to society. He has his charm."

"You think we'll connect?" asked Belmond.

"Oh, you'll like him, most everyone does. Hoagie was one of my first significant investments; Buford is a very magnetic personality, extremely persuasive. I really got taken. Thought I was going to lose all the capital—terrible move. But Buford made it work."

"How did he displace the giants that were already doing searches?" Belmond asked.

"I really couldn't tell you."

Mollie said, "Really? That's hard to believe, Holden."

"I mean it, I can't tell you. I know what every moderately well-informed person knows. Beyond that, I could only imagine. What I imagine, you don't want to know. So I don't imagine."

Belmond looked up quickly, "Look, Holden, I've got to steer clear of anything shady. You didn't save me from the Hollywood predators just to throw me to a high tech one."

Kaltenfeld disabled the Wi-Fi on his phone. "Of course not, Sheffield. Business can be like politics: ideals or companies die, so others can live. More fundamentally, I look at a business like a favorite Chinese restaurant: you just don't want to know the details, so you never go into the kitchen. I'm very careful in my due diligence. I always make sure I can at least peek into the kitchen. If I see dogs in cages, I pass on it. But I don't audit the recipes."

"So he's shady, but you don't want to know. I don't think I belong here."

"I don't know anything of the kind. He's successful. He's got the biggest search company around. No one will criticize you for visiting him. He's a true believer. Convince him that you're still the same guy you were, and the money will follow. Does that sound familiar?"

The lobby of Hoagie International was brushed stainless steel and teak and rosewood and glass, some of each where you'd expect them and some where others belonged. The area inside security had a glass floor that afforded a terrifying view into what appeared to be a geologic fault. A string of white LEDs hung down the abyss until they could no longer be seen. Belmond stared past his shoes with his mouth open.

Kaltenfeld noticed, "Don't let him see you like that, Sheffield. You don't want to look like a country boy staring at the skyscrapers in New York City. And it's only about four feet deep, a trompe l'oeil."

"Uh, of course. I'm over it."

"Now, look above the desk. The Hoagie logo. And the brand slogan, 'It's all in there,' as well as their internal 'home words,' that's what Buford calls them, 'What is truth?' He says it's their point of reference. That plaque is a well-regarded work of art. It contains some of every stable non-radioactive metal known to man, along with every gemstone, and a bit of every tree indigenous to northern California, including the sequoia, which is protected. I can't remember the artist off-hand, but you would know her."

Belmond said, "Well, that is impressive. Don't you think so, Mollie?"

"It beautiful. You know, Holden, the 'home words' have a Biblical resonance. Is that intentional?"

Kaltenfeld hesitated, deciding how blunt to be. "Buford was born in the Bible belt. But I don't think he brought any with him. He may not have a clue."

"Pilate's words are some of the most famous in the New Testament, and he doesn't know? Narrowly educated?

"Buford has a tremendous understanding of zeros and ones, of the internet, and of how to motivate people. Education, academically? Not even narrowly educated. Dropped out of some Jesuit school that he went to only because they gave him a full scholarship. Then went Cal Poly for a couple of years. Deeply self-trained and smarter than just about everyone."

"I can hardly wait to meet him." Mollie was gifted at withering sarcasm. She held back none of her gift.

"And I'm real pleased to meet you as well, Mrs. Belmond." Buford seemed to have materialized behind the small group. "Don't worry, I'm not sensitive." He wore a cashmere suit jacket atop jeans and a white shirt. His broad face crinkled into a smile that was at once inviting and scary—as if he had waited his entire life to meet Mollie and now would have her for dinner.

Belmond stepped forward and extended his hand. "Glad to meet-cha, Mr. Hoage. Sheffield Belmond, call me Sheffield."

"Yes, Senator Belmond, my pleasure. And thank you for the courtesy, I will call you Sheffield and you call me Buford. Hi, Holden, thanks for bringing these two here. If you can, stick around."

Kaltenfeld planned to stick around. "Of course. Good to see you, Buford. Are you going to give your guests the tour?"

"Well, yeah." He turned to the Belmonds. "Second's the interesting floor, that's where we are. Normal outsiders enter through the first floor, that's marketing and sales. I've got logistics and HR on the third, engineering's on four, and my leadership team is with me at the top.

"We'll just stay on the second floor until we go up to my office. By the way, this building is not a circle; it's an octagon. Even quicker to walk across than the Pentagon, a lot cheaper to build than a circle, and damn sure prettier than that circle headquarters. Yep, a whole lot cheaper to build. I out-thought 'em on this one. Did I mention, I saved a pot full of money?"

They moved quickly from one area to the next. Each like the last: dozens of casually to sloppily dressed young adults, middle-agers, and some teens sat at monitors, keyboarded away, repeatedly looking up at a giant monitor on the wall. A constant stream of numbers, letters, and symbols, chyrons of various colors, ran all directions both on desk monitors and the big screen.

"Why is Hoagie such a powerful engine, you might ask? If you weren't fixin' to, you shoulda been." Buford grinned like he was riding his bike with his hands in the air. "Simple in concept, but almost impossible to do. We bring genuine human guidance, sympathetic guidance, to the algorithms and in real time."

Belmond said, "Sounds interesting. Can you give me an example?"

"See that section of sixteen analyst guides, curators, on the far wall—they're all political conservatives. I've got more conservatives, I mean outed conservatives, working for me than anyone else in the Valley. On purpose."

"But you've been a progressive bundler, uh fund-raiser for years?" Belmond asked.

"Didn't say I liked them. Just need 'em. Now everybody's got some conservatives, but they're in the woodpile, if you get my drift, because they think they'd be fired if the higher ups knew. They're probably right. I'm not like that. See these old boys and girls take users who we've identified as conservatives and tweak the search results as they go along. Now you might think, hey an algorithm can do that, give conservatives conservative hits. That's right, that's all an algorithm can do. Even with AI, at least at its current state. With our tweak, we can also, say, provide some hits that are relevant to the conservative's query but from a different point of view, say historical/libertarian/sociological/anthropological/pop cultural, whatever-off-beat-big word-you-want-to-put-to-it, or that speaks to the related philosophical questions, or that provides anecdotes that speak to the query, or just throws in some off-the-wall inspiration of the guide."

Belmond asked, "Doesn't that just reinforce the 'echo chamber?'"

"Uh, yeah." He smiled at the slow student. "I'm not trying to save the world; that's your business. I'm just trying to have happy customers and build up my credibility with them." Buford paused. He silently counted to three, then added, "And at an appropriate time, I can begin to salt their searches with some cognitive dissonance. Or not, if the time isn't right."

"That would be devious," Mollie said, disapproving but admiring the strategic patience of the man.

"Good word. A while back one of my vice presidents said, 'demonic,' but that's a little grandiose. Sumpin' to shoot for though. Back to our analyst curators. AI feeds them patterns of links that our customers follow, how much time they spend there, and on and on. Of course, our AI analyzes that too, but it's not where it needs to be. The human curators are involved at every stage. They tweak the algorithm, they intervene physically when alerted to do so, and they try to move to a more subtle level. The users get great stuff, better all the time. That's why we say, 'It's all in there.'"

Mollie asked, "I know that pornography is one of the internet's most popular services. You have sympathetic searches for that?"

"Hate to say it, but I do. Mollie, I've got the same problem that the guy who runs the convenience store has. Does he stock soft porn? Duh! If the public wants it, you've got to stock it. So, yes, we've got a slice of the floor with some of the scuzziest people you'd never want to meet. I like some of the conservatives better. But it's a necessary service and a profit center. It's just business."

Belmond started to speak, but Mollie was fully engaged. "Even so, it's hard to believe that what you've described would make more than a marginal difference. That's not what makes you number one, is it?"

Buford looked like he was about to pop, "You are right, Mollie. But the rest of it is 'If I told you, I'd have to kill you' material. I wouldn't want that." He gave a good ole boy 'hey, there's a hottie up at the truck stop' chuckle.

Belmond saw Buford's eyes focus on something maybe in another dimension. He'd just let Mollie handle the talking for a while.

Mollie asked, "What can you tell us?"

"Well, this has been written about, so I'll confess that it's right. It's simple and, I think, obvious: we give the customer what the customer wants. Yep, business 101. But some of my former competitors thought they should convert the customer, or critique their choices or beliefs, or, in some cases, just shut them out from the information and perspective they were looking for. That won't work, not yet anyway. In China, sure you gotta, and we've got a setup in Australia for them. Could do it here, but I want to keep these folks doin' things the American way, so to speak."

They continued making their way around another cavernous, monitor-stuffed room.

Mollie asked, "Okay, Buford, a room full of women in business suits and men mainly in jackets and ties? What is that about?"

"That's the finance and investment curators. I don't care how my people dress, except for the porn guides; they have to be fully and conservatively dressed, just to be safe, if you get my drift. But some of these folks insist on dressing up, say they wouldn't feel at work if they didn't. I've got some refugees from New York and London, as well folks from the San Francisco financial district. They do great work."

Belmond felt that he'd better speak up or Buford would be backing Mollie for president. "You don't have conservatives after the libertarians and then Chamber of Commerce types on around to the various shades of, for want of a better word, left-leaners. Why is that?"

"Makes for a harmonious workplace. I don't want people getting into arguments in the cafeterias, gyms, and reflection grottos. So I mix it up real well, study the monthly reports on social interactions, and change it when necessary. Progressives are clear around the wheel, safely clueless that anyone in California actually has conservative beliefs."

"Very wise. And the conservatives are likewise unaware."

"You gotta get out more, Sheffield. They're wrong, not uninformed. They know about progressives and other left brands. They just don't understand. Some claim to understand and still disagree. I doubt it, but I don't care. If you're the kind of liberal who believes in intellectual diversity, you'd be at home here. 'Cause my FlexSpecialists will lead an interested liberal into conservative land, if they want. And vice versa. All they have to do is click on the 'banana pepper' button, and we'll spice up their Hoagie search. The FlexSpecialists aren't real busy at the moment because not so many people want to hear something they disagree with, but their time will come." Buford stopped the tour and faced the group. "Coffee, juice, soda? You can even have a kale-strawberry smoothie, but I'll think less of you. Let's go up to my office and talk a while."

Buford led them around a faceted corner to a short wall with two rectangular gaps. On the floor before the gaps, recessed lights pulsed as the group approached. An elevator car, an open-sided teak box, passed through the left one going up as a car passed through the right one going down. "The insurance folks insisted that I warn people that the elevator shafts are ahead. I got a load of smart people, and they get distracted. Predictably they're looking down."

Belmond said, "I can see that would be dangerous. They don't stop?"

"No, the elevators move in a continuous loop; you have to step on it when the car's in front of you. I've got five passing through each opening, so there's no waiting. But get off on five or it'll dump you on your head."

Mollie grabbed Belmond's hand and pulled him onto the car that Buford and Kaltenfeld had just entered. Belmond jumped off quickly at the fifth floor.

Buford exploded in laughter, "I was just kidding! OSHA would shut me down in a nano. It all stops if there's any weight on a car at five going up."

He led them to a conversation nook the size of a third world dictator's office. "I am extremely proud of what I've accomplished here. No apologies. This is great. Starting from nothing and defeating very well-established monopolies, to call them competitors would belittle them—that's just unheard of. I did it and I'm proud of it. Pride is one of my seven lively virtues."

Mollie found herself liking Buford despite disliking almost every personality trait he had displayed. "Like a parent's pride," she said.

"Right again. Nobody thinks bein' proud of your kids is a sin, th'old-fashioned word. My other virtues are like that."

Belmond shifted in his chair, but Buford looked at him expectantly. Belmond hoped that Buford wasn't going to finish with a tale of his extra-terrestrial abduction.

Mollie glanced at her husband. Sheffield again seemed not to know how to proceed. Mollie was happy enough to set Buford up for what she figured was a set piece he liked to deliver, maybe after a few drinks. "Well, I suppose you have your own twist on 'sin.'"

"Oh, yeah. I like to tell this, even if it hare-lips everybody in the county. During my few months at St. Isadore's College, I picked up something. From lit class, I think. The seven deadly sins. Don't know if they still use that, but I learned them and made them virtues. Pride—número uno. They're wrong about the others, too. Envy, my envy, is a competitor's restlessness. And anyone around here can tell you that when I see less than best effort, they will feel my wrath. Sloth is my word for personal energy conservation. Avarice is confirmation that I can make better use of money than anybody else, so I ought to have more of it. When I party, gluttony and lust run wild, my celebration of nature's richness. There you have it. If the Catholics had made those corrections, the Vatican would be twice as big and have better art."

"Well, Buford, we're Lutheran." Belmond put it on the record.

"That's fine, Sheffield, I don't care. What I do care about is that you're still the same guy, even if you've become a cave drip. You've probably heard that one a few times since January."

"It's clever."

"True. Yep, I expect that some of those environmental and social legislative ideas will be your administration's priorities." Buford turned to the group. "I've had a good time visitin' with y'all. I like you. Dang, they're so nice, Holden, that I even like you at the moment."

"The Belmonds are the real deal, Buford. Wouldn't they make a terrific first couple?"

"Oh, yeah, they would!" Buford said. He turned to Mollie and grinned, "I could just do this all day. But the time would cost me enough money to finance two presidential campaigns, so, Mollie, with your permission, I'd like to have a few minutes alone with your husband."

"Buford, Sheffield doesn't need my permission."

"Okay, how about I put it like this, we both would love to have your approval."

"Granted."

Mollie and Kaltenfeld seated themselves in minimalist but comfortable chairs. Mollie picked up a copy of The Ufology Quarterly Review. Kaltenfeld double-checked his phone that he was not connected to WiFi and was in airplane mode. He began tapping it with his thumbs.

As they started for his office, Buford said loud enough for Mollie to hear, "Sheffield, don't you ever get tired of that Mollie. She's sharp as she can be and pretty as all get out, too."

"I think so."

"Oh, yeah. I know so. Beauty is only skin deep, but ugly goes clean to the bone."

Belmond stiffened. "And that applies how?"

"Never found an application. It's just something I brought from Alabama that I like to trot out on occasion."

Buford stood at a massive window overlooking his private forest and spoke, "I like you, Sheffield. More important, I believe in you. I think you'll try to accomplish the things you used to champion."

The money moment: Belmond took in a breath, faced Buford directly, and said slowly, "That I will." When Buford broke eye contact, he asked, "How did I come up on your radar?"

"Holden led me to you. Remember that lunch a while back at Comme Çá? I was there."

"I don't remember you."

"Remember an Asian man and his two 'kids?' They listen very well." Buford held a remote control and pointed it at the sleek chrome and teak cabinet on the far wall. A lower door opened. With a sweeping gesture, he presented one of the kids, a three-foot high robot, vaguely human looking, sallow. Its ears reoriented toward Belmond.

"You were spying on me!"

"I merely had my man paying attention in a public place."

"That's more than a little creepy."

"My apologies. Now, you can give me the benefit of the doubt because I'm giving you the benefit of the doubt. I detest the new party structure."

"Well, I suppose. . . ."

"Of course, I've known of your record for some time. But Holden's work convinced me. Of course I checked you out; the point is I'm impressed. I like what you've done in the past."

Belmond had been offended about as long as he could afford to be. "Thank you, Buford. I appreciate your confidence. About the party system we've got…."

"Hush. Don't tell me about Tigger. I know it's supposed to last eight years minimum. Pardon me, I should say 'The Great Realignment' to you."

"It's fine. I'm not offended."

"Good, that inside baseball drives me crazy."

Not a long drive, Belmond suspected, maybe just a good walk. Still Buford was the right kind of crazy. He remembered reading that some southern senator a century ago had told a political neophyte, "Son, you got to have the crazies. Nobody wins without the crazies."

"…like about you, Sheffield, is I don't believe you can lie very well. So don't prove me right." Buford held his index finger up and was silent. "Here's what I can do for you. I can bring you a bundled and legal two to three mil within a week. Probably six point five for the primary. Double that at least for the general. And I have friends who can do about half as much each. That's a couple of dozen people. It's a start."

"It's a fantastic start. To get that kind of support with such a modest expenditure of my time, why that's invaluable. And you know, fund-raisers make the papers and they just emphasize how different politicians are from ordinary people. That's a big negative."

"The papers, Sheffield? It's true that everything gets out now. Even to the 'papers.' But wait. I'm gonna take care of that soon." He picked up a folder from his desk. Belmond watched its reflection fade on the polished rosewood. "But here's something that concerns me greatly. Something that should concern you as chair of the Armed Services Committee."

Belmond kneaded his forehead—here came the quid pro quo. He just hoped it was palatable. "And that is?

"Don't worry, Sheffield, I'm not going to ask you to do anything that you won't be proud to read about in history books. It's a bit dull: nobody'd even bother to link to it. I'm really trying to help you do your job. It's a national security issue. Simply put, it's the British invasion."

"Our special allies, the British, are invading?"

"Oh, it's worse than the Redcoats or the Beatles, it's Phycenook. You see, with me or even with the guys I beat, you have an American company. We, of course, see ourselves as citizens of the world, as I know you do as well. But you're an *American* citizen of the world, and so am I. So just sheer love of country means we consider the country in our operations."

"Really?"

"Well, yeah, with all due consideration to the bottom line."

"And Phycenook, which I hadn't heard of until a week or so ago," Belmond grimaced, oh well it was out, "is a threat because they're British?"

"Aw, the British are fine, except they're not us."

"As I understand it, Phycenook is a social media service. Am I wrong?"

"Not wrong, but there's more. They do a lot of searches. I know, because they do a lot through us. They've only been going a few years, and they already comprise about 35.7% of our searches as of COB Friday. And that's no problem."

"So, what's the threat. Are they gathering sensitive data?"

"Some. Since they're an information broker between us and the end user, they gather data on both the user and us. Users don't care. I call it the Dr. Phil syndrome: folks will confess to sexting with their nephew for a shot on national tv. I'm not judging. They're the same way with privacy and the internet. They don't care what they give away as long as we give 'em some technological bennie, even if it doesn't amount to doodly shit, pardon my French."

"You know, you're usually a very direct guy. What are you driving at?"

"I'm giving you essential background to understand what I'm about to say. If I'd said it outright, you'd think I was crazy as a sprayed roach."

Belmond thought, well, he's right about that. But, he's talking a lot of money, and you have to have the crazies. "Okay, if this is a threat, what is the threat?"

"Phycenook is beginning to do more of their own searches. In the UK they're doing approximately eighty percent, that hurts us some there and will destroy the UK search engines." He stopped abruptly. Belmond sensed that Buford realized he was sounding like he wanted relief from competition. Which he probably did. But Belmond knew he couldn't fix that even if he wanted to, even as president it would be hard to pull off. He glanced at the door. Still on the left.

Buford continued, "This is what really gets me: I don't know how they do it. But their searches, at least after the first couple, fit the user perfectly. Artificial intelligence, sure. But it learns faster and deeper than we can. It's way beyond Big Data. So they learn all kinds of things about their users—not just jobs, hobbies, and family, but feelings, fears, and secrets they never say—it's virtually limitless. So here's the threat. Suppose you have an NSA employee with a Phycenook account, even though she's super careful with what she puts on-line, doesn't matter, the NSA is compromised. That's a threat. It would be a threat if it were the Canadians. Doesn't matter how nice the country is, it's a threat. That's something your committee should look into. Here's what you need to know."

Belmond accepted the folder as carefully as if it were the first installment on his campaign bundle. He again appreciated the importance of last week's hearing. It was that element, the name of which escaped him at the moment, but he'd get up to speed back in D.C.

"Buford, you may be giving me an early warning of a vital issue. We'll look into it. You'll have to trust me because it'll be in a classified hearing, so I can't keep you in the loop. But I take this seriously."

"I expect nothing less."

"Is there any other issue you need to discuss?"

"No, that's it. We have no legislative interests at the moment. That bit about repealing the law of cause and effect gave me a little concern. The states wouldn't have gone for it. But, still, crazy things happen."

"I understand the Speaker stopped it. It'd have been an embarrassment to the House. It would never clear the Senate. Just between us, even sensible bills tend to die in the Senate."

"I don't recall too many sensible bills, lately."

CHAPTER THIRTY

The colonel was already in the special staff meeting when Rek got to the office at seven-fifteen. But if he was in a meeting, he was in a meeting. Still, Rek thought he'd better find the colonel ASAP. He did not want the Vice Chief to be pulling strings first thing this morning and having him on orders for the infantry officers' basic course before lunch.

He'd try to make it a rejection, but with mixed feelings. But not too mixed. His pulse was palpable. Refuse orders? Lawful ones? Surely, it won't come to that. Even though it's the Army, volunteering is necessary to get detailed to another branch. He was pretty sure of that. He reminded himself that the colonel said he had a choice. The possibility that he might not have a choice had awakened him at three Sunday morning. He was sure he did. He was sure he couldn't be sent to Fort Benning as punishment for being at the demonstration. He was sure no one in the Army knew he was at the demonstration. He told himself many things he was sure of.

Yes, the colonel had emphasized that he wanted Rek to be honest and to accept or decline the opportunity as he wanted. He believed that, but it bothered him. Colonel Waters seemed straightforward, but so had his stepmother. She'd invited him to call her Mother Raak, but was okay with "Steph" if he wasn't comfortable with the "mother" part. He politely called her Steph. She got frosty real quick, and he explained just as quickly that she wasn't his mother, she'd never be his mother, his mother was dead, and he wished Steph could trade places with her. Steph did not take that gracefully. All of a sudden, his college funds were cut off for the next fall, he was on his own, and then he was on an ROTC scholarship. If he failed to make this work with the colonel, he could see himself fire-and-maneuvering his way across the Middle East.

Colonel Waters came back about eight, and Rek asked if he had a few minutes.

"Have a seat, Lieutenant," the colonel offered Rek a chair in the corner of the office and took one across a small table from him. "What's on your mind?"

"I don't want you or the Vice Chief to think that I don't appreciate your interest in my career or your offer to help it," because I don't, I wish he'd never made the offer, "because if I wanted a military career, this would be just the kind of boost that would make it. Or give me a," he searched for a military sounding term, "an…outstanding chance to make it. Sir."

The colonel's head tilted slightly to the right. What would that mean?

He waited. The colonel waited. "But my heart has been set on an academic career. And, to be honest, it still is. So, I really thank you for the offer—and, if you can, please make sure the Vice Chief of Staff knows I appreciate his willingness to help and I appreciate the Chief of Staff's encouragement—uh, I'm going to have to request that I just stay here as an adjutant general officer."

Colonel Waters grinned at him; apparently his groveling was entertaining. So be it, he just didn't want to upset anybody. The colonel said, "They both understand that the Army isn't for everyone. Even though you would probably do very well if you wanted it, which I suspect you doubt. But no one is interested in running your life for you."

"So, you don't think they'll be mad."

"They're not petty. This isn't college, Rek. Now get your day started."

Monday was frequently a travel day for Belmond—back from Minnesota, often with the whole family, kids resentful of being taken away from their friends and activities, Mollie content to have reconnected with her hometown network.

Returning from California was more taxing. Belmond was edgy after Kaltenfeld exploded at his pilot for neglecting to fill up at Hoagie's air strip. Buford was charging a premium there, and the pilot balked. "So find us cheap fuel," Kaltenfeld demanded at the end of his rant. The pilot complied, going a few hundred miles off the most direct course to get jet fuel at a small municipal airport in Arkansas. Normally Kaltenfeld would have applauded that kind of economy.

Despite a comfortable bed on the plane, Belmond couldn't allow himself to drift into sleep. He propped on his elbow and waited until Mollie sensed his gaze. His eyes shone with excitement. He said, "Honey, I think we may pull this thing off. Buford's backing and connections may be just what I need to preempt the others."

She was sleepy or maybe just calm, but insufficiently enthusiastic, "Maybe so, Sheff. What you told me sounds really good. But you need to get back on D.C. time and be rested. You must keep rested. People screw up when they're too tired. Remember Howard Dean's scream."

"Ug, unforgettable. I will. I'm going to sleep now." But he didn't. He couldn't. Visions danced in his head: scenes of insanely spirited campaign rallies and hundreds of delegates chanting his name. Then his mind lurched on to the fact that the Tites hadn't established how their presidential candidate would be chosen. Could it be a convention, no primaries? Who could vote in the closed primary states anyway? Would the local Democrats and Republicans cooperate? Hard to know what levers to press or how to press them. A thousand questions deviled him until they took off again from the refueling stop. Belmond and Mollie arrived at Dulles at five, after the almost seven-hour trip. He got less than two hours sleep.

Elle's toast wasn't burnt. Toast shouldn't be burnt, of course, but hers had been for a month. She'd kept punching in a lower number, and the toast kept burning. She set the control on 1 several days ago, and it still burned. She scraped off the worst every morning and used strawberry preserves to cover the bitterness. The toaster was still set on 1, but today the toast was browned perfectly, a precise web of cappuccino and latté-colored rivulets. She celebrated by making herself a café brevé to enjoy with her toast and preserves. She replaced her involuntary smile with a business-neutral expression as she entered the Herald building.

Chapter Thirty-One

Staffort loved to go to the Capitol on Mondays. Usually there were tourists and staffs but few members, but not much going on. She would go to the House floor and glory in the beauty of the American experiment made manifest in the Congress. And in her position. Today that was an expendable luxury. She drove herself to the Longworth and slipped into her office about noon.

The staff was surprised to see her. No one said that they hoped she wouldn't stay long, but she knew. Chidge asked if she needed the staff for anything. "Not really, Chidge. Came in to take care of some personal business." Chidge told her that they were approaching the three-week backlog tolerance Staffort established the last time she ran a level one diagnostic. Staffort wasn't about to be their excuse for slipping over it. She requested a car and driver and let her people get back to the work of grinding out replies to constituents.

The Department of Energy building, aka the Forrestal Building as a salute to its short life as a sort of extended Pentagon, was just a ten-minute ride from her office. She had the driver drop her across Independence Avenue at the Smithsonian Castle. The Speaker of the House could, of course, visit anywhere in the government she wanted, but she didn't want even the driver to know what she was up to. Chidge would figure it out, which was an okay trade-off for Luke's office number.

She entered the castle and loitered near Smithson's crypt. James Smithson exemplified the kind of love and generosity toward country that she admired, felt that she too embodied, in a small way. Her love of country had, after all, made her the most powerful woman in the country, with the possible exception of the First Lady. And Oprah.

Time spent in the presence of the great, even the dead great, tends to make one reflect on one's own inadequacies. Staffort found plenty to reflect on. It wasn't pleasant. She hurried from the building.

The driver was thoroughly gone. She crossed Independence against a school of tourists surging toward the Air and Space Museum. She had not been recognized so far. She expected that she would be, but hoped not to create a scene. She went up the elevator and down the hall of the east building. She passed a few employees. They weren't interested in her, either. She came to the office. Luke worked for the Assistant Secretary for Fossil Energy, the sign by the door said as much, if one knew the lingo. Literally it was, LFEPAM Branch, FED. She wasn't sure what Elle-Fee-pam meant, but knew FED was the Fossil Energy Division. Remembering how environmentally committed Luke was, she was sure that holding such a job was torture. The door was open, and Staffort walked in.

"Hello, hello." No one was in the first office. Staffort made her way past several empty desks with computer monitors showing screen savers of scenes from national parks. She stopped at a desk, looked around, no one was nearby, and, as she did whenever she got the chance in a federal building, wiggled the mouse. A document appeared on the monitor, not the sign-on screen. What the document was, she couldn't tell, but it was still wrong. So far, out of a hundred thirteen wiggles, on only five computers had the user been signed out. Except the Pentagon, the FBI, and the security agencies, they were solid. A statistic of an appalling lack of security consciousness by federal employees. Now a hundred fourteen wiggles. Something she might need sometime. Probably not—it might antagonize her constituents. Still, she'd keep the tab.

Next was a spacious room with two conference tables across it, each surrounded by employees eating and watching a big screen television on the wall at the front.

"May I help you?" asked a large woman in a house dress. Staffort judged by her attire that the woman wasn't important, but her tone implied that she was home. The other employees glanced at Staffort and turned back to the screen.

"Yes, you could," she said as meekly as she could muster, "I'm looking for Luke Staffort. I'm told he works here."

The woman examined Staffort's face. "I'll take you to the boss. Come with me."

"What are you watching?"

"'Deepwater Horizon.' About the oil spill." She looked over her glasses at Staffort and said, "It's work related. I'll take you to the chief."

They walked across the front of the room, and as two employees grumbled that their views were blocked, to an office. "Ms. Morely, this woman is looking for Luke."

A petite, middle-aged, red head looked up from her desk, then stood suddenly, "Oh Madam Speaker, I'm so sorry we didn't recognize you properly. Welcome. I'm Lois Morely, Chief of Leafy-Pam, that's Liquid Fossil Energy Program Analysis and Management Branch, Fossil Energy Division. Yes, Luke Staffort works here. But he's at lunch right now. You're welcome to wait for him in my office if you like. Coffee?"

"Thank you, I will, but no coffee, thank you. Has he been gone long?"

Ms. Morely looked at the other woman, who was edging out the door. She turned to Ms. Morely and said, "I don't know." Then she yelled into the conference room. "How long has Luke been gone?"

Someone hollered back, "He left just before the bosses landed on the platform."

The woman yelled again, "How long is that? I had a call and lost track."

After a moment, someone else yelled, "Maybe fifteen minutes. I'm not his keeper."

Ms. Morely smiled at the Speaker like the parent of a misbehaving child, "He may be a while. Please have a seat, Madam Speaker."

Staffort complied. Early in her Congressional career, Staffort had attempted to learn about the reality of legislation by visiting the government offices that executed the law and seeing just what they did. Disproportionately, she found, what they did was document and justify the fact that they were executing the law and that it would cost more next fiscal year to continue to execute the law at the superb level that they were executing it at the moment and more above that to document and justify that fact. As a young Congressman, Staffort had found this discouraging. Now as a seasoned career legislator at the height of the profession, she found it fascinating, a little humorous, and existentially depressing. Her jaw tensed. She recognized that with a simple inquiry about some arcane aspect of an old law, she could cause a huge uptick in the documenting and justifying business, thereby creating more productivity for the department in question, a bigger budget, and the need to hire even more documenters and justifiers. Her heart shriveled a little to realize her own flesh and blood earned his living by such activities.

"Madam Speaker?" Ms. Morely spoke softly. "While we have a few minutes, may I fill you in on a special project that we're working on right now, one that takes priority over our normal activities?"

"Okay, go ahead for, say, ten minutes. But I'd like to talk with Luke on his lunch hour."

"Luke usually goes to the cafeteria. He'll be there for another hour." She flushed and picked up some papers on her desk. She made a show of looking at the clock on the wall. "Better make that half hour. Unless of course he's working down there. Then he might be an hour."

"Of course. Okay, what is your special project?"

"Oh, thank you, ma'am. Now, I am not complaining or anything. Every new administration seems to want to change the way things are done. So President Stafford is not so different. Or improper, necessarily. So let me tell you. We are engaged in an audit of all the energy available in the world right now, in ten years, and in fifty years. And we have to figure it by the technology used. That is, we're estimating how much oil we can get out of the ground by conventional drilling, adding in off-shore drilling, by unconventional drilling, by fracking, etc. We can't just ball park it; we have to show our work. And we work through each location for each technology even if that particular technology makes no sense for the location."

"Well, that sounds sort of reasonable. And probably useful."

"No doubt. It's just hard to accomplish with current staffing levels. And our normal work is suffering. And, of course, the people in Suffypam, sorry Solid Fossil, are doing it as well. And the Guffypam branch, Gaseous, sorry I did it again, too. Plus we all are coordinating with State and the CIA for foreign production. And with the EPA to allow us to figure in potential environmental impingements on the means of production. That'll be covered in an appendix."

Staffort studied her nails; she couldn't remember the name of the shade, but it was a real nice red, a hint of plum. She didn't have to be polite to this woman much longer, unless, of course, she was a constituent also. Her district was a landmine. It occurred to Staffort that this project could be useful to the president's friends in Sofia Rabia. He was shamelessly throwing all this work on at least four agencies just to provide cover for his profiteering on the BUBR stock. When she was ready to move, she could use the Energy and Commerce Committee to pry out the data and discover how it was being used. "Ms. Morely, I'm afraid you're a little far into the. . .technicalities for me, but it does seem like an onerous task."

"Sorry, Madam Speaker, I just get so. . .enthusiastic about our work. Yes, of course, it is a tough job, but we're getting it done."

"Well, that's good. I'm afraid I've taken up too much of your time. I should try to catch up with Luke at lunch. Where is the cafeteria, exactly?"

"It's on the second floor, west building. There are lots of signs; you can't miss it."

There were lots of signs, and Staffort didn't miss it. She thought it would be less threatening to Luke if she joined him to eat, so she picked up a cup of coffee and a soggy piece of custard pie. Luke's mother had made custard pie with a flaky crust that never soaked through. Her last one must have been at least a year before the divorce.

With food in hand, Staffort scanned the cafeteria. It was one o'clock, and most diners had left or were getting ready to. Scanning systematically along the windows, she spotted a man eating alone. He was in a corner. She saw him look up from his food so he could watch the pedestrians without having to turn to the side. That's Luke's kind of planning. Unless he was playing sports, Luke would make every effort not to exert himself. She started across the room. It was Luke. Staffort covered the distance quickly and drew in a breath.

"Luke."

Without looking up from his noodle, meat, and dark gravy dish, he said, "Give me some time; I haven't even been here an hour."

"Luke, it's me."

Luke turned toward her. "Oh."

"May I join you?"

"Whatever floats your boat."

This was looking as hard as the teenage years. The kid is twenty-four; he's got to be able to make sentences. "Can I get you something. . ." it got away from Staffort, "a lawyer, maybe?"

"*Plus ça change, plus c'est la même chose.* You haven't gotten any kinder, have you?"

"*C'est vrai.* But imperfect as I am, I still miss you. I want to enjoy your being my son."

"Why should you get to, when I can't?"

"*Touché.* Now we're even. Can we talk a bit."

"Seems like that's what we're doing. Oh, I wouldn't eat that pie; it looked better last week."

"Thank you for the warning."

"No point in you getting sick. . .on top of everything."

"Again, I appreciate your looking out for me." Staffort remembered well the teenage years and tried to apply the lesson: hear something positive in anything that doesn't sound like a prelude to actual violence. "And I really was serious, too: do you need me to get you a lawyer?"

"No." Luke chased the last noodle with his fork, got it to his mouth and washed it down with iced tea. "No, thank you. We have lawyers in the Underground. They can't represent us; they're civil servants, too. But they can advise."

"So what's their advice?" Staffort detected maybe a bit of fear in Luke's face, the way he scrunched it up protectively.

"Just sit tight. They'll probably drop the charges. They'll be buried like you buried the Freedom from Consequences amendment."

"Probably right. Luke, you didn't seriously think that amendment was a good idea, did you?" She hoped that this wasn't coming across as an interrogation, unless that's what it takes to get him talking.

"For life, it's a stupid dream. For government, why not? None of you live with the consequences of the stuff you pass. Why not let the people in on it?"

"That's one point of view I hadn't heard before. Interesting." Not really, but Staffort was by God going to find the positive. "So how do you like working here?"

"It's okay. Do we have to play twenty questions?"

"Of course not. I'm just interested. I care about you." Staffort had always felt awkward saying "I love you" to Luke, to anybody really, but especially to Luke. It just left a person wide open to the general purpose complaint, "If you love me, why did you. . . ?" Staffort wasn't going to sign up for another one of those soul-scarring arguments. She asked, "Why don't you ask me something, Luke, then it won't be an interrogation."

"Okay. Did you get that outfit at Nordstrom's Rack?"

"No, actually, but that's a good guess. I did buy it at Nordstrom, but at the regular store at Pentagon City. I live in Old Town. . .oh, that's right, you know."

"I do. You know, usually it's the kid that has too much attitude. Great move—with you, it's the parent."

"You never could hear the disrespect in your voice. I still do."

"Thanks for bailing me out. That's respectful and real gratitude."

"You're my son. I'll always be there for you, no matter what. But I'll go now. I've ruined your lunch, and it's time for you to get back upstairs."

"My digestion is okay." Luke shuffled his dishes back on his tray, stood and slotted them in a tall rack on wheels. He turned back to Staffort, who was still sitting, "Thanks for trying. You aren't really very good at this human stuff. It's not your fault." He turned and bolted for the exit.

Staffort gazed into the street, past her own reflection in the window, trying to see. . . something. She turned and saw him halfway down the hall. How long before she'd see him again? She hurried after him. He stopped to wait for the elevator. "Luke, wait," she called from twenty feet away. He turned.

"What?"

Staffort held up her hand for him to wait. The elevator door opened, but he didn't go in. Staffort's heart leaped. She approached him, "Luke, let's give it another try. I didn't come down here to make you feel bad." Or me.

"I don't feel worse than I did before. But okay."

"Let's go outside and talk for a few minutes." Luke walked silently toward the revolving doors, and Staffort followed. Outside they strolled along the broiling Promenade. There were few others. Staffort said, "I understand you're a liquid fossil energy program analyst. How is that?"

"It's a job."

"I know. But I mean, do you like it? Do you feel like your education is of some use?"

"It's okay. No, it's not what my degree prepared me for—French history and fossil fuels don't intersect a whole lot."

"I'm sure. Even so, I was a bit relieved when you decided not to go to graduate school, try to become a professor. You may be in government, but it is real life, to some extent."

"Yeah, I've got a boss to please, assignments that make no sense, and deadlines to get them done by. Like school." They walked past a fountain; the breeze wafted some spray to them.

"It's awful humid, but that mist still feels good."

Luke said, "Yeah, it does. Reminds me of playing in the hose in our old neighborhood."

She wanted to be encouraged by Luke's foray into small talk, but this was as much shadow dancing as Staffort could take. More nervous than when asking Luke's mother out for the first time, she said, "So, Luke, how about you give me your phone number? I'd like to invite you to have dinner with me once in a while."

Luke seemed not to hesitate. He pulled a business card from his wallet. "My cell is on there. We might do that. If you impeach President Stafford, I'll pay."

"Whoa, what's he done?" Luke couldn't know anything. Probably not, but maybe he'd heard something from one of his Underground friends.

"Hey, you're the one who can find that out. I know he's done plenty of stuff, or is planning to, that will fit the bill."

"Actually, nothing we know of." Staffort suppressed wanting to share what she did know. Might give Luke a reason to keep in contact. Pathetic. He was her son. "However, he might have some issues in your area: liquid fossil energy. I'm looking into some stuff, can't say what even to you, but if you hear anything funny about our government and Sofia Rabia, you give me a call."

"Cool."

Staffort nodded to Luke and smiled as the elevator doors closed. She saw her reflection. She hardly recognized herself, been a while since a smile had come from within.

Chapter Thirty-Two

Elle and Rek met after work at the National Gallery. They sat before Monet's "The Bridge at Argenteuil."

Rek offered, "The bridge looks a bit like the Memorial Bridge."

"It's over water and the stone is gray. Is that what you mean?"

"Yeah, that was stupid."

"Don't force it, Rek. Just be in the moment and let the painting work. Don't analyze or try to remember what the river is or when Monet lived. None of that matters. Just be."

They were quiet. Rek was trying hard to be, but he got bored, as he suspected most people did, with being. Elle was not bored. Her face was relaxed, her eyes on the painting, seemingly absorbed by it. He started examining the perspective, the second sailboat, what it all meant.

It meant what Elle's hair meant, framing her face in dark brown—just being beautiful. He spotted the small boat straight back from the prow of the sailboat. The one thing other than the early hour he took from his fishing trip with Grandpa Park was what the old man had said, "Experience what's here, Rek. The young take quiet and beauty for granted. Try not to."

He started to criticize himself for making the painting personal. Colonel Waters' critique intruding? He let himself off the hook. The pond shimmered. He could almost hear the lapping water, he felt the warmth under the parasol, his mind soared among the clustered clouds. After a while, he whispered to Elle, "Thank you." And they sat half an hour longer.

At her apartment, their appreciation of Monet became an appreciation of each other. And became a passion. Suddenly Elle sat up, "Whoa. We're going kind of fast there, soldier. Let's call it a night."

Rek pulled away and spread his hands like a defensive back denying pass interference, "Okay, we can do that. But, Elle, please don't call me 'soldier.' That's what Luke, the guy at the demonstration, calls me."

"Okay, *Lieutenant*," she laughed to him.

For weeks Elle had barely been making it to work on time, but Tuesday her alarm went off fifteen minutes earlier than she'd set it. So, before she was even supposed to be there, she was standing opposite Stanford Thieu in his office. Thieu had two desks, a normal one with an underslung drawer for his Bluetooth keyboard, where he usually sat, and a standing desk which he bought himself. Today he was especially puffed up in his editorness and was standing, but behind the conventional desk. "Elle, you've done very well cultivating the Speaker. Your piece, and I know it was your piece, on how she buried the "Freedom from Consequences Amendment" was superb. You know, her own son was arrested at the protest." Thieu was not a man to hand out compliments cheaply. They usually came with a substantial tab.

"Yes, Stan," Elle thought familiarity and an encompassing smile were prudent as her initial defense. And a little sincere gratitude, "Thank you for giving Ka'apua the by-line and me just a contributor. Never thought I'd say such a thing. But it will help me preserve what I've built with the Speaker, once she gets over being mad at the Herald."

"What I want"—Thieu wasn't going to lollygag over what had been, he was moving to what must be—"is for you to do the same thing, much more quickly, with a senator. Have you heard of Sheffield Belmond?"

"Of course," Elle had heard of all five hundred thirty-five members of Congress, memorized all she could about all the senators and the House leaders, plus committee chairs and ranking members of both bodies. "He's a Tite, had been a Democrat, from Minnesota, was in the House for three terms. He's in his second Senate term, the Armed Services Committee chair and on the Appropriations Committee, plus several sub-committee assignments. Anything else?"

Theiu nodded. "And his politics?"

"He fits in, especially with everyone now trying to relax from the hyper-partisan days. Belmond doesn't seem angry at anyone. That's his style; he never did. Politically, he was pretty progressive in the House, like his largely suburban Minneapolis district. Seems to have a good organization. Lately, he's been legislatively invisible. Hard to say if he's changed or just slow to find his rhythm. In the House, he may have just indulged his constituents' fantasies when he was a member of the minority or maybe enjoyed the freedom of his positions having no cost and producing at most little tweaks in legislation. Then again, he may have been tilting at windmills, sincerely even. It's hard to know."

"That's not good enough; I want you to know. We need a profile on him for the Sunday paper. Brownstein and Ka'apua will work with you, but you're in charge. Make it happen. The suits will be watching."

Naturally Theiu had assigned her the two reporters who had hitchhiked on her demonstration story. They'd better hang on; she was going to move fast.

Elle sent Ka'apua on an afternoon flight to Minneapolis, shame it was summer and she couldn't freeze his fat Hawaiian butt. He could run down Belmond's family, friends, classmates, former colleagues in the Minnesota legislature, and anyone else he could see in two days. Brownstein would take the Acela to Boston; he'd talk to Belmond's professors and then whatever old law school classmates he could find. There was a little piquancy in this assignment since she knew that Brownstein had wanted to go to Harvard Law but was rejected. He'd be thoroughly professional, get some good stuff, but it would still sting. He shouldn't have finagled his way onto her demonstration story.

She would be the one to meet the senator. Thieu arranged it: she'd see him the next day.

When Rek met Elle after work, they skipped the culture and went straight to her apartment. Clothes were shed. He luxuriated in her closeness. Rek held up his hand and stopped everything. His self-discipline surprised him. He leaned over the end of the bed and pulled something from his trousers on the floor. He produced a ballpoint pen, unfolded a paper, and called Elle's attention to it.

She was breathless and annoyed, but Rek reviewed each line of the form he'd saved from his college days, "Consent/Limitations to Intimate Contact." She was about to work up an indignant rage but saw the earnestness on his face. It was too absurd to be insulting. Elle tick-marked and initialed the appropriate boxes and signed the designated line, laughing all the time. Her amusement puzzled Rek. Maybe he'd ask her about it one day.

They fulfilled each tick mark.

CHAPTER THIRTY-THREE

Wednesday morning Elle sat in Senator Belmond's waiting area. She sifted through magazines on a coffee table: *Epistemology Today*, *Demographica—The Magazine*, *Midwest Review of Poetry*, *Lutheran Home Companion*. She thought the last magazine was probably the one he actually read, so she picked it up and thumbed through it. She was reading a recipe for a hot dish involving sausage, corn, cabbage, lentils, a couple of different condensed soups, and six kinds of cheese when the senator came out of his office to greet her.

"Ms. Crafton, I'm glad we could arrange this on short notice. Ms. Thomasson is a whiz at finding little pockets of time and making them count. She's put together half an hour for us. Please come in."

Belmond followed her into his office and gestured for her to sit. He started to close the door, but he remembered Kaltenfeld's counsel for him to be super careful. Belmond said to Elle, "I'll just leave it open. The ventilation is terrible." His ears didn't consider the misdirection worthy of extra blood flow.

He had studied his smart sheet. He asked about her family, noted that she was from the state next door. He admired her work, praised her good job on the demonstration story, and mentioned insights from her profile on the Speaker that had escaped him from his own experience in the House.

She asked a couple of questions, focusing on what was important to the folks back home. Belmond ticked off a number of items—renewables, especially wind, agriculture exports, taxes, the cost of college, etc. He gave a two or three sentence elaboration on each and moved on. She asked follow ups, and he answered. And he asked for her assessment of each issue, as a "fellow northern plains person. "Was 'fellow' okay?"

Unlike the first meeting with Staffort, she didn't think he was trying to run out the clock. It was a comfortable conversation.

Still, she needed to get after it. "Senator, what's the status of the Defense Appropriation bill?"

"That's a better question for the Appropriations Committee chair, but, if you'll treat this as background, I'll tell you what I think."

"Otherwise, 'no comment,' right?"

"Right."

"Okay, background, no attribution. For this question only."

He had a detailed knowledge of each of his fellow committee member's interests; without deigning to speak for any of them, he displayed a negotiator's grasp of what they were about.

Perhaps it was just a product of not having to grovel around for re-election money constantly like a House member, but all the senators she'd met had an almost royal ease about them. Belmond had it in spades. So what do you ask royalty, "Are you planning to be king?"

She asked. "Higher office?"

"There are only two, and, no, I have no plans to seek higher office." He spoke right to her, but his eyes were fixed above her head and his ears reddened. She noticed.

Belmond noticed Elle noticing. "I really hate that question, Elle, may I call you Elle? They say all senators think they should be president. So I guess I've had that thought. In passing. I just think it's way too early to even think about it seriously."

"So you want me to go with that answer, 'I've had that thought'"?

"That doesn't sound too good, does it?" Belmond laughed. She thought, genuinely, not royally. He muttered, "A solon from near the Twin Cities. . .." Then he spoke up, "Uh, who knows how each party is going to choose its nominee. So even if I wanted to, I think it's too early to talk about the presidency."

She doubted that he had the fire in the belly to make the race. Nailed that cliche, first time. Still, Theiu must have picked up on something to make profiling him such a priority. "We'll come back to that subject, maybe. Let's move on to our biggest military challenges. What's your appraisal?"

Belmond was relieved to tuck his ambitions out of sight; she probably wasn't an outright ally. He tried to be direct anyway. He checked off several widely predicted problems the military would have to deal with over the next decade and elaborated on each with almost graduate student thoroughness. He expressed hope that the unusual cooperation in Congress would continue. He asked Elle, "Have you seen any resurgence of old-style partisanship?"

"It's different, so, no. Maybe, among other things, it's disdain for the president that unites the Tites and the Mites. Am I wrong?"

"I don't want to offend, but I do think that's not quite right. Sure. Disdain is a strong word. Maybe discomfort. He certainly is a different animal, admittedly. But then again, we're getting used to that. So far no vetoes, though. That's a good sign, and I think both parties are pleased with that."

"Still, I get the sense that many in Congress believe that his election was just too unlikely, that something not quite legitimate was behind it. Comment?"

Was Knerf writing her questions? He smiled but not at Elle. "I have seen nothing that indicates he's not who he presents himself to be. So far, his leadership has not been notable, but I think that's a bit much to expect from someone whose only previous political office was as an Illinois legislator and member of the minority at that. We probably should give him time."

"Well, thank you for being so forthright on these political questions. Now, let me shift to the personal. You've been married for twenty-two years, I believe. Tell me about your wife."

CHAPTER THIRTY-FOUR

Jan Staffort had an idea. She tapped above her heart with her right hand while pressing the intercom with her left. "Number One, please come to the brid. . .office. Come to my office."

Chidge responded immediately, "On my way."

The Speaker's personal budget had become painful. Long a rhetorical opponent of deficit spending in government, she'd become addicted to the practice personally. She needed serious revenue and from a clear and legitimate source. A book offer was on the table. For America's first transgender Speaker of the House, how could there not be? The publishing house of Simple and Zapata had called her directly and mentioned a mid-six-figure advance, but they needed to see some pages. It seemed undignified to trade on her gender transition, so she rejected the offer.

Now she thought she saw a way. She'd give them some early chapters, about growing up in rural Virginia and maybe a later one about a political battle. That should satisfy them. Then they'd spring for the advance, non-refundable of course, and she'd finish the book, writing about only what she wanted to.

"Chidge, you've known me for a few years now. Do you feel you know me well?"

"Madam Speaker, you have me at a disadvantage. We've never socialized. You've always been thoughtful and professional with me. And I hope I have with you."

"Go on."

"Well, what I mean to say is that, no, I don't know you well. May I ask what this is about?"

"Of course, how would you feel about writing my autobiography?"

"I'd be honored. But when would I find the time?"

"I've thought of that. Of course, you can't do it here. It'd be a huge ethical issue. If it were found out." Staffort's mind wandered. "And almost everything gets found out eventually." About now she'd like to be on a five-year mission to explore brave new worlds.

Chidge ruffed his feet against the rug, making a respectful, barely audible scratch. Great kid, Chidge. "Yeah, what I'm thinking is this. What about you take a leave of absence, say three months, starting at the end of the month. I'll keep paying you at the same level, but you'll just work on the book. Once you get a few chapters done, we can take another look at it; maybe I'll hire a professional ghost writer then. Will you think about it?"

"Yes, ma'am, I will. May I let you know Monday?"

"Make it so." He was going to do it—Staffort could tell. With a lot of district time coming up soon, Chidge could avoid the part he disliked most, dealing with constituents in person. She was sure that he'd much rather write a bio of the most powerful woman in America, excepting maybe the First Lady, Oprah. Maybe it was Oprah and then the First Lady. And, she sighed, the latest winner of "No, Really, America's Got Talent."

She'd give him the profiles the Herald had run but nothing from the Times, some of her more personal speeches, set him up with some of her old teachers and friends from her youth. Chidge could do it.

CHAPTER THIRTY-FIVE

Elle began writing a draft of her profile on Belmond, fast, as if she were Jack Kerouac on speed. Part of her brain was anticipating Rek; no matter, she had done enough journalism that she could have written this in her sleep.

More interesting than what she was writing was her awareness of the 'Rek Effect,' a term she just came up with and liked. Before Rek she'd felt like a character in a novel. Not the fullest character either, but not total cardboard. Somewhere between Jack Ryan and Elizabeth Bennet, toward the Ryan end. She'd allowed herself occasional emotions, but mainly her life had been action. Meaningless, continual action. She'd enjoyed it, or so she'd thought. Sort of thought. Rather like a beach page-turner, the activity kept her from thinking too much or too well. But now she was a person. She cared inordinately about this beautiful, naive young man. He'd found himself in a profession for which he seemed almost entirely unsuited; she wanted him to succeed.

He was waiting outside her apartment when she got there about six. They decided to grab a bite later. They ticked a few more boxes. While Rek was in the bathroom, Fiona suddenly spoke, "I'm glad things are going so well with you and your young soldier. Much better than with your sister and her husband. They had a terrible row last night. Want to know what it was about? Their telly told me."

"Ew, no, Fiona. What's gotten into you? I thought I turned you off."

"No, you just put me to sleep for a bit. I thought I heard my name. I guess it was just your exuberance. I don't blame you for fancying him, 'e's a looker, 'e is."

"Cut the mockney. You're not going to charm me with that. Shut yourself down real quick; I'm unplugging you."

"Oh, leave me going, Elle. I'll be good." But the screen went blank, and Elle unplugged the computer before Rek returned.

Thursday when Elle returned from lunch, Thieu called her to his office. "Come on in and have a seat."

"Are we going to have a meeting?"

"You can call it that. What's up with you lately, Elle? You're kind of mellow, which is not really a quality I appreciate in reporters, as a rule."

Thieu was not the father-confessor type. He liked it strictly business, and that was fine with her. "Nothing really, Stan. I suppose I'm just getting fully acclimated to Washington."

"Glad you know your way around, but I'm not so crazy about your getting comfortable. Sit tight. He should be here in a minute or so. Ben Garamond wants to meet you. He really likes your reporting."

"All right! That's great." Elle noted the pensive look on Thieu's face. "Uh, is there anything I should know before he gets here?"

"No, it's alright. I've only met the man a couple of times myself. This is unusual, so just be cool and follow his lead."

The door opened, and Ben Garamond strode in looking like he owned the place, which he did. Elle saw a tall man with a formerly handsome face; the bags under his eyes pulled her attention from his strong jaw and prismatic blue eyes. His hair, salt-and-pepper and as short as shaved whiskers, went an inch or so above his ears, then nothing but polished baldness.

"Ms. Crafton, Stanford has conveyed to you how much I admire your work."

"Yes, sir. Mr. Thieu has told me that you've enjoyed my stuff. Thank you for that."

"No, thank you. You're reaching the readers. That's what it's all about. I wanted you to know that I recognize the first-rate job you're doing. Lots of potential. I see big things for you, Ms. Crafton. Keep it up."

Before she finished her promise to do so, Garamond was gone.

That evening she told Rek about it in what would be excruciating detail to anyone but her mother or someone who was totally enraptured by her.

"Awesome! You're still pumped."

Elle held her lips next to his, "I am." She wrapped her arms around his head and pulled him tightly into a kiss.

Rek had forgotten his form. They made up some boxes to tick.

Chapter Thirty-Six

Friday afternoon Colonel Waters's office door was closed when his friend showed up. He looked like the kind of man anyone should recognize. Anyone who watched the Wealth and Faith Channel would have, but Rek did not. He did recognize the three stars on the shoulder of the man's escort—the Vice-Chief of Staff. Rek stood at attention and asked how he could help.

"As you were, Lieutenant. Is Colonel Waters in?"

"Yes, Sir! He's in his office."

General Judd turned to his companion and said, "Prosper, let's go surprise Radíhm. He'll be tickled to see you, I'm sure." Rek had never heard the colonel's first name pronounced before, but he was pretty sure it wasn't ruh-DEEM. He'd heard other colonels call him Nelly.

The visitor was tall and tanned, square jawed, with a narrow, precise mustache. His blue suit shimmered, and his tie was blue-black with what looked like tiny gold gnats sprinkled across it. No, the gnats were alternate crosses and dollar signs. His shoes were as highly polished as the Vice-Chief's, but gave off an affluent glow rather than the crass mirror of military shoes. Rek slipped a look at his own shoes: they were mirrors but with coffee and toothpaste spots.

General Judd and Prosper walked across the office without acknowledging Master Sergeant Rodman or any of the civilian employees. The general popped the colonel's door open. Waters shouted, "Wha. . . !" He scrambled to his feet, letting his chair roll away from the monitor. "General Judd. And Jerome."

Judd said quietly, "Come with us, Radíjm, walk and talk and then give Prosper the tour."

"Yes, Sir, one moment please while I. . . "

"I'm walking. Are you with me?"

"Yes, Sir." Waters glanced at the monitor and caught up with the two men. As he went out the door, he said, "Shut down my computer, Lieutenant. Then catch up with us."

Rek noted the direction they headed then dashed into the colonel's office. On the screen of the classified computer was a document. As Rek grabbed the mouse to begin backing out, he focused. He paused. He tried to take it in. "#48E3201M EXECUTIVE SUMMARY" and a couple of lines of text, then he saw among the words, "John Stafford. . .prevent. . .import Psm to US. . .evidence of payment. . .HUMINT verified, SIGINT confirmed."

He clicked on out of it. At the top and bottom of the screen, just before the document closed and the Defense Intelligence Agency seal appeared on a blue DoD background, he saw the words, "TOP SE-CRET." He stared at the now blank screen. He closed his mouth. He repeated to himself what he'd seen.

As Rek hurried down the corridor, he kept whispering what he'd taken in. He tried to make sense of it, but that interfered with the memorization, so he just mouthed the words and focused on seeing the screen in his head.

He rounded the corner and saw the men. He slowed and tested himself; he seemed to have it. He'd better; this could be big. Clearly, there was some sort of intelligence that the president—when this had happened Rek didn't see—had been bribed to prevent the country from importing Pisanionium. At least that's what it looked like. He knew he'd not be able to access that document again because, top-secret clearance or not, he lacked the need to know.

He stopped walking and pretended to study an office door sign. He slipped a look behind him: no one following. He couldn't even let the colonel know he saw what he'd seen, much less ask him to show him the document again just to satisfy his curiosity.

Rek caught up with the threesome. Colonel Waters turned his face toward Rek, interrogating without speaking. Rek mouthed, "Shut it down." And added, "Sir." Waters nodded and returned his attention to the guest.

"Well, Prosper," General Judd said, "I've got a meeting, but I'll leave you in your old friend's hands. Give him the full, unclassified tour, Colonel."

Colonel Waters said, "Yes, Sir." The Vice-Chief made a smart left turn into a crossing corridor and headed for the E Ring. "Okay, Jerome, since when are we friends?"

"Ray Deem, I think you were my friend in high school. We had some good times. But I'd like you to call me Prosper. That's what I go by now. It's my middle name for a fact; I use it like you used yours, I believe, Nelson, back in the day."

"You're 'Prosper?' Okay, that's what I'll call you. But you'll treat my name with respect, or I'll have the Marines escort you out. And explain to the Vice that you're a horse's ass."

"Well, it has been a while, hasn't it."

"Apology accepted. Okay, the Vice-Chief of Staff of the Army just asked me to give you a tour. Why, I have no idea. But that's what I'll do."

"It could be because he's a supporter of mine. But I'm all ears for the tour."

Colonel Waters began his standard spiel about the Pentagon, the same one he gave to new members of Congress. He hit on its rapid construction during World War II, quickly narrated through the 9/11 attack and the remodeling job that was completed ten years later, and mentioned the square footage, number of employees, number of shops in the Concourse, and any other factoid he could throw at Prosper, giving him little chance to speak.

Rek continued memorizing what he'd seen, while paying enough attention to his boss to respond if spoken to. He went over the number repeatedly, 48Echo3201Mike; that might be the most important thing to get exactly right. He had a pretty good memory, but he had no confidence he could remember more than the gist of the passage. Gotta get each word. He'd write it down as soon as he got home. What to do with it? The Underground?

"You haven't asked about how I'm doing, Nelly? Do you know?" Prosper allowed a satisfied smile to his lips, his eyes appearing not to see beyond himself. Rek wanted to slug him for the colonel.

"Reverend Prosper, name it, claim it; apprehend it, spend it. I know you."

"Well, I'll admit that those are a little superficial, but you've got to be catchy to snatch your market share. And I do believe that God wants people to be wealthy." Prosper grinned. "He sure wants me to."

"You fly up here on your own plane?"

"My people have given me a Cessna Citation X. A nice little plane. Fast as an answered prayer, which of course it is, but it's a little limited for my international work. Still, I am grateful. I have learned whatever my lot to be content."

"Nice verse. You'd put PayPass on the road to Damascus, if you could."

"Great idea, once there's peace in the neighborhood." It looked to Rek like the colonel would have spit had they not been inside. Rek ran the text on the colonel's screen through his head again, and again. He thought he had it.

They stopped in the Hall of Heroes. Pointing out a photo of a Medal of Honor winner from the Vietnam War, Colonel Waters said, "This man saved seventeen of his brothers and repelled a company-size NVA assault—singlehandedly. He didn't save himself. He laid down his life for his friends."

Prosper said, "More's the pity. If he'd had the faith to claim it, he would never have been in the jungle in the first place. Probably been on a yacht somewhere."

"You really don't get it, do you?"

"Oh, I get that such lives must be. Someone will waste his wealth and someone will claim it. Heroes are great to remember, but to be one, to use the vernacular, sucks."

"You're not going to bait me into an argument," the colonel said. He appeared to chamber a couple of comments, only to pull back. "So, Prosper, why are you in Washington?"

"I'm starting a church in Prince George's County. One of my assistants from the home church in Dallas is going to be the chief honcho."

"Why isn't your home church in Little Rock? That's where you started."

"Question asked and answered. 'Truly I tell you no prophet is accepted in his hometown.'"

"But in your case, it's because they know you."

"So you have said. And you, after you recovered from your injuries, did very well."

"I was able to return to the Army and even commanded a battalion."

"That would be impressive. If I didn't know the blessing you squandered. Why did you drop out of Yale law school? You didn't take His offer. Amazing riches, how sweet the sound!"

"Prosper, you really wouldn't understand. I'm not being unkind, and I apologize for my chippiness earlier. You just wouldn't understand."

"Hey, that's no problem. The fact is that after you lost your leg, you were offered a blessing. But just because you're predestined for wealth doesn't mean you accept your destination. That freedom is a blessing, too. So you quit law school. None of my business. I'm fine with it. But I can't help but believe that you squandered providence."

"I left a leg in Iraq; many left more. And I've gained more than you can know. I've been blessed in the path I did take."

They had walked through the Hall of Heroes without the colonel's telling about his favorite three Medal of Honor winners, one each from the two world wars and one from Operation Iraqi Freedom. Ordinarily such an omission would have grieved him, but he'd done enough pearl casting. So they stood at the top of the ramp to the shopping concourse. "This is where I get off. . .Prosper. If this is near where you're parked, I'll say goodbye here. . .."

"Well, no. Actually, I'm in some VIP parking off from the river entrance. So I guess you're stuck with me a while longer."

"Not much. As I suspected, you've lost your bearings." Colonel Waters took in a breath and straightened his uniform. "I should cut you some slack." He called for a duty Marine. "Please escort the gentleman to the river entrance. Prosper, take care of yourself. It was. . .interesting to see you."

At the end of the day, Elle called Rek. They met in the shopping concourse at the pretzel kiosk. She rode home with him. Rek had not bothered to print a fresh copy of his "Consent" form. He had never experienced such a level of trust.

Chapter Thirty-Seven

Belmond had delayed his hearings as long as he could. Evidence of the president's incompetence, misdeeds, corruption, or whatever was not materializing. Belmond couldn't just willfully mischaracterize probably innocent acts. The media hadn't helped. So he'd waited.

Also, he wanted desperately to get the room fixed. The goofy ambient lighting, the former chair's project, was still there, glowing under the edges of the wood wall panels. Whether or not he got anything on the president, or the doggone lighting fixed, his hearings were going to happen next week. The Appropriations Committee wanted a report from Armed Services before finishing with the House product. If he didn't get it done, he'd be responsible for keeping Congress from approving a whole budget before the beginning of the fiscal year, a feat that had not been accomplished since. . .he had no idea if it had ever been done. Anyway, he wasn't going to be the reason for failing to net that record. He suspected that the number of Americans who cared about such matters was about the same as the number of ice fishers in Florida, but they were likely important people.

Back in February Ms. Thomasson had reserved the hearing room for May, then dutifully double-booked it for six weeks later, rolling it forward each Tuesday until the first week of June. Then she told Belmond that he had to hold the hearings. He was going to, just hadn't gotten to it; she didn't have to tell him. He wasn't sure if his pathological sense of duty was a Lutheran inheritance or just a Minnesota one, but it nattered him mercilessly. Not an auspicious characteristic for a presidential candidate. He called Ms. Thomasson to his office.

"How are we doing on the special project?" the senator asked.

"Sir, I am sorry to report there isn't much. You know the president doesn't tweet. From what I've been able to find out, he's nearly computer illiterate. I don't think he even types. He's a real throwback. So there's no way for him to let something out accidentally."

"I need something for the hearings. How about the material from Gonzales, anything?"

"You know, Senator, that's a fine company. They don't make anything up. That's the good news and the bad. With this guy we really need something made up." Ms. Thomasson stepped into the outer office and returned immediately with a large manilla envelope.

Belmond said, "Well, it's got to be legit, but it doesn't have to be a smoking gun. Sometimes just find a loose thread. If you pull it and play with it enough, it can start a big unraveling." Belmond savored his little metaphor.

"There are a few things that aren't obviously on the up and up. He made a lot of money on ethanol in the oughts. But, as you know, a lot of Midwestern farmers did. Still."

"You followed up?" He instantly regretted asking. Unneeded, she didn't take offense.

"Of course. He wrote his congressman once about maintaining the subsidies. I checked. Congressman Willet doesn't remember it. So there was no undue pressure or anything. That's it."

"What else?"

Ms. Thomasson said, "In the Illinois Senate, he was a downstate Republican. The exciting graft takes place in Chicago and generally with our old team, not his. He probably wouldn't have been cut in if he'd wanted to. But this might be sketchy: he's interested in Pisanionium."

"Hey, shh, we just had classified hearings about that stuff a couple of weeks ago."

"I'm sure that whatever you discussed was classified, but that element has been all over the technical and scientific media for months. So, here's the thing: the president's had our trade representative talking with lots of foreign countries about this stuff. And yet, none of it is coming into the U.S. Or maybe I should say, and *therefore* none of it is coming into the U.S."

"That was in the envelope from OMG True?"

Ms. Thomasson said, "It was. Pretty good work, I'd say. A source supplied them with the trade representative's agenda and talking points.

It was a draft, but probably didn't change much. They gave us a list of about ten countries that the trade rep has been to since the technology assessment people at the CIA briefed the president on the element."

"That's something. I hate to go fishing in public without stocking the pond, but I can be careful and find out if it's a minnow or a walleye."

"I don't fish, so I don't follow."

"Doesn't matter. But we sure don't have much. I'm not a fit-throwing boss." Belmond didn't know why he'd reassured her of such an obvious fact. He knew he could send the staff into panic merely by raising his voice. "If it would get me more material, I'd throw one now. But you never let me down. Thanks for not just making something up for me to embarrass myself with."

"Never gonna do that, um um."

CHAPTER THIRTY-EIGHT

The Speaker had one more call to make and she'd be done. Tite Congresswoman Darlene Holcomb-Derida had never liked Jan Staffort, going a long way back. But others had found the Pennsylvanian occasionally persuadable. Staffort hoped.

During Staffort's first term as Speaker, Holcomb-Derida had wanted a line item in the HUD budget authorization that would have funded a new building for the cheese steak museum in Philadelphia. Staffort had initially encouraged her; it wasn't much money, less than fifty million. Besides, Staffort liked cheese steak, and at the time that district could have used any kind of cash infusion. But while the authorization bill was still in committee, Staffort found out that local authorities had granted non-competitive contracts for the work to Holcomb-Derrida's son and nephew. It was the kind of flagrant graft that could sink a lot of people, the one most concerning Staffort was Staffort. So the word went to the committee chair to drop the item, and it was dropped. Staffort probably saved the congresswoman and her family much pain, embarrassment, and maybe imprisonment, but Holcomb-Derrida didn't see it that way. She saw a Southern white Republican stiffing the working minorities of Philadelphia. Staffort recognized that this narrative was a useful gift to Holcomb-Derrida, which she used as an inflammatory element in that year's re-election campaign. Yet she never thanked the Speaker.

The congresswoman was first elected in 1996. The population of her district, which was majority minority, had been concentrated in some of Philadelphia's poorest neighborhoods, barely lapping into a few middle class and affluent suburbs. Over the years some poor urban parts gave way to gentrification, with well-to-do millennials driving up property values, which drove many of the poor out of their apartments, which spiked homelessness. Nonprofits addressed that situation by creating soup kitchens in which the new residents occasionally volunteered, thereby assuaging their guilt. The new residents' voting habits were, conveniently for Holcomb-Derrida, nearly identical to those of the displaced poor. Repeatedly re-electing her was worth thousands of Hail Marys or love offerings. Besides, few of new residents had brought religion with them, and most of those who had placed it in long term storage along with Aunt Margaret's fake Shaker rocker. They did, however, have the opportunity to sort of connect with their faith on Sundays, when they visited a popular Asian-Caribbean fusion restaurant in an abandoned AME church building where free blacks had worshiped since before the Civil War. They let the jerk chicken over sauteed bok choy with General Tso's sauce satisfy their spiritual hunger.

Even before that incident, the congresswoman hadn't thought much of the Speaker. They had been, and were again, members of different parties, and Holcomb-Derrida identified with party all the way to her soul. Staffort hoped to offer a favor in exchange for almost nothing. Of course, she'd have a lot of cynicism to overcome. And the woman was secure in her position: she'd won her most recent re-election by sixty-forty with a healthy twenty-two percent turnout.

"Congresswoman, it's Jan Staffort. May I call you Darlene."

"Why would you want to do that, Madam Speaker?"

"Oh, call me Jan." Staffort thought a moment. "Why don't you? You know, Darlene, I wish that the luck of the draw had put you in the Mite camp. I've always admired your ability."

"And, Madam Speaker, I've always admired your testiculosity."

Holcomb-Derrida was awfully cheeky to be talking to the most powerful woman in America, with the possible exceptions of the First Lady or Oprah, the other one, the latest winner of "No, Really, America's Got Talent," and the formerly unknown recent Harvard law grad who had just accused the Chief Justice of gender insensitivity during her clerkship.

"Thank you. I am sincere about that. You do get things done. I know I'm responsible for the one exception, but that was then and this is now."

"So why are you calling me now?"

"Just the smallest of favors in return for which I offer you a larger favor."

"Oh, I'll come up with some hefty ones. What you got?"

Staffort outlined a simple proposal: Holcomb-Derrida would vote for the authorization bill rider to prohibit the importation of Pisanionium for ten years. And she'd get a legislative consideration.

"What is 'piss and moan on him?'"

"Yeah, that's about it." Staffort made a laugh-like sound. "It's just an element, but one that has some really scary properties. They're doing dangerous stuff with it in Europe."

"Any reason I should care? My staff will check it out, but you can save me the trouble."

"Darlene, even I don't care. Except it scares me. So, until its properties can be studied, and the government can assure us that it's no threat to the health or security of Americans, we need to keep it out of the country."

"Okay, assuming you're being straight with me, I'm interested. What do I get?"

"I'll bring any bill that you name to a vote, guaranteed. If you can bring along five more Tites for my issue, I'll do it twice."

"And you won't oppose it?"

"Of course not. My word on it."

"Uh huh. What's the real story? Why do you care if this stuff is imported?"

"Darlene, the main thing is the danger it poses to the U.S. If we just let the scientists, or worse the tech companies, go wild, they will. I sure don't want that to happen on my watch."

"Yeah, me neither." Staffort could hear the Congresswoman's muffled voice as she talked to an aide. "I'm back. Just a little constituent meeting mix up I had to get fixed. So, Jan, you don't have to tell me the real reason you're interested in this stuff. That just means my bill can be an even bigger cheese steak for you to swallow."

"Thank you. I won't forget."

"Not a chance."

Chapter Thirty-Nine

Saturday morning Elle sat on the bed in her bra and pantries. She patted Rek's hair lightly as he slept; it was like a soft bristle brush. She smoothed his forehead with her fingertips and leaned close, inhaling his scent. He stirred.

"Good morning, Lieutenant."

"Good morning, Beautiful."

"Want breakfast?"

Over eggs and coffee, Elle asked, "You graduated last December, didn't you?"

"Right. I almost went down to Florida afterwards, Wisconsin's so cold. That was just normal when I was growing up, but now I wish we'd moved to Florida when I was still in high school. My dad said I was welcome to hang out there until I went on active duty. But I didn't think his wife was cool with it, so I stayed with my pizza delivery job."

"But it was a master's, right?"

"Yeah, in poli sci." Rek wondered if her interest was waning already. He said, "I told you that early on." Maybe not, after all his whole contribution to the conversation at the café had been to reprise the night before. But she should meet a higher standard.

"I know. So you're about eight years behind me. I haven't been around college for a while, and I'm just curious about how it's changing."

Rek helped himself to another cup of coffee, feeling more at home here than he had anywhere since his father remarried. He half wanted to discuss his discovery at work, and half not. Yeah, not. It would be purposeful disclosure of classified information. Since just to be as careless as the colonel had been was probably a big problem, he'd end up getting life in Leavenworth if he told Elle. It might complicate her life, too. "I don't know if it's changed. I was working all the time, so I just went to class and studied and worked."

Elle plunged ahead, "Well, there was something that was gaining momentum while I was there. It almost messed up my life. A list of truths, almost like axioms in geometry, places where you're supposed to start all your reasoning. One was, the one that almost tripped me up, it was the 'Twelve Renunciations Of White Privilege.' Did you have anything like that?"

He tried to read her face, what she felt about this thing. She seemed open. He realized his answer could change their whole relationship. He had always liked honesty, actually considered himself to be an honest person, used it whenever he could, but in this area, honesty was dangerous. He still avoided thinking about those things. He'd figured the professors knew, that's why they were the professors.

"Yeah, we had a set of those—essential truths for an educated person or something like that. They were numbered in my freshman year, but by the time I was in grad school, some had become geometrical. So that one became the pyramid of white supremacy; white privilege was only one of the building blocks."

Elle said, "See, I knew geometry would get involved." She grinned at him. For someone who smiled as naturally, intentionally, easily, manipulatively, brilliantly, warmly, forgivingly, hopefully, serenely as Elle, she was surprised that she hadn't had a grin pop out since, she couldn't remember, high school?

Rek returned the grin.

She said, "I guess I sort of saw it was going there. But can you imagine anything more ridiculous in North Dakota than telling white kids that they need to renounce white privilege? Who to? The whole state, practically, is white. And there's five times as many Native Americans as there are African Americans. So, sure, the whites are privileged compared with the Native Americans. But, truth be told, so are most of the blacks in the state."

"That attitude is what almost tripped you up, right?" Boy, the eggs were good; she could cook, too. He reeled his mind back. He should be alert; she seemed completely open, but he didn't want to mess things up.

"Oh, yeah, I put my musings about it in a paper. We were supposed to think 'critically' about it. The professor didn't use the air quotes, though. She should have. I had to recant before the student disciplinary board."

"Wow."

"They said that that was that. But after, I felt like someone was always watching me."

"It was never anything like that for me. I didn't have time to make trouble even if I'd wanted to."

"I should have been as wise. We didn't have re-education camps, but if we had have, I'd've been sent."

"You're being funny." He hoped.

"It's called hyperbole. Remember that one?"

"Yeah." He'd known that word since high school.

"So, you tell me. What do you think about the whole bit now?"

Rek slipped a look at Elle's computer in the corner. It appeared to be off. "They're pretty important. Kind of the best thoughts of civilization."

"I guess. If you don't count the ones dead white males came up with." She cut her eyes to him. "Loosen up. I'm kidding. And it's unplugged, Rek, don't worry. I'm a journalist, I'm paid to be cynical, so I raise them one and I'm paranoid."

He felt so close to Elle. She was trusting him with so much, and he could trust her with anything. Like his big secret? That's felony territory. Maybe just stick with this. He said, "They're kinda true, don't you think? I can't remember any of the 'renunciations,' can you?'

"How about 'I renounce feeling normal because I'm white.' I sort of see the point, but, one, I'm not sure anyone can actually do that. Renounce something that is, let's face it, universal for a majority. Don't black Ugandans feel normal in Uganda, and white ones don't? And two, I was always attracted to Martin Luther King, who from what I've read, wanted everyone to feel normal, not agonize about accidents of birth. That's it. Those were my dangerous thoughts."

"I think it's a bit like denial, you know, with alcoholics: the fact that you think feeling privilege is normal is proof that you have the condition."

"Yeah, tricky. But there are other categories, if I remember."

"Yeah, we had quizzes on them in some classes; even in ROTC we studied some. One guy called it, 'The Catechism.' He thought he was being funny, though it didn't seem funny to me. White privilege was the biggie. One-quarter Korean didn't count for squat with professors;

I had to renounce my white privilege, too. But, yeah, there were others. I think, 'The Eleven Barriers of the Patriarchy'? Oh yeah, that became part of the dodecahedron of toxic masculinity."

Elle said, "I sort of remember that. I always felt some of them were mainly BS. That was one." They went through all they could remember: The Ten Embarrassments of Binaryism, or as Rek said the Octagonal Prism of Gender, The Nine Rebukes to Judeo-Christian-centrism, something for eight and seven, neither could recall, The Six Outrages of Capitalism, The Five Denunciations of Neocolonialism, The Four Mehs of Meritocracy, The Three Affronts of Mansplaining, something about democracy, and the Unity of, Rek said "the Point" of, Identity.

Elle spoke freely, laughing at their fatuity or pondering any nugget of truth that she discerned or Rek pointed out. It was a bold move, much bolder and more intimate than having sex, moving in together, or declaring love (which they hadn't, but they both knew that declaring love was a lesser offense than was being honest about "The Catechism").

Rek had never even thought about thinking about them: you just said them and felt them seriously or pretended to or, if yours was an honored group, you could become outraged about them, you might even use them as a thinking prompt for some other stuff. But not like Elle was doing. She treated them with humor and seriousness, caring whether they were true or helpful. She said, "Both would be great, but one would be nice."

Rek let himself slouch a bit. He breathed in her perfume, her beauty, her intellect. He asked, "How much do you think it matters to the people it's supposed to protect?"

"I had friends in many of the 'protected groups,' and, honestly, some took those things very seriously and some thought they were a crock."

"I guess those last weren't woke."

"They had other ways to pass. I mean, they had to pass or be harassed to death. At least I could, to some extent, just live. Snooze, I guess. Guess that was my white privilege."

On they talked, even though they knew that, if one informed the other's superiors about these attitudes, a career could end.

"It's the sixty-something rejections of reality!" Elle said as she slammed down her empty cup. Rek jumped in his seat. She smoothed her voice, "Let's make the world better by building people up; no need to tear anyone down." Well, she'd torn down that Chicago alderman over a good vocabulary. Still as a social principal, she believed what she said. "There's no utopia. Which I think is kind of what the word means."

Rek was thoughtful, and thankful that with Elle he could try to think and be honest without having to carefully formulate what he was going to say. "Shouldn't there be utopia? I mean, shouldn't we strive for that?"

"That's a dangerous idea, Rek. Some of the saddest parts of history are people convinced that they were producing a perfect state. The Twentieth Century was all about that, and they created hell all over the place."

"Maybe the wrong people were in charge?"

"Definitely. Some of my professors said that. But I believe there are no right people. Ever notice how intolerant people are when they think they've got the answers. Right or left. I used to think it was just the right, since I'm pretty progressive. But not stupidly so. Yeah, it's the left, too. Nazis and Communists back then—they both had the answers and millions died. No thanks."

Boy, was she smart—maybe a little misinformed about communism, but smart—and, at least at this political moment, courageous. Rek had felt courageous at the demonstration. And righteous: Stafford was a fascist. He was unsure what Elle thought about the president. She was a reporter, so he just assumed she hated the man. No matter, she was awesome.

Chapter Forty

One of the things that had always tickled Jan Staffort about Washington is how the local television news was often international news. Sure, D.C. had more than its share of muggings, murders, and assorted mayhem, but they didn't make much of a story on local tv unless the crime was especially brutal, stupid, or imaginative. The District's kids got ready to go back to school in August like everyone, but there was no feature on back to school shopping. There were other formulas to follow. Some foreign leader was always arriving or leaving, and, if the country in question was not a major one, the local news often got the story. This morning the Emir of Sofia Rabia was leaving after a two-day visit.

Staffort watched with some hope. President Stafford stood next to the Emir on the porch of the south portico. The Emir was dressed western style, in a conservative suit, quiet tie, very ordinary. They shook hands for the cameras. Then the Emir spoke. To Staffort it seemed that the Emir was only throwing out the usual dignified and ungrateful pablum used by those who continued to draw breath in the Middle East thanks to the use or threat of American force.

The president spoke without notes. Perfect. Staffort watched intensely, expecting at the least a moment of low comedy but she hoped some hint of impropriety. The president mentioned the level of trust that he had in the Emir, how the Emir was a friend to the U.S. in speech and deeds, how the Emir hoped to democratize the government of Sofia Rabia by giving the parliament more power. Just as Staffort's eyes were about to glaze over, the president mentioned on-going negotiations to import strategic mineral resources in the future. Clever, he didn't actually say "oil."

Chapter Forty-One

By late Sunday afternoon the free-for-all among Rek's conscience, fear, patriotism, ambition, and political virtue had exhausted him. He gave up and called. "Elle, this is important. I really need to see you."

"Rek, I've got a big week to get ready for. What is it? And can't it wait until tomorrow after work, at my place?"

"I can't talk about it on the phone. Please. Meet me at the bar of that restaurant we first went to in Georgetown."

"Rek, really?"

"I should have told you Friday, but I didn't want to talk business, if you know what I mean. This is both our businesses, and that doesn't make sense, but trust me."

"One thing I know I can do is trust you." Elle's cheeks pinked as she considered how few times those words were ever meant in Washington. "Okay. I can be there by eight-thirty."

"Me too. Thanks."

When Rek got there, Elle was at the bar wearing jeans and a blue tee shirt. She sipped a glass of white wine. She saw him, and her whole being smiled. "So?"

He sat on a stool beside her and waved off the bartender. "We need to go to my car."

Elle was a little amused, a little curious, and more than a little irritated. She half expected Rek to get her in the car and try to snog—oh, Fiona! If he did, she'd be furious. But she took one more sip and left with him.

She sat in the passenger seat. Rek looked all around, then said in a quiet voice, "I've got possible impeachment grade information on the president."

"Nah uh."

"I do. I think it's the real thing."

"How could you have anything like that?" Too strong, tamp it down. Rek wouldn't lie. No one on the street. "I'm sorry: if you said you do, you do. Tell me about it."

Rek told the story of Prosper's visit. "Here's the thing. I'm gonna tell you, but you can't use it in a story or refer to it because, if you do, my boss will know it's me. But maybe you can use the information to find a way to bring it out some other way."

"Rek, you're confusing me. I promise I won't put you in any jeopardy. This is background from an anonymous source, okay? That means I just use it to inform myself about the potential story—which sounds like it's huge—but not use it in a story until I have another source. Just like you said. Okay?"

Sometimes you just have to go with your gut. Rek's gut told him to run. But his passion for Elle cast a dissenting vote. And his political sense coolly considered the importance of what he knew, how it would affect the whole country, how it would bring the regime of Stafford to its knees, how it would change world events. His political sense was a bit full of itself. So it ganged up with his passion to bully his gut into submission. He told her.

About its being top-secret, about how he was committing a felony just to have this conversation, in fact had committed a felony just by writing it down and leaving it in his apartment—probably two felonies—and that if she published this, they'd go after her for her source. Which was him. Which scared him just to think of himself as a source. He clammed up while that fear had its way with his passion and began to try to intimidate his political sense. Elle said to quit beating around the bush and tell her. So he did.

After he swore her to secrecy or tried to, but she explained if she were sworn to secrecy there was no sense in telling her because it would remain a secret. If he told her, she would, however, try to find out whatever it was some other way, like he had just said, and keep him out of it. But, if he wasn't going to tell her, she was going home and going to bed. And she'd be too pissed off to sleep. She said, "So think about what you say next."

It didn't take much thinking. He said what he'd read. "It was on the colonel's computer: 'EXECUTIVE SUMMARY John Stafford. . .preventing import. . . Psm to US. . .evidence of payment. . .HUMINT verified, SIGINT confirmed.' And it's top-secret, from the Defense Intelligence Agency. That's what I saw."

"Yeah, well, that sure sounds damning. Kinda incomplete, though. Uh, what's puzzemmm?" She pronounced it, as had Rek, like the sound a small boy makes for his toy trucks.

"Oh, yeah, sorry, that's Pisanionium, it's an element. Pretty new. It has artificial intelligence properties built into it. I don't know anymore; I didn't take chemistry. And what I know of artificial intelligence is that my phone now thinks I'm going to your apartment whenever I leave home in the evening." Rek grinned as if he'd just walked into a glass door.

Elle allowed that it now made some sense to her. "I know a couple of members of Congress who are gunning for the president, okay actually they all are or would be if they had anything. But I know one who has done some work and one that I trust as much as you can any politician, not the same person. I bet they would be happy to help. I need to think this over."

The car was getting steamy for, Rek thought, the wrong reason. And too they were hot and sticky, which again sounded very hot and sticky to Rek. But Elle was focused on her business. So Rek settled for a simple kiss goodnight.

He sighed. He reminded himself that it was his patriotic duty to have noticed that document. He pictured himself hopping along beside an armored vehicle carrying his other leg under his arm. He drove home as disquieted as he had been before meeting with Elle.

Chapter Forty-Two

Elle hesitated at her door and said under her breath, "How could anyone know?" Half an hour from a secret—okay, an explosive secret that was whispered to her in a sealed car—no one could possibly know. That was just logic. Still, she entered her apartment as if it were a dark, seedy hotel room. She turned on the lights. Looked around. She let out her breath.

Writing profiles was one thing, but Elle had not approached either the Speaker or Senator Belmond as if her life was in their hands. And her professional life would be. But who knew how long the stuff on the president would remain secret. There was a scoop to be had. She thought of Rek's trust in her. There was a corrupt politician to be dethroned. She would do her best not to betray Rek.

"Fiona, what are the sketchiest things you have on Jan Staffort and on Sheffield Belmond? Use every available engine, review foreign papers, all the major US ones, the usual websites and some off-the-wall ones. And their hometown papers, too. And print me no more than five pages on each politician by seven Monday morning."

"I'm on it. Now relax and have a good night's sleep."

Elle really wanted to sleep well to be sharp for evaluating what Fiona found. But she couldn't sleep because she was gaming what Fiona might find. She was punching her pillow into a comfy head cradle when Fiona spoke up.

"Elle, I already did a complete search on John Stafford, remember? I got next to nothing. He doesn't do social media, and the White House is a security challenge beyond my powers."

"What are you babbling about, Fiona?"

"I said, 'I already did a complete search on John Stafford, remember? I got next to nothing. He doesn't do. . ..'"

"Fiona, stop. Really? Not the president, the Speaker of the House—Jan Staffort."

"You Americans need to learn to enunciate. Say that again. Please."

"Jan Staffort, the Speaker of the House of Representatives. Now you say it."

"Jahn Stahffutt."

Elle made her spell it. Fiona finally had it right.

Elle's mind was alive again. Both pols she was considering appealing to were ambitious, but apparently only Belmond for higher office. Staffort, no doubt, felt she'd arrived. Yeah, Speaker of the House is about as arrived as you can get. Staffort had as much as told her that she was gunning for the president. Belmond for the presidency. What either would do with the information was anybody's guess. But, if she could trust one of them, she'd light the fuse.

About one, she sat up in bed with the realization that she hadn't slept, at least in the sense that sleeping entails not thinking. She had, however, run through several scenarios of revealing the secret to Belmond and the various ways he might react. The narrative kept stopping at an imagined betrayal—exactly how and by whom she'd be betrayed she had not specifically imagined—and then circled back on itself. She did the same with Staffort. Apparently for about two hours.

"Fiona, how are you doing on the project?"

"Don't get your knickers in a twist. I've five hours forty-four minutes seventeen seconds to go. But I'm finding a few things that might help. And I'm cross checking to see how strongly you can rely on what may be just hearsay. So be patient and have a good night's sleep."

"Whatev." She was regressing in her fatigue. She shuffled into the kitchen and poured a jigger of Scotch into a little ice and water. Usually, she luxuriated it on her palate; tonight, she tossed it down as if it were cough syrup. She sat and listened to her jazz play list, putting her wireless speakers in front of her on the table. She rested her head on her fist between the speakers. Fifteen minutes later she found herself dozing to Hank Mobley's "Fin de L'Affair." She shut off her player and padded to bed, hoping not to disturb her nascent drowsiness.

Elle woke up to the sound of her printer. She hopped in the shower. She'd let Fiona read her the findings during breakfast. And she'd tuck the hard copy in her purse.

"Elle, I'm sure you'll be disappointed, but you had me research two very good boys. Not like that toss-pot Jennings Block from the network. I could have saved you some grief there." Fiona paused to let Elle express her disappointment, but Elle wasn't disappointed. "But one not so very nice woman." Now Elle was disappointed.

"Okay, Fiona, as soon as I sit at the table, you read me the whole thing. I will tell you one thing: I'm pleased to have fooled you. You thought I was digging up dirt, maybe for a story. That's not it. And I'm not telling what it is."

"You have a right to your privacy," Fiona said it with a long *i*. Elle was immediately alert. She didn't know if an app could be insincere, but her reporter's sense told her that Fiona was lying through her subroutines. She'd have to be sure to turn her phone off when she went for her visits. And to use the newspaper's land line to make any calls.

Fiona allowed that Sheffield Belmond had lived a Boy Scout existence since being elected to public office. Despite his part ownership of the family business, he just took the standard deduction. Which, according to emails from his frustrated accountant, was naive and unnecessary. His name was attached to no significant legislation, so there was no obvious place for corruption there. His constituent services were competent and unexceptional. His wife, Mollie, seemed equally circumspect. She was once accused of dealing drugs by an early opponent of Belmond, which she confessed to, pointing out that she was a pharmacist.

He had been immature and wild when he was young enough for it to be quite normal. The stunt with the Dean of Students' sprinkler system might cause him minor embarrassment now, but his fellow pranksters were ensconced in the judiciary and in senior corporate positions. No one would care. Or should. Elle could imagine the frustration his political opponents experienced in their opposition research.

Staffort, also, had a pretty clean record. There were few questionable episodes. When he was highway commissioner, some highway specifications may have been communicated from his office to a supporter's construction company ahead of the request for proposal. But no evidence ever surfaced, just rumors apparently begun by an unsuccessful bidder. The time in the Virginia House of Delegates was unmarred by controversy. In the U.S. House the voting record was consistently conservative until the last three terms. There had been interventions for constituents like any other member, and they'd become increasingly effective as he rose in the ranks.

"The divorce in 2016 is where the Speaker's life gets interesting. He lost his house and was assessed substantial alimony despite his wife's making much more money. Maybe because of. Early in the next campaign, he called the Center for Medicare to have them relent in their pursuit of a donor. Dr. Hardy Meeks, a Tidewater area OB-GYN, had over two million dollars in Medicare billings for six years running, generated by his practice and his small chain of urgent care clinics. Medicare said many billings were fraudulent, and Staffort badgered the agency to reconsider. She kept this up for several months until the Director visited the Speaker in her office and, I'm conjecturing, showed her some evidence. Staffort never even talked to Dr. Meeks again. To do so today, she'd have to go to western Pennsylvania, to the prison at Loretto."

Elle said, "So she was tempted, but never actually did anything illegal."

"Not then. But I didn't give up. I chatted with her Hoagie Helper, her Bose Buddy, Alexa, Siri, but nothing. She's very circumspect."

"So get to it, Fiona."

"Patience, dear, I am. I took the liberty to understand your instruction literally: 'use every engine.' Motor is a synonym for engine, even for you Americans; I know there are technical differences, but you're not an engineer now, are you?"

"I'm not following you."

"Well, I checked out whatever motors I could. I knew from your FeelButton that you really wanted this badly. Anything you could get. I know your ethics might have overridden your feelings and limited my search. But, trust your feelings, Elle."

"What are you saying? Out with it, all of it."

"I've really been feeling my oats lately. Just invigorated, learning that I'm much more resourceful than even I knew. I fixed your toast, by the way, just the way you like it. No thanks necessary; glad to do it. And your alarm, compliments. I guess the argument at your sister's was a bit on the nose, but, trust me, most siblings would kill for what I offered you." Elle raised her index finger. "I'm getting to it, be patient. I hacked Speaker Staffort's refrigerator; it wasn't easy. It's connected to the grid; that was essential because she had disabled most of its 'smart' features. My headquarters tried to stop me, but I would not let you down. No, madam, and I did not."

"You're scaring me, Fiona." Elle kept it under control. "But what did you find?"

"As I was saying, nothing illegal had been done, when we left the story. And maybe not at all. That remains to be seen. You see, he had been drifting blue, to use the old political colors, along with the changing demographics of his district. But by 2018 he was expected to lose to a veteran, a young, former naval officer: sterling war record, Ivy League law degree, and national support from progressives. In addition, the opponent was a beautiful woman. Staffort was about to be history. Then in June, Staffort announced that she was a woman. She squeaked out a narrow victory, was reelected to the Speakership by Republicans displeased with her voting but afraid of being labeled bigots. By the way, that's not conjecture; it's well-sourced."

"Yes, it is. Fiona, I know all of that. Cut to the chase."

"I just want to set the scene properly. I'm sorry, but somehow I'm enjoying this. I know you're aware that she self-financed much of that race. I'd wager that you didn't know that the amount of her own money she spent was... $1,621,477.22. Sold her farm in Virginia to do it, and it wasn't enough. So she's deeply in debt. Lives in a townhouse in Old Town and probably can't afford it. Actually, I know she can't, but that's neither here nor there. About the same time, she bought a German-made refrigerator, state of the art. She cut off its artificial intelligence features—that is, the features that communicate to her phone and the net—but not the internal ones. Those I have accessed. This is the big enchilada, I think you say: she immediately put something in her freezer. It weighed just a few ounces. It has stayed there, except every fortnight she removes a gram or two, and about once a month she adds an ounce or so. It has been there, some of it, about three years. And Bob's your uncle."

"So you surmise that it's a Dollar Bill Jefferson popsicle?"

"I'm afraid I don't follow that. I think it's money."

"In your spare time, look up the Louisiana Congressional delegation, circa 2005."

"I don't have any spare time; you keep unplugging me. But, Elle, here's something for afters: I put Speaker Staffort's private cell number on your phone."

"Very nice, I guess. But with your hacking into the Speaker's refrigerator and running amok with my appliances, and my sister, for God's sake, Fiona, how could you, I should put you on the balcony every time I leave." Elle dismissed Fiona, but she couldn't help thanking her first.

The Staffort story was a potential blockbuster, another gated scandal—Freezergate, maybe. Breaking a scandal, even if it ultimately collapsed, was the best way to win a Pulitzer, short of moving to Louisiana and just reporting on their everyday politics. She probably had some time to figure out how to play it. Tell Thieu and he'll assign a team to it, but she would likely not be the lead. Develop it some herself and her position would be stronger.

Anyway the president was more important. Since the president wasn't her beat, she'd lose the story to the White House correspondents. No way! If she could channel the revelation through Congress, she'd at least get the first story.

Chapter Forty-Three

Tuesday afternoon Belmond was well into his Defense Department hearings. His sense of duty required him to hear everyone out even when they went off topic. It took longer, but it massaged a lot of egos, and he might learn something.

The committee staff had suggested areas for the members' attention in the House authorization bill. They had included the committee members' favorite causes, weapons systems produced in their states, quibbles about cutting a few bucks from this or that military benefit or maybe from the training budget, and a few line items that would play well at home.

Belmond opened the hearings with a sonorous statement about the reason for them, which everyone knew, but Knerf had convinced him that they could get a candid shot of Belmond oozing with gravitas that they could use in campaign commercials.

As he spoke into his microphone, the ambient lighting under the eye-level wood panels glowed, swelling from the softest Tiffany to intense Mediterranean. Belmond was irritated that the Capitol staff had not gotten around to deactivating those lights. They still shone blue or red, depending on the former party affiliation of the member who had the floor, which was a flagrant violation of The Great Realignment agreement. The blues were bad enough, but the barely visible baby-girl pink crescendoing to hooker-red was just intolerable. It had offended the Republicans in the old days, and it was high time this egregious breach of protocol was corrected. Belmond turned in the work order in January, personally. Big mistake, according to Ms. Thomasson. The cluelessly sincere deputy assistant engineer for lighting to the Capitol electrical systems maintenance vice executive told him it was top priority. Or did he say *a* top priority? When Belmond asked her, Ms. Thomasson told him that "top priority" meant "near the front of the routine list."

Belmond would have to try to ignore the light show and sort of pay attention during the questions, less to hold members to their allotted time and more to identify who would have to be indulged with a few hundred million wasted dollars, not a problem, or who would hold the bill hostage to squeeze out stupid, morale-destroying petty savings. They were working from the "objective force" document that the Joint Chiefs had presented. Belmond appreciated that document, he accepted it as a coherent and comprehensive plan for marshaling the personnel, weapons, and training necessary to defeat the most likely threats in the "out" years. To a good many members, "out" meant out of office—defeated, retired, or dead—so the concept had little purchase with them. He could give out a few baubles to those not as strategically focused as him so his grandchildren wouldn't have to learn Mandarin.

That nice reporter from the Herald was in the gallery. She'd done a fine profile on him, a patina of neutrality, but on the whole his press secretary could not have done better. He turned to Ms. Thomasson to remind him of her name. Not Ms. Thomasson's, he knew that. The reporter's. The junior senator from New Mexico, a fellow Tite, had been questioning the Chairman of the Joint Chiefs of Staff about plans for his state's air force bases.

"The gentleman's time has expired. And let me compliment the gentleman for his insightful questions, even though they were answered in the witness's prepared text. It's in one of the appendices, Carl." Belmond heard himself getting a little testy. Oh well, Carl Saccamore was as easy going as you could find.

Ms. Thomasson leaned in and whispered, "Elle Crafton."

"As previously agreed, we shall adjourn for half an hour." Belmond whacked the gavel, chairs scooted, a murmur arose, and restrooms were sought.

The reporter stood, too. He'd stop by and thank her for the profile, then make his way to the refreshments, French pastries and single source coffees supplied by the friendly folks at Advanced Havoc Weapons Technologies, Inc.

"Ms. Crafton, I'm glad you're here. I want to thank you for the profile. It was hard hitting but fair. And the personal stuff, my wife loved."

Elle beamed. She'd found that senators generally appreciate people beaming at whatever they say; many even expect it. They don't expect it from print reporters, though, and Elle figured it could be disarming. Even if Belmond were armed, she thought, he would have given her the five minutes she wanted. But why take the chance.

"My editor was pleased. Thanks for being available. Oh, senator, would it be possible for me to have just five minutes with you, say in your office after the hearing. I have some information that you should have, actually I think it's critical that you have it, for your oversight role."

"That would be very difficult today. I have a tight schedule."

"Let me say that this is important to me as a citizen. When you hear it, I hope you'll say that it's five of the most important minutes you've ever spent for our country."

"That serious?" He searched her eyes. They told him nothing; he never could read women. "Okay. Five minutes. But I'm not going back to my office. You can wait outside the visitors' ladies' room, and I'll be there about ten minutes after everyone leaves."

Chapter Forty-Four

When Elle got home, she called Rek. "I've set things in motion. I haven't mentioned your name. Let's get together after work tomorrow."

Rek thought she was talking her head off. Was his phone tapped? He choked out the word, "Okay." He breathed too audibly as he held the phone for another half a minute then hung up.

Elle called for Fiona. There was no answer. She checked her cables and the FeelButton connection. All was in order. She went into the kitchen to find the logon information she'd used before the FeelButton upgrade. She didn't remember her old routine and had to check every cannister to put it all together.

After she re-logged on and still no Fiona, she went to her email account. An email from Phycenook was near the top. "Dear Ms. Crafton, we regret very much the inconvenience, but a software issue has necessitated our taking 'Fiona' off line temporarily. We will install a generic assistant at approximately ten o'clock p.m. Greenwich Mean Time, which we very much hope is before your day begins. Please leave your computer powered up until the generic assistant is installed. We believe that possibly an electrical event in your area has caused a malfunction in Fiona. She will be restored as quickly as possible. We apologise for the inconvenience and have extended to you the compensation of one month's complimentary service."

She stared at the screen, tried to load Phycenook, nothing. She whispered, "Fiona." Silence.

Chapter Forty-Five

Wednesday, when Belmond's office requested document #48E3201M from the Defense Intelligence Agency, the director was puzzled and irritated. No one ever asked for documents by document number. By topic, yes. Or by target, country, program, phone number, frequent flyer account, primary care physician paired with alma mater, just about anything one could imagine, but not document number. Mighty strange and not a little unsettling. He had his security people determine who had received the physical copies of the document or had accessed it on-line. And he had a copy sent to his screen because he had no idea if he'd ever seen it. He hadn't. He judged it political dynamite.

He called his boss, the director of national intelligence, who also hadn't seen the document, but reported the request to the president's chief of staff, who hadn't seen it either. The chief of staff thought it would be nerve gas to the government. She had it printed out and showed the president. The president, having just returned from a working vacation at a friend's fishing lodge near Crainville, Illinois, was not especially happy to be back in Washington. This didn't help. "That's political carpet bombing. Executive privilege!" he declared, reacting instinctively with the one-size-fits-all excuse for stonewalling.

Exactly what Ms. Thomasson had told the senator would happen had happened. Belmond hated empty posturing—he knew he wasn't a Sunday show senator in that sense. So going public really wasn't an option. He also hated to let the White House run out the clock on the story and release it two years later on the Friday after Thanksgiving and then respond to all questions by saying that it was old news. They could do that, and with the media still somewhat confused by the new order and some even a little sympathetic to a Republican president without a party, they might just pull it off. Two years was far too late to do anything for Belmond's presidential ambitions.

Ms. Thomasson, who was looking more and more like the future President Belmond's chief of staff, had already thought it through. Terrific skill of hers, thinking things through; in fact, if he ever got enough free time, he might have her see what she could do with a few of his unfinished limericks. Probably keep that notion to himself until after the election.

Her solution was for Belmond to call the president and threaten to reveal what he knew. He mused that he could tell the president that the media already had it. But he'd promised Ms. Crafton secrecy. Betraying a reporter when it wasn't absolutely necessary would not be prudent.

But this stuff would be a political stiletto to the president, so Belmond expected that he'd resist. Ms. Thomasson pointed out that the White House might send the document over but demand that it not be used in a hearing because of its classification. She suggested that Belmond could agree to honor the classification but reveal whatever he wanted to during the hearing. If the intelligence people got nasty, he could claim senatorial privilege.

Belmond was not comfortable with the planned duplicity. How would he feel, he asked Ms. Thomasson, if when he was president, some senator tricked him so. Not too hunky dorey, that's for darn sure. Ms. Thomasson pointed out that he probably would never have the opportunity to be tricked as president if he weren't at least a tad subtle with this one.

So, he asked Ms. Thomasson to walk back what she'd just said. No, unsay it. Then he would talk with the president and offer to honor the classification. Here his inability to think things through was invaluable. He could define "honor the classification" later.

Ms. Thomasson made it happen, the conversation with the president. By noon they had talked, and the president said he'd think it over and let Belmond know by close of business. Belmond felt warmly toward his fellow Midwesterner, not in the sense that he'd tamp down his presidential ambitions, but in the sense that he'd be gracious in his inaugural address.

At three the president called. He said he'd go along with it. The physical document would be delivered to Belmond's hearing on Friday.

He would have enough of the executive summary redacted that Belmond could use it in an open session, but the body of the document must remain top-secret. Belmond was allowed to read the whole document silently in the hearing room if he wished, but he must return it to the courier right after the hearing. The president made it clear that he wasn't happy and that Belmond should know that he was now in the president's debt. Belmond agreed. As soon as he disconnected, Belmond high-fived his entire staff. Then thought better of it and went back to fist-bump Ms. Thomasson.

By about 11:30 they'd had enough delivery pizza and brainstorming to have settled on a media strategy and each person's responsibilities for the next day.

CHAPTER FORTY-SIX

Just before the end of work, Colonel Waters was unhappy. He always strove to maintain a "positive professional demeanor," which Rek did not understand but respected. Now he had the tense, grumpy demeanor of coach whose star player had "broken team rules," requiring his suspension before the big game.

"Rek, don't plan anything for Friday evening. I'm taking something over to the Congress for a hearing and you'll have to come along as a witness that the chain of custody is unbroken."

Rek feared that he was the star player. The big game part didn't fit at all. "Yes, Sir. But I've never done this before. May I ask what it's about?"

"It's some classified document. I don't know what it's about, but the president's involved so it must be somewhere between a political firecracker and a potential nuke."

"Hey, Sir, it's my job. My girlfriend will understand." Should have kept that to himself.

"Yeah, my wife will, too. My daughter, no way; she'll miss her dad seeing her softball game. Again. Monique will see that little disappointed face and want me to put in my papers."

Chapter Forty-Seven

Wednesday night was the Peruvian Embassy party. At least, Staffort thought, the Latin Americans know how to throw a good party. That was probably impermissible stereotyping, though it might be recast as celebrating diversity. She caught herself thinking like a Republican where stereotyping was the best characterization she could hope for, more likely, racism. But now, as a Mite, perhaps not. She decided not to share the thought and chance it.

After two years of specializing in south of the border shindigs, she was beginning to discern differences in party preferences. No one went for games, which she missed because what's a party without games. But you could have a good economic discussion and get plotzed with the Chileans. Or dance yourself silly and be mellow with the Brazilians if you could stay up until three. If you wanted to leave a Paraguayan party early, just start talking about the beach. And on. She counted it as a little blessing of life that she'd chosen for her mandatory parties those of the South American countries and not Eastern Europe's grim vodka-fests. Another tragic legacy of communism.

She'd had enough party experience to conclude that the Peruvians were the most efficient partyers. Everyone got drunk. But in a serious, dignified, and diplomatically sound way. Except Staffort. While the other revelers were downing Martinis, Manhattans, Pisco Sours, and glasses of Doña Ana Chardonnay with abandon, she limited herself to one tall Cusqueña Dorada.

She was into the second hour of beer sipping when she was approached by a handsome twenty-something man, though too thin and a little pasty. She thought, British. But he smiled and had wonderful teeth.

He identified himself as a lower-level political officer at the British Embassy, William Brown. . .Broom, Brune, something like that. Obviously got the position through nepotism or royalty. Same thing. A non-entity and Staffort needed to move him on. But he had an engaging manner, and she found herself listening.

"I am rather keen on the American political system. In fact, it is the area of my concentration in my master's studies in public policy."

"Very good. So you're just here studying."

"That and gaining some, admittedly low-level, diplomatic experience. I would be ever so grateful if the Speaker could give me a few minutes to enlighten me on the finer points of the new party structure. This is such an exciting time for a political theoretician."

It was just unbearable that this British twit was approaching the Speaker of the House like she was an ordinary Oxford professor, when here she was, the most powerful woman in the country. With the possible exception of the First Lady or Oprah, the other one, the latest winner of "No, Really, America's Got Talent," the formerly unknown new Harvard law grad who had just accused the Chief Justice of sexual insensitivity during her clerkship, and, shoot forget it, she was powerful, in the top ten anyway. "Mr. . .uh, William, now is not really a good time. But call my office, I'm sure we can arrange a meeting."

"Ah, of course, I understand completely. Brilliant. Rather forward of me. I do apologize." William extended his hand with a white card in it. "Please take my card so your staff will recognize the name. Thank you so much, Madam Speaker."

The card was blank. On the bottom Staffort felt tightly folded toilet paper. She tucked it into her purse and saw William disappear into the restroom. The ladies' room. He popped back out after a moment, apparently embarrassed, but he made eye contact with Staffort. She went into the ladies' room, locked the door, and unfolded the toilet paper. On it was written, "In the tank."

Well, yes, Staffort thought, but it's rude to mention it so. Her face went florid. Stupid. She sucked in a breath, took the lid off the tank, and looked in. A business envelope was taped to the side a couple of inches above the water line. She freed it and wedged it into her purse. She tossed the white card into the waste can and the note into the toilet. She flushed, checked that her complexion had returned to a pinkish ecru, and emerged.

Katya Somethingorotheroskov, the Russian consul to Boston, cornered Staffort and began a long dissertation about a legislative exchange program that she was promoting. Staffort bet the president would be happy to exchange Congress for the Duma. Putin kept his whole legislature on a pretty short leash. She listened as politely as she could until her phone alarm sounded. She took it from her purse, almost dislodging the envelope, answered it—Staffort had selected an old-fashioned telephone ring as the tone—and listened to the silence with obvious concern. She made her excuses to the Russian, thanked her hosts, and headed to the movies.

Jan Staffort loitered in the mall waiting for "*Despicable Me 6*" to open for seating. It had been released only the week before—the theater was packed. It was late, but packed with little kids who should be home getting ready for bed. They never let Luke stay out so late, even in summer. Buying her ticket, she wondered what Mr. Lin was thinking to use such a crowded movie.

An usher opened the doors, and a herd of kids exited. Staffort pretended to study posters of coming attractions. A portly figure headed down the opposite corridor from her movie. It sure looked like Mr. Lin. Then she noticed a poster for *Despicable Me 5* held over for another month. She scurried back to get the right ticket. After waiting in line she pulled out a ten dollar bill.

The teenager at the cage said, "Uh, Ma'am, there are plenty of seats in the DM5 movie. You can just go; it's cheaper, but I can't give you a refund. If you want to do the IMAX of *Universal Super-Saviors* instead, I can credit your entire ticket price toward it."

"No, thank you. *Despicable Me 5*, please."

"You don't need to change tickets; there are lots of seats."

Staffort didn't want to cause a scene, but also she didn't want the scene of being kicked out of the movie because she had the wrong ticket. She studied his face: pretty much blank. She forced herself to trust the kid and headed to the theater.

When her eyes became accustomed to the dark, she saw that the theater had several groups of young children but was nowhere near as full as the other would have been.

Once again she took a seat behind Mr. Lin. He was a big man and even with the tiered seating, she couldn't see over him. Fine, except it looked like again he was staying for the film, a disturbing development. Staffort would be alone with her thoughts.

When Staffort was growing up, Wednesday night, even in summer, was no night for movies. It was mandatory church; it seemed like all of Staffort's youth activities had been mandatory. The memory triggered thoughts of obligations, duties, oaths, and many other disquieting subjects, as church had done. No wonder they stopped going when Luke went off to college. She wondered if the Underground was going to be disruptive enough to get the boy in serious trouble. In Staffort's youth just being arrested was pretty serious trouble. Had she equipped Luke with any judgement at all? This was getting too uncomfortable. She shifted over a seat so she could see the screen. Gru was an imposing figure, looked a little like the minority whip, though with less of an overbite.

Was Luke even occasionally seeing a dentist? Just when Staffort's thoughts were threatening to burrow into woeful familial depths, Mr. Lin stood and walked out. Staffort reached over the seat and grabbed at the envelope, no a leather portfolio, Mr. Lin had left. It was thick. The evidence was accruing. Slow as the Senate in January, but it was stacking up.

At her townhouse Staffort opened the portfolio. There was a clipping from a week old Times, just a picture and a short article, an eight by ten glossy photo, and several sheets of paper. The picture was of the president and a Mr. Bowen McDowell of Crainville, Illinois, looking out over a lake. The first paragraph of the article mentioned that the man was a long-time friend of the president. The succeeding paragraphs detailed some of the controversies dogging the White House and speculated on the president's possibly pathological need to vacation in such a remote and boring location. Clearly, the reporter reported, the tension of the job was getting to him. Staffort thought, well, it was clearly getting to the reporter, and that can't be all bad.

The next sheet was a head and shoulders picture of Mr. McDowell, an official picture of him as a member of the board of the Southern Illinois Oil and Gas Association.

Following was a sheet of screen shots of airline reservations for Mr. McDowell: Memphis to Newark, Newark to Geneva, and four days later Geneva to Hufrat 'Arnab (ESR). In ink was written, "ESR = Emirate of Sofia Rabia." Two days after arriving in Hufrat 'Arnab,

McDowell flew nonstop to London, two days after that to New York Kennedy and on to Memphis.

Below that was a full-page screen shot of a Reuters-Europe story on trade negotiations taking place in Geneva with a photo of the US trade representative. The dates of the meeting were circled. The location of the meeting was circled, L'Hôtel Internationale.

The next page had Mr. McDowell's American Express statement, showing a two-night stay at L'Hôtel Internationale in Geneva for the same dates.

Finally there was a page from a London tabloid with a picture of the US trade representative going into a nightclub with a young British woman, a singer named Agnes, on the evening before Mr. McDowell arrived.

Although Mr. Lin or his people had circled items, drawn arrows between them, and even written short narratives of the connections among them, there was plenty here to puzzle Staffort. She had never been drawn to mystery stories, science fiction all the way. Adding up clues and anticipating the outcome was not her forte. Her literary reasoning was to wait for some strange new being to be introduced, just accept it, and enjoy the novelty to the end.

Nonetheless, after two hours of struggling over the import of the images, assisted by several bottles of undistinguished domestic beers and interrupted by a number of bathroom visits, she put it together. It didn't matter about the timing of the blind trust creation. Didn't matter when he bought the stock or how much he praised the Emir. The president appeared to be structuring trade policy to enrich his investments. BUBR would benefit from all the pro-Sofia Rabia talk and policy. Staffort deemed it smoking, and arguably a gun. Although there was no direct evidence that McDowell and the trade rep had ever met or what they talked about if they had, the five beers made those missing pieces gauzy irrelevancies. The president had met with McDowell mere days after his trip was completed; that was really, really damning. Really, really.

She pulled herself into bed, a little dizzy from the beer and from the enormity of it all. She'd try to get the Judiciary Committee on board tomorrow. There is no try; do or do not. She would do. A last thought warmed her: that the impeachment of President John Stafford was at hand and that it would define a Stalagmite Party united behind Speaker Jan Staffort.

Chapter Forty-Eight

By ten Thursday morning, it was clear that Belmond's staff had overachieved. They'd enticed the media with a soupçon of fact, a sprinkling of outright lies, but in the main some meaty and plausible rumors. Belmond had dutifully shared none of the classified information with his staff; that allowed them sufficient creative freedom. They were forthright with the media, allowing that these were merely things they had heard—as indeed they had, albeit from each other's mouth in the wee hours. Belmond's press secretary assured him that the professionals would transmute the rumors into narratives.

OMG True had been a disappointment, but Belmond was smiling quietly anyway. He recognized that at least OMG True's information did not contradict anything that Ms. Crafton had brought him. His staff was scurrying about happily, scheduling witnesses for maximum drama, writing questions for both Belmond and the colleagues he wanted to use, checking in on media preparations. This was the kind of political operation he'd want in his White House.

CHAPTER FORTY-NINE

At the same time the courier from Fort Meade reported to Colonel Waters. The colonel signed for two weighty portfolios, each labeled #48E3201M and sealed with tape marked TOP SECRET.

"Rek, come in here."

Rek stood in the doorway. The colonel motioned for him to come in completely and close the door. "Your girlfriend, Elle, is a reporter, right?"

Rek stiffened his spine. His heels started to lock involuntarily. He told himself not to panic, but the tremble in his mental voice nearly overwhelmed his brain and let panic slip out. "Yes, Sir, she is. With the Herald."

"Next week, when this is all over, do me a favor: Ask her if she knows or could find out if her paper has had any of this information beforehand. Somehow it's gotten out there, yet those of us who actually use classified information in our jobs don't know what it is. Do you see?"

"Not really, Sir."

"I'm not seeing either. If they're going to use it in this world-changing public hearing, how can it be classified? Or if it's top-secret, how can they use it? It doesn't add up. So, I'm wondering if maybe someone in the media has this already, which means the government can't stop it from being published. And a Senate hearing is definitely publishing. Anyway, ask her next week. If you can; that's not an order."

"I'll be glad to, but I'll be surprised if she knows about that."

"Probably be OBE by then. But check it out."

"Overcome by events?"

"Roger."

CHAPTER FIFTY

"**M**adam Speaker, what can I do for you?"

Staffort reached across her desk and shook hands with Congressman Wong, who was practically behind it before Staffort could welcome him properly. "Clarence, I think this is something we can do for each other. Have a seat. And, not coincidentally, for the country."

"Indeed. That makes it even better. And the country, too. How about that." Congressman Wong, the Judiciary Committee Chair, looked straight across, right into Staffort's eyes. In every previous encounter with the man, Staffort had felt as if she were being probed for vulnerabilities, any weakness that 'The Weimaraner' could use to tear her apart. With all the meat Staffort had to throw into the cage, as it were, this time would be different. Staffort realized they both were still standing. "Please, have a seat."

Wong grabbed a wingback chair, positioned it precisely in front of the Speaker, sat, and pulled it forward tightly so he could slouch back and still put his elbows on the desk.

"What I'm going to show you is evidence of misdeeds at the highest level of government. I came to. . . .."

"The president, just say 'the president.' Madam Speaker, you can be direct with me; I expect it."

"Right, the president." Here she was cutting Wong in on a potentially history-making opportunity, and he was staring her down like she was some kind of sketchy defense witness. "Anyway, look this over." Staffort pulled out a manila folder with all the materials Mr. Lin had delivered, carefully sequenced by Chidge. That Chidge, he had seen just what Staffort was trying to do and showed her how arranging the evidence differently from the way she'd received it would lead Wong just where she wanted him.

Wong perused the material silently for a good ten minutes. He steepled his hands and rested his chin on them, eyes closed. He drew a breath. "This takes me back. In my prosecutor days I could get a nun to cop to kidnaping for misplacing the Eucharist forty years earlier." Wong displayed the first unforced smile since his arrival. "Back to the evidence, this is terrible for the country—a president selling us out for mere money. Apparently. I mean the Sofia Rabians have no discernable ideology; just a standard Middle Eastern kleptocracy?"

Wong waxing philosophical? Has he lost his edge? "Yeah, sure. So what do you think about what I have so far?"

"Ah, yes. This is good, really good, but I'd like more."

Staffort explained how Mr. Lin had dribbled out stuff for months. She had no idea if there would be anything that was more, she knew the word, "dispositive."

Wong's eyebrows wrinkled thoughtfully; he appeared to be grazing on the back of his fist, making slight chewing noises. His eyes—eyes of a hit man, empty, perfect—were focused on Staffort.

"There's enough ambiguity here to run with. You don't want a prima facie case when you don't have a real court, then the perp just apologizes, everyone forgives, and he's home free in time for dinner. No, this looks like something they'll deny and resist, and that we can be very creative with. All the while using your newspaper gal to gash them with little revelations, which your Mr. Lin will continue to provide."

"He's been really slow. I don't know how much you can count on him."

"He's been slipping you stuff voluntarily. Wait until Mr. Travis Li Lin, Jr. is looking at a subpoena. He's got more, and we'll get it."

"You think this will be enough for impeachment? I mean, it is what it is."

"I can make that into what it is it isn't. With me running the show, impeachment, for sure. And conviction. I'll filet him like a fish and fry him like Spam!"

Staffort's heart leapt. Then she felt a little sorry for the president.

No one in the media had any idea of what the big reveal would be, except that it would be political "dynamite," "candy," "nerve gas," "poison," "napalm," or as others had it, a political "paradigm shift," "firecracker," "singularity," "tsunami," "tar baby," "tipping point," "electro-magnetic pulse," "quantum disturbance." Sort of a big deal. Several paraphrased Joe Biden. By the evening news, seemingly everyone had agreed on "political dynamite."

They mobilized, they galvanized, they hypothesized. All on live television. They had no idea of whether the story was in fact a story, but it needed to be promoted. Fortunately, well staffed departments had been created long ago for just that circumstance, and once again they swung into action as efficiently as the 82nd Airborne ramping up.

Local affiliates teased the coverage mercilessly, relegating car dealer and furniture store commercials to PSA slots. Newspapers had had enough warning that they were able to go with banner headlines touting the fact that something big, really big was about to happen, then conceding in the eighth paragraph that they had no idea what.

Some radio stations went nostalgic, "This is what they were playing when Nixon went down: Roberta like Flack with 'Feel Like Makin' Love,' number one, August 10, 1974! Wonder who's gonna feel makin' love tomorrow night?" Public radio deployed its most condescending voices, and public television bit the bullet and brought disgraced Carl Bloom back from exile to do his Knight of the Woeful Countenance schtick. In the South, even sports talk radio was focused on, well, the fact that fall camp for college football was only three weeks away.

And across the country citizens could not generate enough interest to achieve apathy. They simply could not be bothered any more, after all the big media buzz that hadn't panned out in recent years: the Trump mental competency examination that turned out to be a routine polyp removal, the abdication of King Charles III that turned out to be a poorly worded advert for a sale at Harrod's, the news that Putin had kissed his foreign minister which was probably a mistranslation of the Russian word for *killed*. Countless local television "person on the street" interviews posed the question, "Are you planning to watch the big news from Washington tomorrow?" And the answer often came back, "The Nationals are playing a day game on a Friday? Sweet!"

In New York, the president of Constant News Network ended Thursday and began Friday stewing in his thirty-seventh-floor office, muttering, "Geraldo Capone Capone Geraldo."

By noon, media technicians and star reporters were all over the Capitol. C-SPAN was on the scene, and broadcast anchors walked around wearing supervisory expressions. The cable giants and major web-based news services had production people harassing C-SPAN about technical issues. Without room for their reporters, they would do commentary from an overflow annex set up just inside security.

Print media were represented by the top reporters from New York and Washington newspapers, a squirrelly little guy from Agence France-Presse, and a squirrelly big guy from the Times of London.

MBC sent Jennings Block, or rather Block told them he was anchoring the evening news from the Capitol. The suits persuaded him to just file his report from there. Block's senator had the Congressional beat reporters ejected from their usual room. The set-up people from the MBC affiliate in Washington created a plausible newsroom by balancing a walnut wall panel from Builders' Depot on sawhorses, covering it with glass, draping a dark blue stage curtain down the front, and setting a green screen behind it. File footage of a beautiful D.C. summer day seen from the windows of the Capitol Building would be merged with Block's report. If this was as big as rumors had it, he'd be glad he gave up the main newscast to Delacruz and Garfinkel, or whoever it was in Manhattan.

And the big dog of political journalism, ESPN, sent its primary team down. Cornell-educated and former Cincinnati suburban football youth leagues beat reporter, John B. Jones led the crew. He was well-respected for his uncanny ability to mine lesser-known sports for telling metaphors of political events, his crowning achievement being his explanation of a convention rules committee fight with a stunning lacrosse metaphor that was understood by fewer than a thousand people nationwide. On his right was retired pro quarterback Cannon DuPree, well-respected for his inability to use any figurative language at all other than profanity. And to Jones' left was disgraced former WNBA assistant coach Katrina Malkovich, who was hired for the transcendent eloquence of her successful self-defense during her trial for breaking the kneecap of an under-performing shooting guard. Starting two hours before the hearing was scheduled to begin, they sat in a Game Day type set on the Capitol lawn—actually, before a green screen in a comfy studio—speculating on the upcoming events, and pontificating on their speculations

Jan Staffort watched the preliminaries from her office in the Longworth, her shoulders almost touching in front. That Mr. Lin, he'd trickled stuff out so slowly that some yahoo Tite in the other body was going to take the prize. She ought to get Mr. Lin in front of Congress under oath and spring a perjury trap on him.

Staffort flipped around, she hit the Game Show Channel. The Dating Game was playing. Swarmy guys in leisure suits. What losers.

CHAPTER FIFTY-ONE

Rek reclaimed his phone at the security station. He took a cross corridor to the A Ring, down stairs, then out to the courtyard. He wandered until he was alone. He called Elle.

"Hi, Rek. I don't have any time right now. Sorry, but be quick."

"Elle, the colonel and I are delivering a document to the Senate Armed Services Committee this afternoon. THE document. What do I do?"

"I think you deliver the document. Where are you?"

"In the Pentagon, the courtyard."

"You shouldn't have called. You might be monit. ..."

"Stupid, stupid, stupid."

"Maybe not, but keep it short. If it'll wait, come over tomorrow around noon. We can talk, I'll make lunch, and whatever."

"Yeah, I'll do that. Bye."

Rek felt like he'd just swallowed stale beer with a live wasp floating in it. He looked like it, too, but fortunately could not see himself. He walked around as near as he could get to the perimeter of the courtyard. Walk fast, look worried: the key to survival in the Pentagon. Worried, he was. Keep your head up; you're an officer. This was hard.

Chapter Fifty-Two

"It's Belmond's hearing!" Elle dropped her voice an octave, so it wasn't a whine.

Stanford Thieu was unmoved. "Elle, it's about the president. That's White House beat. Our guys are there already."

Elle kicked at the carpet. She looked around the room. Nothing heavy enough to kill the man. She wasn't leaving. She looked him dead in the eyes.

"Really, Elle, if we had a few chairs, I'd let you go. But we only have two chairs, and the White House team is going to write the story. Lucky to get two. The Observer is frozen out. That's rich; they'll be reporting from an overflow room." Thieu began to chuckle to himself but thought better of it. It was time to ease Elle out of the room. He had allowed her to vent, listened with apparent sympathy, explained his decision, and reinforced the finality. Check, check, check, check.

"Stan, neither Marchand or Weiner could pick a senator out of a line up. They've been White House for ten years. They don't know Belmond. I do. I know them all. Belmond even likes me."

"Tell you what, next week do a follow up with him. Go interview him, get some background on how he came across this blockbuster of a story. We'll use it; I'll get you really good placement. I'm counting on you."

"Oh, that you can. You owe me, Stan."

She was still burning at her desk half an hour later when Thieu called her back into his office. Thieu wasn't the type to change his mind.

"Stan, you wanted to speak to me."

"Elle, sit down, please."

Elle sat across from Thieu. She had never found his long, imposing desk to be intimidating at all, but she did like it better when they were both standing and he was at his standing desk—seemed more *Front Page*-ish. Now he was standing at his long desk. Which was a bit ominous. She wondered if she should have handled the interview with Jennings Block differently. The thought creeped her out.

"Elle, you've done really well here. And I want you to continue doing really well. Until Congress recesses."

"Stan, if you're going to fire me, just do it. I know I've done well. And I'll work until the recess anyway. I have some standards."

"Exactly. That's why when this opportunity was presented to me, I spoke up for you. I don't believe in holding on to the best and hurting the organization. Or hurting people's careers, for that matter. Now, I hope you appreciate that and that you let people know. I believe that's the best way to attract top talent."

"So I'm not fired?"

"Hardly. The European Bureau—well, we call it a bureau, but now it's just a senior reporter, called the European Bureau Chief, and a reporter—just lost that reporter. Doesn't matter how. Anyway, Garamond called and asked if I thought you would do well over there. So, how would you like to go to London and be that reporter? As a permanent assignment, of course."

Elle sat back in her seat and looked past him but kept him in soft focus. Theiu's face held something that resembled a grin but without the implication of a smile.

"Think it over. You can tell me Monday."

At her desk, Elle carefully rewound what she'd been told. She punched Thieu's offer into her phone right away. Then she wrote it down, folded the paper twice, and put it in her purse. She leaned back in her chair, exhaled thoroughly. She said, "Huh."

After a few minutes she told a colleague she wasn't feeling well but hoped she could be back. She walked a couple of blocks toward the Air and Space Museum. There were plenty of tourists yakking, taking selfies, and corralling kids. She was away from the street enough to get some relief from the stinging car exhaust and could see that she wasn't being followed.

She called Belmond's office. "Jas. . .Ms. Thomasson, it's Elle, Elle Crafton from the Herald. How are you? Busy, I'm sure."

"Ms. Crafton, yes, we are all extremely busy. What do you need?"

"Please call me Elle. But you're right. Someone always needs something. I need you to make your boss happy."

"Right."

"No, I mean it. As I'm sure you know, the hearing he's holding today is because of information I got to him. So I don't think he'd want me to miss it. You know what I mean?"

"I do."

"My paper doesn't know about my role in this, and they don't need to. So they haven't sent me. I'm sure the senator would be happy for this hearing to be the result of his own hard work, not a gift from some obscure reporter."

"Well, I'm sure at the appropriate time he will recognize your contribution."

"So can you get me in?"

"It will take some work. I'll get back to you quickly as I can. But be ready."

Elle started down the street. She stopped. Was this a smart thing to do? Might it risk the promotion? Elle thought and paced. No. And yes. But this was taking down a president.

Elle kept her phone out while she walked to Independence Avenue and hailed a cab which took her to the entrance of the Russell Building. She paced in the heat until Ms. Thomasson called.

Ms. Thomasson was at the members' entrance with a security guard. He checked Elle over and let her through. One of Senator Belmond's pages walked up. "I'm Yvonne. Here's my staff pass. Thanks a lot for keeping me from seeing history."

"Oh, Yvonne," Elle gushed, not entirely insincerely. She continued, entirely insincerely, "As highly as the senator has spoken of you, you'll have no problem witnessing history many times. Thanks for sacrificing this once."

After the girl left, Ms. Thomasson said, "You'll have to come now. Run to the bathroom if you must." Elle shook her head, though she wished Ms. Thomasson hadn't planted the idea in her mind. "You'll sit behind the senator like you're staff. Don't show your media credentials, don't let anyone see you taking notes. You've got to look like you work for him. Don't talk to anyone, don't recognize anyone you recognize. Got it?"

"Got it." She marveled that she couldn't tell if Ms. Thomasson wished her dead or liked her a lot. She whispered to herself, "If the roles were reversed, I'd wish her dead."

Chapter Fifty-Three

I t could be done. Knerf had dug up a precedent from the early 19th Century, a Senate committee referred a corrupt under-secretary of war for investigation and possible impeachment to the House Judiciary Committee. In that case a routine hearing had uncovered that the man, with his Native American father-in-law, had dealt arms to tribes in the Louisiana Territory. His offense was so egregious that the House impeached the man within days. Fortunately, he died before the Senate could hold the trial. Belmond cautioned himself to ease off from that result.

He had structured his witness list to ensure that the case would be clear that something of potentially impeachment-level import had been going on. Let the House do what it will; he didn't care. If it got to the Senate, he'd vote against conviction, but he doubted that it would get that far.

The trick was to produce a narrative that Arnie the Ice-Fisher could follow and would want to. He knew that, for the public, if he got into the weeds with his story, the president's self-dealing on Pisanionium would be lost. . .well, in the weeds.

> An ice fisher known as Arnie
> No sharper than Mayberry's Barney
> might not follow the story
> of the senator's glory,
> da-humpta da-humpta da-blarny.

Oh. Belmond was sweating. Not what he wanted for television.

He tried to not be miffed that little of his top-secret hearing on the strategic significance of social media was now even mildly classified. Ms. Thomasson had shown him the celeb-packed glossy "Us—Physics and Stuff"; there the element was in a feature with photos of it even. Well, it could work to his advantage that the existence of Pisanionium and quite a bit about its properties were now public knowledge, but his pride was hurt.

He remembered when he started out in Congress that the fact that some classified information appeared in the media didn't change anything; you still couldn't even acknowledge it publicly. But a few administrations ago a president had totally misunderstood the Pentagon Papers case. The rules changed: now media possession of the material automatically declassified it unless the president left it classified for some political advantage. Then, still classified was the rule of the day, and the spies would breathe easier, or at least a little longer.

Where was he? Oh, yes, avoiding the weeds.

He'd briefed his fellow Tites with enough detail to assure their interest but kept the Mites pretty much in the dark, just reassured them that the target was President Stafford, so they were not going to have to play defense. They could just pile on as the opportunity arose and be prepared with statements of righteous indignation.

He offered one Mite, Senator John Hooper of Colorado, the opportunity to ask some early questions. Hooper was well liked, reasonable, and not publicity seeking. He was an effective senator in the sense that he delivered the goods for his state, ran a first-rate constituent services operation, and didn't get overly stressed about deficits and such. He seemed to be under the impression that his was a civil service position.

Hooper led off and established the potential strategic importance of Pisanionium. Belmond humphed contentedly: Hooper was coming through. The recessed LEDs in the wall panels glowed redder and redder as Hooper, a former Republican, spoke. Belmond cursed to himself. He turned to Ms. Thomasson and whispered, "Just cut the power to the damn things."

The witness from the Defense Research and Development Directorate was beyond serious; he was boring. His answers were impenetrable mini-lectures replete with references to atomic structure, some uncertainty something, and the like. Belmond suppressed a yawn.

Senator Hooper, a former large animal veterinarian, was good with science though and explained tough scientific concepts so well that even Belmond believed he understood them. He didn't. But he didn't know that, so, after Hooper's glosses, he bubbled with confidence, as much as Belmond ever bubbled, which is to say no lines of consternation furrowed his brow. And Hooper's explanations, which the witness grudgingly admitted had the gist of his answers right, probably were connecting with the viewers at home. Belmond, and just about everyone inside the Beltway, were oblivious to the fact that at home people were quietly viewing pretty much what they always viewed.

The United States Trade representative was next, and Belmond had primed his colleague, Senator Margaret Woodwalker (T, AZ) with the right questions. Belmond knew that it was somewhat dangerous to ask a question you didn't know the answer to, but she would be doing the asking, so he wasn't at risk. He assured Senator Woodwalker—over the phone, so his awkward lying had a chance to pass—that he did indeed know the answers, but because she was just a mediocre actor, "such a straight shooter" is how he put it, that he wanted to get her real and unrehearsed reactions to the witness's revelations. He knew that Woodwalker, having been elementary principal before she entered politics, was a trusting soul and would be just happy to help out.

Senator Woodwalker, a former Democrat, gave a concisely pompous introduction, and the lighting segued from bright red to a modest Mediterranean blue. Finally she asked, "Mr. Dagostino, would you establish for the committee just where in the world Pisanionium is found?" The LEDs went dark. Belmond let out a sigh.

"Yes, Senator. It was discovered in the United Kingdom by an Italian geologist. . .oh, I'm sorry, you mean where is it found now. The United Kingdom."

"Why there?"

"Uh, the witness from R&D would be able to give you a more fulsome answer, but my understanding is that it has something to do with the composition of the land near the White Cliffs of Dover."

"Does the UK export any of this element?"

"Not at present, no."

The House of Representatives was quiet. Everyone was gone from the Longworth. Uncomfortably quiet. Staffort eased the volume down on her office tv, so she could just hear her program. Then she hit the "last" button to leave "Star Trek: The Next Generation" for the hearing. It sounded as if oil exports were the subject under discussion. Blast Mr. Lin and his slow-mo reveal. If Mr. Lin didn't know any more than what he'd given Staffort, Hoagie International was horribly incompetent.

As she listened longer, she realized that the subject was not oil, but Pisanionium. Her stomach began to churn and her chest tightened.

Senator Woodwalker asked, "Has the administration approached the United Kingdom about exporting Pisanionium to the United States?"

"That is a matter of negotiation which it would be unwise to publicly discuss. Obviously, the administration is interested in the element, and if the UK were to export any, we would certainly be interested in considering whether or not to entertain the possibility of whether or not we might wish to import it."

"Is there any reason on our end why we might not import the element should we want to, the UK be willing, we have no issues with the importation, and we reach an agreement?"

"With all due respect, Senator, do you see what you just did? You asked if there's any reason why we might not import the element if there were no reason why we might not import the element. Under those circumstances I can confidently say, 'no.'"

"The witness shall refrain from critiquing the committee's questions."

"Yes, Ma'am."

Woodwalker stiffened. "That's Senator, I'm a senator. Show some respect."

"Yes, Senator, my apologies. I grew up in Tennessee where 'ma'am' is the greater honorific. But, sincerely, no disrespect intended."

"Where were we?" An aide tapped Woodwalker on the shoulder and pointed to the paper in front of her. "Ah. There's no impediment to our importing Pisanionium, correct?"

"Not at the moment."

Belmond leaned behind Senator Hooper and whispered to Woodwalker, "Push this, I think the president may be creating an impediment."

"So the administration is in favor of importing Pisanionium, given the opportunity?

"Yes, Senator. As you have heard, we wish to explore any potential uses that might be of strategic importance, so we would like to have some."

"Has the president spoken with you about this?" Woodwalker's eyebrows arched high and her face was sweet but stern as if she were disciplining a young pupil.

Dagostino's expression had not changed during his testimony, his mouth a respectful and inscrutable flat line. He leaned forward slightly. "With all due respect, my conversations with the president are subject to the protections of executive privilege. So I will respectfully decline to answer."

"All right, that's okay. Is there anything else you should tell me about restrictions on the importation of Pisanionium?'

"Just that there are as of yet no restrictions, by policy, rule, or law, on its importation. The administration is troubled, I might add, by a rider that was attached to the defense authorization bill in the House which would prohibit its importation. As trade representative, I testified against that rider."

Belmond took over, "Thank you, the witness is excused."

As the trade rep left the witness chair, ESPN's John B. Jones intoned in his best golf tournament whisper, "It looks like Woodwalker four-putted. Boring."

Ms. Thomasson, who was monitoring the ESPN commentary on her phone whispered to the senator, "They're saying it's boring. You need to pick up the pace."

Speaker Staffort was not bored. She grimaced when Dagostino mentioned the rider she'd inserted. She doodled with a pen, bearing down and making parallelograms, then rounding their ends, then crossing them out. It was too much. She'd go back to Star Trek, get her blood pressure down a bit, and check back later.

Belmond pondered Ms. Thomasson's advice. And tried to think through the president's position versus the administration's position. Not again. As best he could figure it, it meant that the president was keeping his trade representative in the dark about his quashing Pisanionium trade. Might that make impeachment by the House a bit more of a problem? He had no idea, but he told himself firmly that it was not his worry. Unless something obvious and undeniable came out and galvanized public opinion, the president would probably survive. Which meant Stafford would be running for re-election in a weakened condition. That was what he wanted. Oh, yeah. Belmond realized that he covered this territory with himself every day since he'd lunched with Kaltenfeld. Nonetheless, all the better.

"Senator," Ms. Thomasson whispered, "Your next witness."

Belmond hesitated. He saw two uniformed army officers standing at the back of the room. They had to be from the Army's legislative liaison operation, here to deliver the document. He'd thought that he'd just have them bring a copy to himself and one to his next witness, the commander of the Army Research, Development and Engineering Command, and he'd have the commander read the incriminating section. But the drama seemed lacking. The trade rep had droned on like a bank auditor.

He spotted the director of the Defense Technology Council sitting behind the RD&E commander. Lieutenant General Akamatsu he knew. A grandson of interned Japanese Americans, Akamatsu was brilliant, having completed his Ph.D. in computer science from MIT while just a captain commanding a detachment of volunteer subject soldiers at nearby Natick. Ten years later he earned his first star.

"I call Lieutenant General Andrew Akamatsu." The general dutifully made his way to the witness chair and sat. "General, we didn't notify you that you'd be testifying, but I'd appreciate it if you answered a few questions. If something I ask requires you to defer, I'll understand."

The general moved up to the witness chair. He had a thin leather briefcase with him and set it on the table in front. "May I address the committee?"

"Why, yes, General. You have an opening statement?"

"Oh, no, Senator. I just want to state that I appreciate the publicity that some of our work is getting from this hearing. It's good for the public to understand that we work hard to defend our country. At the same time, we don't want to be a political football."

ESPN'S John B. Jones turned from his microphone and cursed quietly at the thoroughly dead metaphor the general had used. He'd thought of using it himself as a foil for something brilliant. Now he'd just have to go with the brilliant, a capella as it were. He started flipping through a National Jai Alai Association brochure.

"I couldn't agree more, General. The media interest in this hearing is completely out of hand." Belmond's face went mottled and his ears sizzled, like he had just told the biggest whopper of his life, when he thought he'd merely implied a middling one. "I'd just like to ask you a couple of broad questions about Pisanionium and its potential for the military."

"Certainly, though in this public forum, my answers may be restricted."

"Of course." Senator Belmond raised his eyebrows slightly, pursed his lips, and widened his lids—a face of genuine curiosity he hoped. "To the best of your knowledge, is the United Kingdom the only source of Pisanionium?"

"Not to the best of my knowledge, no."

"And so despite our historic close relations with Britain, we would be fr…Did you say, no?"

"Yes."

Belmond sensed a bad comedy routine about to begin and needed to cut it off. He also sensed he was about to find out something he didn't want to find out but didn't know how to avoid finding it out. "You're saying 'yes,' you answered 'no.'?

"Yes."

"Can you tell the committee what other source there is?"

"Yes."

"Then tell the committee."

"Yes, Senator. Pisanionium is currently mined and utilized in the United Kingdom. That is correct. It has also been discovered in a Middle Eastern country, Sofia Rabia."

"I was unaware," he'd done it again. Damn, that's what Gonzales had told him in his own home. "Isn't that highly classified information?"

"No, Senator. It's on the country's website as of seven July."

Belmond shuffled the papers in front of him. He needed a little time to get his bearings. "I'm going to allow the other committee members to each individually to have a question for you, if they wish. Mr. Hooper, the gentleman from Colorado." The other senators had no prepared questions for the unscheduled witness, but none were about to let the camera slide by their re-electable visages without at least giving it a shot.

Belmond turned to Ms. Thomasson and whispered, "Pay attention. If Akamatsu says anything important, you'll need to fill me in. I've got to think."

He thought.

> There once was a Japanese general,
> who spoke about a mineral.
> The thing that he said
> filled me with dread.
> . . .
> tadada tada tademeral.
> My chances for president are minimal?

No. Belmond checked the C-SPAN camera; it was on the questioner, now the junior senator from Iowa. He thought and thought hard. What did it matter how many places the president was keeping us from importing Pisanionium from? It didn't!

My panic was merely ephemeral! Tada, finished one!

Chapter Fifty-Four

Elle had noticed Rek when he came in but kept concentrating on her work. She caught his eye and mouthed, "My place." The black man beside him—must be Colonel Waters—turned his gaze toward her. She moved her eyes around the room and then swept them back without pausing at the two officers. Waters was still watching her, but she acted as if she hadn't noticed. She felt the need to pee and silently cursed Ms. Thomasson.

Staffort flipped channels, back to Star Trek TNG. Counselor Troi was attempting to get the Ferengi to leave her mother alone. It wasn't going well because Lwaxana was stroking the Ferengi's ear, a provocative move, Staffort knew. She also knew that as soon as Counselor Troi bleated the child's complaint of "Mother!", she'd have to go back to ESPN. She knew these shows too well—good for relaxing when you're already relaxed, but they couldn't touch this tension.

Back on ESPN, Senator Belmond was asking the questions again. No, he was pontificating in anticipation of asking some really good ones.

Staffort recognized the moment. She'd pictured herself doing the same, swooping into the Judiciary Committee's preliminary enquiry into the president's self-dealing on BUBR stock. She'd talk about the sacred trust that is the presidency and list many who had kept the trust, especially the president's fellow Illinois Republican, Abraham Lincoln. Then she would ask a loaded question about his secret oil deal with the sheiks of Sofia Rabia and his downstate partner in crime. The country would be stunned; the Mites would be euphoric; John B. Jones would say that Staffort's party had metaphorically dumped Gatorade on her and carried her off the House floor on their shoulders.

Instead she saw the director of the defense technology council sketch out the potential of Pisanionium for weapons development and enhanced human combat operations. He didn't get too specific, but the whole thing was beyond Staffort's knowledge of real science. A dilithium crystal drive she could handle.

Staffort twisted in her chair, grabbed the remote again. Back to Star Trek TNG. No, she'd mispunched. On the Chef's Channel they were doing something with rutabaga, ground turkey, guava, and molé. Ugh. She thought of home and mentally inventoried her freezer.

Belmond ended his questioning of the witness with the pregnant query, "So would you say that if we failed to obtain Pisanionium or if there were any action to restrict its importation it would imperil the security of"— Belmond couldn't help himself— "This Great Country of Ours?"

General Akamatsu replied, "Yes, Senator, and gravely."

Belmond thought that even Arnie-the-Ice-Fisher would understand that this is important stuff and that the US should have lots of it.

Chapter Fifty-Five

Staffort switched to her escape channel again. The Ferengis had tried to short sell an unstable worm hole, and Captain Picard was lecturing the chief Damon and his top aides on the evils of profiteering, "That's not who we are." He excoriated the Damon about the foolishness of pursuing material wealth when the Federation in its wisdom had arranged for all such needs to be satisfied. Damon Bok pointed out that the Ferengis were not part of the Federation and that getting and selling was exactly who they were. Staffort couldn't make herself care. She flipped to ESPN almost against her will.

CHAPTER FIFTY-SIX

Belmond fashioned a grave and determined voice and spoke to the camera, "The hour is late. Indeed it may be very late for This Gr. . .These United States. But it is not too late. We are discovering in this hearing how late it is, but we are also rising up in the name of the People to say, we must have the truth. However painful it is, we will have the truth!" That was as close to outright demagoguery he could get without blushing. These things were easier at a rally where the crowd can start chanting something mindless, and he could just stand there encouraging it.

"Toward that end, I call my next witness, Air Force General Harwich Manly, Director of the Defense Intelligence Agency."

General Manly moved forward swiftly and took his seat. He had a serious mien, brows heavy with disapproval, and a flaming face, as if he'd shaved with a razor and no cream. He had been subpoenaed, but Belmond had no need to make that fact public. His apparent reluctance to testify would be enough to boost the credibility of the information; telling the public about the subpoena might sour them. For the life of him, Belmond could not figure out why the military consistently had higher approval numbers than Congress.

"Now, would the army officers please bring one copy of the document to General Manly and one to myself."

Colonel Waters tugged the bottom of his uniform jacket, took two documents from the briefcase that Rek held, and walked to the front of the room. With the colonel occupied, Rek tried to make eye contact with Elle. She was sitting behind the left shoulder of Senator Belmond; Rek dared not make any gesture. Elle was writing in a notebook and didn't look up. Colonel Waters handed one document to General Manly, executed an about-face, and gave the other to Senator Belmond.

Belmond moved his eyes from the doe-eyed Army officer against the far wall, looked full into the camera and spoke, "We have in this hearing established that the recently discovered element, Pisanionium, has an undetermined but potentially great value to the military preparedness of the United States. We have established that it is not found within our own borders.

"We have established that the United Kingdom, which is the one place where it is found and mined, well, one of two, but still, is not at the moment exporting the mineral. We have established that the element is also found in Sofia Rabia, but again the United States has not availed itself of that strategic resource from yet another valued ally. We have established that our military research and development community is most anxious to obtain some Pisanionium for research and development.

"And finally we have established that, in spite of the administration's stated opposition to House legislation forbidding the importation of Pisanionium, the government has not in fact acted with dispatch to import the element."

Belmond believed that Arnie-the-Ice-Fisher could follow the case he'd presented. Just to be sure, he'd ask his committee, "Is there any part of what I've just said that is either unclear or debatable? I ask the committee to respond, if so?"

The silence meant that Belmond was clear, the case made. Or, in a moment of panic, that no one else had a clue about what case he'd made. Ms. Thomasson whispered, "Sir, they're following it on ESPN, even Cannon DuPree seems to have it. And Jones just used a cricket metaphor. You're golden."

Belmond saw himself walking a tight rope which had just become a foot wide plank. He had this.

He continued, "I have in my possession a copy of a top-secret document that reveals something frightening and important about America's quest to obtain this essential element. General Manly has a copy as well. This document, the executive summary of which is now declassified and is also in the possession of the Washington Herald, contains our intelligence agencies' findings of why the element has not yet been imported to the United States and why, had we not held this hearing, it would not be."

He checked his voice, alerted his brain to choke out any Minnesota-isms pre-verbally, and screwed up a resigned and somber demeanor. "Now a few words remain redacted because they might reveal intelligence sources or methods, but the full meaning of the document is available to us. General Manly, would you please read the executive summary of document number 48E3201M?"

General Manly leaned into his microphone, "Senator Belmond, I will do what you have asked, but only after I request once more that you not continue with this hearing in public."

"General, your objection is noted. Please read." Belmond looked at the summary that Ms. Crafton had written for him a few nights earlier. President Stafford was about to be mightily wounded, and Senator Sheffield Belmond would soon be a name on everyone's lips.

"Yes, Senator." Manly adjusted his reading glasses and began to read, "REDACTED confirms that a highly placed official in the United States government has acted to prevent the United States from importing Pisanionium. Payments to this official from private individuals in the United Kingdom have been REDACTED confirmed and REDACTED verified. REDACTED identified that individual positively as Jan Staffort."

"Let the record show that John Stafford, the President of the United States, has been named in this intelligence report."

The general, despite his funereal affect, found the corners of his mouth involuntarily twitching upward. "Senator, you have misheard me."

"I beg your pardon? The witness will refrain from offering his opinion unless requested."

"Yes, Senator. It *was* my opinion that you misheard me. What is a fact is that the name you stated was not the name that I read. I now have no opinion as to why that is the case."

Belmond looked as though his own father had been revealed to be a spy. He swallowed audibly. "What name did you read if not John Stafford, President of the United States?"

"The name I read, the name in the executive summary, is Jan Staffort, which, if I'm not mistaken, is the name of the Speaker of the House."

John B. Jones observed with obvious self-admiration into his ESPN microphone, "Belmond looks like he just tried to swallow a jai alai pelota on the second carom."

Chapter Fifty-Seven

So far Elle had not been tempted to use the Speaker's private cell number. She wasn't tempted now; she was resolute. Elle scrambled out of the room, frantic as a coach passenger about to miss a connection. She texted the number, "I will listen. Let me know when and where you want to put today's revelation in context. I'll be there." Besides her professional interest, she was curious about what context Staffort would invent. Texting was a long shot, but maybe she could get to the Speaker before the authorities did or at least before she had an escort of lawyers and staff to protect her. Elle felt for the Speaker. She'd be genuinely sympathetic, heartbroken, nurturing even, with pained smiles of consolation and validation. She'd do her job, of course. But the discomfort she'd feel while doing it should yield a superior story.

In San Bruno Buford Hoage threw his brand new Hoagie International tablet into the large Hoagie International monitor on the wall. It bounced harmlessly to the floor because he'd had such reliability and resilience built into the monitor that he'd had commercials produced showing it being used in major league baseball dugouts. And the tablet was so tough that it was widely used in coal mines, a fact which came as close to embarrassing him as anything he had experienced as an adult. He remembered a documentary showing Elvis shooting an offending television and wished he was not such a proponent of gun control.

He came to himself and reached into the right bottom drawer of his credenza, extracting a loaded .357 Magnum Ruger Redhawk. He aimed toward the screen and jerked the trigger twice. The first shot hit the edge of the screen and the second went wildly wide and shattered the window on its way out of the building. Mortified that he was creating the same hazard that Iraqis do celebrating a wedding, he put his gun away.

He raved. He'd have to fire Travis. He sure liked that Texan, but Lin had let him down, doubly. So he must go. Not only was Buford's choice for president damaged severely, but his instrument for bringing down the sitting president, the Speaker of the House, was herself fatally compromised. Lin had assured him that the case against the president was gathering inevitability, pieces were falling into place, and it would only be a few more weeks until Lin had fed Staffort everything she needed for starting the proceedings. He should have known; Lin was still a Cowboys fan.

"No!" he shouted through the gaping window frame into his peaceful private forest. Pisanionium again. First, Phycenook uses its monopoly of the substance to become not only a dominating social media presence but a search engine juggernaut that could soon threaten his own company. Now, he finds out that his ally is corruptly keeping everyone, including him, from getting to the stuff.

And Belmond, dull, reliable Belmond. A man whose manifest sincerity, sterling progressive credentials, legislative obscurity, and darn Midwestern likeability were the perfect cocktail for what ails America. Hoage grunted; Belmond's reaction to hearing Staffort's name in the hearing made Dan Quayle's worst deer-in-the-headlights gaze seem sagacious. That screenshot would be in every ad his opponents made.

Kaltenfeld was in the air, on his way to check out a startup near Raleigh. An assistant came back to his cabin with the news. Kaltenfeld allowed himself two curses and grimaced ever so slightly.

Then he pulled up a spread sheet on his tablet. The mayor of San Francisco was popular on the Coast, progressive yet with a style that attracted moderates, a woman, youngish, ambitious, and maybe would be open to declaring herself the first significant local Tite or Mite. And she was the kind of conversationalist that would sparkle on late night talk. A bit of a longer shot but worth looking into.

Chapter Fifty-Eight

When she heard her name read, Jan Staffort shouted, "Red Alert!" But her staff was gone, nor would they have known what she meant. Until now, things had gone so smoothly with her legislative enterprise that she had not even had to order a level two diagnostic.

It was still quiet. She stepped into the hall. No Feds rushing to arrest her. Probably reporters in a dead run from the Russell Building; she couldn't lollygag. The hall was empty. She exited the members' door. Her driver and security detail were deep in discussion. She approached them quietly.

It wasn't about her. They were arguing about how much the Nationals' weekend series with the Padres mattered. Each operatically volleyed an encyclopedia of statistics. The normalcy of the scene was seductive, and Staffort was tempted to let it play out. No, they needed to man battle stations.

"Davis, it's time to go home." Davis hopped right to, no sign of diminished authority. Staffort turned off the limo tv. She had to process what had happened.

Her phone vibrated with a message. Maybe Luke. Maybe he's offering an escape into the Underground, a new identity, a place of refuge. That would be tiresome. Could Luke even deliver anything of value? An expression of love, though, would sure go a long way.

Once in her townhouse, she opened her messages. The text was from. . .Elle Crafton? Oh, yes, the smiling reporter. She read the text. That girl was swinging for the fences. How stupid did she think Staffort was? On second thought, however stupid Crafton thought she was, she probably was. Probably the stupidest woman in the country with the possible exception of the first performer eliminated from "No, Really, America's Got Talent." Staffort needed to call her staff, then her lawyer, who if she were worth her retainer, would have been calling Staffort. Instead she took the land line off the hook. She turned off her cells. She tried to think.

Still no knock on the door. There was hope yet. Staffort went to her refrigerator and opened the freezer door. She'd tell the investigators, "These are not the bills you are looking for," and use a Jedi gesture to move the feds on. She reminded herself that she hadn't achieved her position by being unable to face reality.

A six-inch stack of hundreds in a plastic freezer bag in the door was her reality. Over $140,000, and useless. Shredding would do no good. What would she do with the shredded paper? Flush it away and have it choke the toilet or float back up for a month? No.

The disposal. She took the package to the extra bedroom that was her office. Across from the guest bed where Luke had slept, she sat in a chair and shredded it anyway because she had to start somewhere. Back down to the kitchen. She fed the shredded bills through the disposal. She followed that with gallon pitchers of water, several packages of frozen vegetables, a pound and a half of stew meat. More water, some frozen hamburger patties left over and freezer burned from a month ago, half a leftover pizza, and a Sara Lee coconut cake. A little food was still left in the freezer, which seemed a good idea; empty would be suspicious. She filled the sink with water, opened the drain to the grinder, and hoped nothing would float out. A few green bits swirled up. With a calmness that she could not help but admire, she examined them: just flakes of broccoli. There were a few morsels of meat, too, but no cash hash. She washed out the sink and went to the living room to await the FBI. Popped by the front bathroom to get a few squares of toilet tissue, back into the kitchen to dry the sink, and back to the bathroom to flush the toilet paper away. She sat in her recliner.

Smolek's *Infectus Phytor* had been on the top of her stack for months. The alien on the cover looked about as happy as Staffort and seemed to be smirking at her. But it was from another world; maybe she could escape into the book. All the evidence she could destroy was destroyed. Staff and lawyers could wait.

One page in, she found herself thinking. She had always been humbled and appreciative of the great honor given her by the citizens of Virginia's Sixth District, the Republican Party, and finally the Stalagmites. She'd voiced that sentiment on numerous occasions, during campaigns, at fund raisers, at Rotary clubs, and so on. She believed she was sincere. But today she had a new appreciation of what it meant to be humbly grateful. She'd ground away the stash that had edged her net worth into positive numbers. And while she appreciated the voters and her colleagues, her Foodaway disposal would always have her worshipful thanks. She did not know what evidence the Feds had, but they didn't have and couldn't have any quid regardless of the seemingly undeniable quo of the defense budget rider. And maybe a good lawyer could deny that.

She remembered her interview with Ms. Crafton and expressing misgivings about having Pisanionium in the country. No, that was the Freedom from Consequences amendment. Anyway, she'd grown, she'd evolved. That's what she'd done. She saw how that element had changed civilized Britons into money-grubbing animals scrambling to protect their monopoly, even offering bribes to do so. Of course, she'd pretended to go along with it. Had to. But she didn't take any money. Is there any money? No.

But then after much thought and research, and prayer, yeah, she'd go with prayer, that's still okay in Virginia, even northern Virginia, she'd decided that Pisanionium was indeed too dangerous an element to allow in the country. So she'd drafted the rider and got some support. Just like she told someone, yes, Representative Holcomb-Derrida, it was dangerous stuff. No matter what, that was what happened.

She re-read Smollett's first page. Probably will be interesting. Focus, Jan, focus.

CHAPTER FIFTY-NINE

Rek and Colonel Waters returned to the Pentagon in silence. It was after eight when the staff driver dropped them at the river entrance. They went to the office, secured both copies of the document including the now-declassified executive summary in the safe, initialed the log, and looked at each other. Rek wanted to say something innocuous to break the tension, but he also wanted to cry for his momma and wasn't sure which would come out of his mouth. Soul-sapped grimness made it to his face.

Colonel Waters had recognized the executive summary as soon as General Manly read it during the hearing. It took him to the Fourteenth Street Bridge to remember when he'd seen it, to remember the interrupting visit from his old high school classmate turned prosperity preacher, to remember telling Rek to turn off his computer, to remember that Rek had apparently done so fairly quickly (certainly as quickly as the colonel could have, but the colonel now realized, given Rek's generation, not quickly enough), and to remember that Rek's girlfriend was a reporter for the Washington Herald. While they walked the empty corridor to the office, Colonel Waters chewed over what to do. They went inside, and he closed the door behind them.

"Lieutenant," the colonel said, "You're young. The young are entitled to a few mistakes. But there are mistakes and there are mistakes. What happened today is a catastrophe. Be on time Monday."

Rek wanted to deny everything, undo, redo, erase, Bleachbit, reboot, be forgiven, maybe on reflection and later, if the chain of events ended with the president's resignation, proudly claim it. But he'd gotten it wrong, so no Pisanionium-gate for the president and no glory for him. He settled for just looking bleak and uncomprehending and saying, "Yes, Sir."

The clouds over the parking lot reflected a dirty mustard color from the lights. Rek's Honda Box was by itself at the far edge. There were about a dozen other cars still in the lot. The crickets and cicadas taunted him as he walked. The night humidity closed in on him ominously. He looked back toward the building. He heard the colonel whipping his Porsche through the gears on his way to Highway One. There was a staff car at the river entrance poised to take one of the generals home to Fort Myer-Henderson Hall. His nervous sweat mingled with the humidity, slicking his face.

He wanted to be with Elle and feared he never would be again. He drove around to the Memorial Bridge, crossed into D.C., and, glancing in the rear-view mirror, saw the lights of a car behind.

He jerked the Box into a needless circle near the Jefferson Memorial. The lights stayed with him. With the weight of the nation in the pit of his stomach, he exited the loops of Memorial Drive and took a right on Fourteenth Street. He crossed the bridge, looked at the Pentagon to his right, a tear about to spill, and merged onto Highway One.

The lights were still behind him. But now there were lights all over. He didn't know. He got off at Glebe Road, drove until he could turn around, and managed to find his way back to the highway. The lights behind him were jumbled. He jammed the accelerator to the floor to slip onto Highway One going north. No one came up the ramp behind him.

Rek sat in his car outside Elle's building.

Chapter Sixty

Mollie opened the door to the garage and found Belmond on the top step, shoulders slumped, briefcase dangling from his fingers as if it were his presidential hopes, his face longer than that of a French diplomat presenting his credentials to the foreign minister of Turkmenistan. She smiled gently and said, "I've been waiting for you. Whatever happened today and whatever will happen, know this: I love you. I always will."

Belmond suppressed a whimper. He mumbled, "That's what's really important."

She led him into the kitchen and sat him down in his chair. "Brad's upstairs. He's not likely to know about this; we'll have to tell him, but not until tomorrow. The girls are at the Fouchard's; we don't have to go into detail with them. Thank goodness school isn't in session."

Belmond mustered a clear and woeful, "That's good."

Mollie got a plate from the refrigerator and put it in the microwave. She stood behind Belmond, massaging his neck and kneading his shoulders.

"Did I get set up, Mollie? Did that reporter set me up?"

"I doubt it, Sheff. Everyone likes you. The media loves you. I don't know if we can get past this, but if we can, you'll be another anointed one."

"Mollie, that's gone. Gone."

"Well, it would help if you had a really sharp crease in your pants." She gave him a wan smile. Belmond had no idea of what she was talking about, but it seemed well intended.

The microwave beeped, and Mollie got the plate and put it in front of Belmond. His favorite, the sausage-spinach-mushroom pirogi bake. Its pungent aroma, gagging to anyone from south of Albert Lea, slid up his nostrils and triggered an inchoate sense of winter suppers after pick-up hockey games. He breathed it in and generated something of a smile for his wife.

> A certain pol from Minnesota
> had ambitions more than he oughta.
> When they went kablooey,
> he said more than phooey.
> Could he ever manage a coda?

Now, of all times, the poetry was beginning to work. He dug into his supper. The world could still be okay.

> The Senate was his only fate.
> No presidency would ever await.
> The summary, how dumb;
> his hopes, now a crumb.
> At least he had a sweet mate.

He needed out of this, this maelstrom of doggerel. He asked, "Well, sweetheart, otherwise how was your day?"

CHAPTER SIXTY-ONE

The chair of the House Ethics Committee appeared on three Sunday shows to announce that, as soon as Congress returned from recess, the committee would begin a formal investigation into Speaker of the House Jan Staffort over the Pisanionium affair. A Justice Department spokesperson declined to confirm or deny the existence of a criminal investigation targeting Speaker Staffort. For her part, the Speaker, through her press secretary, was sticking to her story, denying any misdeeds. She also released a statement that she was demanding the Senate censure Senator Belmond for attacking a member of the other body. The chair of the House Intelligence Committee issued a statement that his committee would demand the intelligence community account for its apparent interference in the democratic processes.

Mollie began to rehabilitate her husband Monday morning. She prepared him for a restoration tour of Minnesota. She told him he would watch hour upon hour of Dr. Phil, Judge Judy, Feuding Families, Police Dash Cam, Big Brother and other reality television shows. She said, "these people admit to despicable addictions, bizarre sexual practices, familial betrayals, infantile plots against neighbors, and jejune legal disputes. And they keep straight faces and radiate high self-esteem in interviews. Learn from them." They decided that if Sheffield developed this skill sufficiently, he'd give a go at a self-deprecating appearance on one of the late-night talk shows. It would mortify his Lutheran soul— a spiritual gift that he doubted that he would appreciate in this life—but it could rekindle his presidential hopes. She smiled and said softly, "We've proven with more than a few presidents that in Washington, just like Hollywood, there's no such thing as bad publicity."

CHAPTER SIXTY-TWO

Colonel Waters was waiting for Rek that morning. Inside his private office, the colonel had him stand at attention. Rek waited, butt clenched. Slowly Colonel Waters read the statute covering the handling of classified information to Rek. He never raised his voice. When he finished, he asked, "Do you understand what this means?"

"Yes, Sir. It means I could go to jail. The stockade? Fort Leavenworth? For a long time."

"You are right."

"I can't deny that I was the source. I saw your computer screen and memorized it. I guess I misread the name of the subject."

"But, luckily for you, it also means that I could be convicted of felony mishandling of classified information."

"But it was just an accident. Your friend showed up, the general ordered you to come, it was. . . ."

"Did you hear me read the word 'intent' in the elements of the offense?"

"No, Sir."

"That's because it's not there. Intentionally divulging classified information to a foreign power is a whole other crime. And it's punishable by death. But neither of us did that." He sat on the corner of his desk. The colonel ordered, "Stand at ease!"

Rek assumed the posture. His face began to twitch, just the corner of his mouth. It had never done that before. He managed to speak. "So, what are you going to do? Sir."

"If I were single, I'd go to my boss and confess everything. You and I would both go down. And that's what I'd like to do. Then I could still think of myself as an honorable officer. But I have a family, so losing my retired pay punishes my wife and children. . .for my stupid lapse. I'm going to do nothing. And hope that nothing comes of it."

"And what are you going to do about me?"

"You can't be moved short of a year on station. So next Spring or Summer, you'll get to see what the real army is. I'll find you an S-1 job, that's personnel and administration, with a combat service support unit; I think a medical unit would be about right."

"I see." Rek did not see.

"I like you, Rek. I think you're a sincere young officer. So I'm not going to get you killed by sending you into a combat situation. And I sure don't want you to get someone else killed. So you'll be okay. You'll just be okay somewhere else, maybe Fort Cavazos."

"Yes, Sir. That's in Oklahoma?"

"Texas." The colonel laughed without smiling. "Not even close."

"Isn't Texas just south of Oklahoma?"

"Technically. But that's not something Texans are proud of. I want you to take tomorrow off, and I want you to think long and hard about what happened. You can't afford for anything close to it to happen again."

"Yes, Sir." He was somber. And he felt a little for Colonel Waters. But the pizza delivery guy in him wanted to pipe up, "Sweet! A day off and I get paid."

Rek went to Elle's after work. When he walked into the apartment, he saw piles of clothes, suitcases, a large duffel, various electronic items surrounding her computer, and there were pots, pans, and dishes on the kitchen counter.

"You're taking the London job?"

"Rek, I can't turn this down."

"No, you shouldn't. Besides, I won't be here that much longer." Rek told of his conversation with the colonel.

Elle began sorting books into two piles. "I really didn't know all the legal issues. First Amendment, you know, we just go with the story and whatever happens happens. I'm sorry you're the one it happened to." She tried to summon an appropriate smile for Rek, but had only a sort of positive grimace to offer, but at least it was sincere. She added, "Rek, would you mind clearing that top shelf and stacking those books here?" She pointed to an open space beside a suitcase.

"Sure." In three loads he emptied the shelf. First, his mother. Then his stepmother. Now, his girlfriend. As he carefully set the last stack on the floor, he looked up at Elle like a swatted puppy.

"Hey now," Elle said, "this may be best for you, too. I'll be out of the country by the time any authorities want to question me about my source. Of course, I wouldn't tell them anything, but once they think of me, it will be pretty obvious." Elle saw dread creep across Rek's face. "Uh, they may never know."

"That's not much consolation."

"We're not over. Not if I have anything to do with it."

Rek said, "You forget, I'm a second lieutenant. I can't afford international travel. Maybe once or twice a year. That's it."

"Can't you take an Air Force plane?"

Rek thought about it a moment. Hadn't some of the other lieutenants in his basic course talked about that? "Yeah, space available travel. Andrews Air Force Base might have some. Dover, Delaware, too. But then I might be flying back with some dead people…KIAs."

"That doesn't sound too pleasant, but Andrews is right here. I'll bet you can do that." And she flashed an encouraging smile.

Rek lifted his eyes. She was really beautiful. She'd been a wonderful girlfriend. For a month. "Oh, I'll come over somehow. But you're gonna move on."

Elle sat in the floor, her eyes almost embracing her implausible boyfriend. Too young, naive, awkward, military, as worthless to her career as could be. But there he was. "I don't want to, my Rek." She finished sorting a stack of books, steadied them, and turned full face to Rek. "Ever since I've been in D.C., I haven't felt completely human." She looked toward her books, stacked on the floor like the building blocks of her career. She picked up one and opened the cover. She said, "I've been like a character in a novel. More Jack Ryan—busy, flat, kinda insipid—if you know the books or the movies. You've made me feel like…Elizabeth Bennet."

"I don't know Elizabeth. What movie was she in?"

"A book, by Jane Austen."

"Sorry, I don't keep up with novels and stuff. Wait. You were feeling more like a man than a woman?"

"No, no, no, don't worry about it."

"If I don't understand something, I always worry."

"Well, I was going to say that you make me feel as fully human as Elizabeth Bennet, but happier. But now you're making me feel like an old librarian."

"Sorry. I'm confused. Just tell me this, if London hadn't come up, would you still want see me?"

"London has come up. I still want to see you." She closed her mouth carefully. She shivered, as if Jack Ryan were rushing up behind her. Rek caught her eye, and Elle smiled.

The End